LOVING AND GIVING

Juliet was quite breathless, having to wipe
her damp face with her handkerchief, by the
time the Peugeot reached the wrought-iron
gateway of de Maureville's house. She looked
with rapture at the magnificent old Château
once they reached it and the car came to a
standstill.

So here she was! Whether the Comte de
Condine's warning and insinuations had any
real meaning or not, she was here — for better
or for worse.

Marino opened the door of the car and Juliet
stepped out, clutching bag, gloves and the
book she had brought to read on the journey
but never opened.

Loving and Giving

Denise Robins

CORONET BOOKS
Hodder and Stoughton

Copyright © 1965 by Denise Robins

First published in Great Britain by
Hodder and Stoughton Limited 1965

Coronet edition 1968
Second impression 1969
Third impression 1976

Printed and bound in Great Britain for
Coronet Books, Hodder and Stoughton, London
by Cox & Wyman Ltd, London, Reading
and Fakenham

ISBN 0 340 02922 6

Friday's child is loving and giving

Chapter One

"My whole life," said Juliet Browning, "seems to have been spent in saying good-bye to *somebody* – and mostly to *you*!"

The tall grey-haired man who sat opposite her at a corner table in the Grill Room did not speak for a moment. He was lighting his pipe. Puffing at it for a few seconds he looked through the smoke at the face of his daughter. It was not a sad face although there was sadness in her voice. It was the face of a lovely girl on the very threshold of a radiant womanhood, one who should have been happy and, thought Alan Browning with much concern, so much more fortunate than she was.

At last a deep sigh escaped him. He took the pipe from his mouth and said:

"It's a rotten business, Ju, and somehow I feel it's my fault."

Immediately Juliet denied this and gave him one of her wide gay smiles; the sort of smile that could always cheer him up. Now, he thought with even greater concern and regret, she looked really beautiful and so like her mother. The same wide apart eyes, darkly hazel with a fleck of gold, thickly lashed. The same short nose (he used to tease poor Molly and call her nose a 'snub' . . .) a sprinkling of freckles left on nose and forehead from last summer, and a bright pink flush colouring the attractive young face, as it always did when she was emotional. The same firm dented chin and big laughing mouth. Juliet was not strictly a beauty, yet so warmly attractive. Her hair – thick, bright brown, crisply waving – *that* was inherited from him he thought (feeling a trifle sorry for himself now as he passed a hand over his balding head). Once *he* had had that same hair.

He was always the proud father when he took Juliet out; convinced there was never a nicer looking girl in the room. Not quite tall enough for model clothes, perhaps; on the petite side, but Juliet knew how to dress well on her slender means; made most of her own clothes, and made them well. She had an eye for colour. She had inherited that from her mother. Once poor Molly was artistic – used to paint.

Alan Browning stuck his pipe back between his teeth and

scowled because he felt a stinging sensation behind his eyelids. Good lord – he mustn't get all worked up like this. His darling wife had been dead for two long years. He had suffered hellishly at the time – so had poor little Ju. So deeply fond of her mother – so furiously indignant against the fate that had stricken down such a splendid person with that fatal illness that none of the specialists could do anything about yet.

Remembering Juliet's words about *'always having to say good-bye'*, he could see that it was true. She had been only eighteen when forced to bid that long farewell to her mother. Then there was that only other member of the family, Alan's son, Nicholas. Nicky was in the Merchant Navy. Only two years older than Juliet, already on the high seas – never home for long.

There were these perpetual good-byes where both brother and father were concerned. Mr. Browning was an established, and not unsuccessful, representation of a big oil company in Iran. Nearly always abroad – and not in the sort of places where Juliet could conveniently follow him. What sort of life was there for a young girl in one of those God-forsaken countries where he had to spend most of his time in the desert, lengthening pipelines, or drilling for oil?

Always bidding good-bye to somebody! Somehow those words struck a forlorn note. With all his heart Mr. Browning loved his daughter and he could not bear her to be unhappy.

She had quite a good job just now as a trainee in a home for Disabled Children in Wandsworth. She loved children and she wanted to go on looking after these tragic little creatures who needed so much love and attention. She had been doing this ever since her mother died. After Nicky had gone to sea, it hadn't seemed a financial proposition for them to keep up a home. They had the little house in Highgate where they had lived so happily together, but had decided to let it furnished. It brought in a moderate income which they divided.

But now, to Alan, it didn't seem right that Juliet should have no home.

"Tell me about Luke," Mr. Browning said suddenly, trying to switch the conversation into more cheerful channels.

Juliet's cheerful expression altered to a more serious one. She hunched her shoulders, sat back and let the waiter place their coffee cups in front of them, and pour out some of the strong black liquid from a round glass beaker.

8

"Oh!" she sighed, "*Luke!*"

"Aren't things going right with him?" asked her father.

"Oh, it's just going to be another good-bye," she said.

"But why – you know I never like to probe but—"

"You never do," she broke in, "you're a tactful old darling. And I'm perfectly willing to tell you all, although there isn't much to say."

Alan had heard quite a bit about her latest boy-friend, Dr. Luke Farrell. A young, newly-qualified physician who helped with the medical care of the children in this Home where Juliet was working.

She hadn't said too much about him in her letters – only that she liked him and found him an admirable character – absolutely dedicated to his profession; the only son of a widowed mother who lived down in Somerset. Juliet had also informed her father that she had been out to several meals with Luke, and one or two theatres. Alan had felt pleased that a nice young doctor should have supplanted that other boy-friend of Juliet's ... (Chris Some-one or Other) a TV film actor. For a time he had been afraid that Juliet had got it badly about Chris. It had been her first real affair. Finally she had woken up as her father imagined she would (she was such a sensible girl) to the realization that Chris was no good. Conceited, selfish and out for fun rather than marriage. Juliet wasn't all that modern in her outlook. She belonged to the set who believed in decent living; in saving one's kisses and caresses for the right boy. Nothing of the prig or prude about her; too warm-hearted and generous by nature for that – but idealistic.

Alan had hoped, maybe, that this doctor might come up to her ideals.

This evening, however, she had no such good news for him. The awful truth was, she said, *Luke was beginning to bore her*. He was so self-righteous – so smug.

"I seem to have hit the exact opposite type in him to Chris," she admitted with a rueful laugh. "At first I thought Luke was wonderful because of his medical work. But he is *dull*, Daddy! I take a dim view of the way he is so ready to criticize other people, too. You know I don't hold with the way some people behave, but I do try to understand why things go haywire at times, and I don't think any of us have got a right to be too pompous, or to adopt that *holier than thou* attitude. You never know what temptation is going to do to *you*."

9

Mr. Browning puffed at his pipe. Remembering some of the temptations of his own youth, he nodded.

"How right you are, my darling!"

"There's been trouble at the Home lately. One of the women I work with – ten years older than me actually – found she was going to have a baby. The man walked out on her. There's been an awful scandal. She's left us now but I was awfully sorry for her. Luke said she must have made herself jolly cheap and that it is always the female's fault, and so on. You know I don't lose my temper often, Daddy, but I did with him. We were having a meal together and I walked out – I was so furious. I don't myself think girls ought to go the whole hog before they are married, but if they do, who should cast the old stone? There may have been a lot of reasons why poor Vera couldn't stand up to this man. And she trusted him. I told Luke that I thought it was his fault – both their faults if you like – but he was all on the man's side and against Vera. I'm sorry nobody knows where she has gone or I'd go and see her and try to help."

"You're a kind little thing," murmured her father.

"A softie," Juliet grimaced. "Anyhow I got tough with Luke and just before I came to meet you this evening some flowers arrived from him with an apology. I think he's in love with me, Daddy."

"I bet he is. And you?"

"No," she said. "That's the awful part of it, I'm not. Luke says love will come later. He's sure of me, but I'm far from sure of myself. Perhaps I live in a dream-world but I don't believe I have met the man who figures in those dreams just yet!"

Mr. Browning smoked his pipe and wished to God that he had enough money to retire and set up a comfortable home for this adored and adorable child of his. How he hated being impecunious and having to go off to Iran tomorrow. His firm had some sort of agreement with an American company there.

He wondered what Molly would have done about Juliet. How she had doted on her pretty little daughter! There flashed into Alan Browning's mind, suddenly, the memory of Juliet's sixteenth birthday party. Before Molly fell ill. Juliet's happy and proud parents had looked at her as, flushed and laughing with her teenage friends, she had cut the cake. They had held a buffet supper party for her. Molly and Juliet, to-

gether, had made all of the 'eats'. Molly had whispered to him:
"Do you remember that Friday when she was born, Alan?
We were so pleased that we had a little girl, as we
already had our son. And she's turned out to be a typical Friday's
child. Do you remember the verse. How does it end?
*Friday's child is Loving and Giving. Saturday's child must work
for its living* . . . etc. . . ."

Alan Browning's eyelids ached again. He remembered it all as
though it were yesterday. And it was so true. Juliet had proved
generous and affectionate; *Loving and Giving* described her. And
she had to work for her living too, he thought with a sigh. Still –
everybody did that now. Work was good for one; it was just that
he wanted her to find the right *man*. With her sweet nature it
would be murder for her if she accidentally married the wrong
one. For her, marriage would be a sacred tie for life.

It was not in the nature of either Juliet or her father to stay
gloomy for long. When they left the Grill Room they were both
laughing at a joke they had shared. Mr. Browning hailed a taxi.
He insisted on driving Juliet back to Wandsworth. He knew it was
extravagant he said, but he didn't come home on leave all that
often, and he wanted to spend some money on her. Now that the
Spring had come, she was to go and buy herself a summer outfit
at his expense, too.

"You're a darling," she said, and laid her head on his shoulder.
The Home in Wandsworth looked large, dark and dreary, on
this May night. He wished her life could be a little more glamorous. But when she kissed him good night she assured him that
she was perfectly satisfied.

"You're not to worry about me, Daddy. I'll be all right," she
said.

But he was not to know how worried she really was about herself and the future, and how when she got back to her little room
in the staff quarters of the home she felt very much like bursting
into tears. Not even the pleasure of having Daddy in London for a
day or two, or buying a Spring outfit at his expense, could compensate for the news she had received this morning. She had not
told him. He was an awful old worrier, and if she had said one
word, he would go off to Iran in absolute misery. Men, Juliet
decided, were really far more vulnerable and easily worried than
women. Women were the stronger sex!

The Children's Home had been a real home to her since

Mummy died. One month from today it was closing down. Matron had explained that it was something to do with new Government Planning. They were going to pull down all the houses in this road and put up a huge block of Council flats. The Home had two country branches. The Wandsworth children were being divided between them. A few of the senior trained staff would go with them. Juliet and the other Trainees must find other work.

Juliet had shed quite a few tears over that notification this morning. She felt a sinking feeling in her heart tonight as she prepared for bed. What *was* she going to do in the future?

Luke, of course, had offered a way out in his letter of apology. He had proposed marriage to Juliet.

But she didn't want to marry Luke. Once or twice when he had taken her out, she had kissed him good night and he had tried to set the stars alight for her. He was nice. Not unattractive. She had even imagined for a few seconds that she might respond to his passion. But it was a failure. It wasn't the real thing; she was sure now that she couldn't marry Luke, even in order to get a home of her own. A pity in many ways; being a doctor's wife would have suited her.

At one time she had thought that after Mummy's death she should have started training to qualify as a hospital nurse. It had perhaps been a mistake not to do so. On the other hand, after long weeks of indecision, she had been forced to the conclusion that she wasn't really cut out for hospital life. She could look after crippled children, but she didn't really want to be a professional nurse. She wasn't very proud of the fact, but she just wasn't made that way. She was too emotional and imaginative. Hospitals didn't want martyrs – they needed dedicated women and Juliet Browning would never make a good nurse. She was not stoic enough. She had the highest regard for the born hospital nurse, but she ended up by taking this job with the disabled children in Wandsworth. So far it had suited her – hard and exacting though the work was at times.

Juliet decided to turn out her light and try to forget her worries in sleep. She and Daddy had had fun together at the Grill – eaten a jolly good dinner. It would be nice to lie and think about that. Poor old Daddy! Life must be a bit lonely and uncertain for him. If only Mummy hadn't died and left them all!

Juliet moved across the room to open her window and suddenly noticed a square envelope with a foreign stamp lying on the carpet.

She picked it up, surprised. This must have come after she left the Home. The draught from the window had blown it from her table on to the floor.

The address was typed. The postmark was the *Alpes-Maritimes*.

Turning it over she saw a name and address written on the flap of the envelope.

From Mrs. Ingram, c/o Mme de Maureville, Château de Roquemont, Nr. Cannes.

Juliet stared at this – her pulses quickening. Then she climbed into bed, tilted the shade of her table-lamp and opened her letter.

So the day had not yet ended; this was a fresh surprise. The letter was from her godmother, Juliet Ingram, after whom she had been named. Juliet was very fond of Mrs. Ingram, she had been at school in Paris with Mummy. Although a bit brittle and a 'socialite' she was really quite sweet. Mummy once told Juliet that the older Juliet had been different when young, but got spoiled after her marriage to her millionaire American – Bob Ingram. About the same time, Mummy had married Daddy – a very much smaller and less glittering affair.

After Mummy's death, Mrs. Ingram had been very kind to Juliet and sent her a cheque and box of clothes (they had the same petite figure). Juliet hadn't seen her for over a year. She lived in New York. But the older Juliet never forgot to provide and post some delicious luxury present from New York on her godchild's birthday and at Christmas.

Now it appeared that Mrs. Ingram was in Europe staying with another friend of her youth – a French woman – in Cannes.

There were four sheets of this Continental notepaper, written in Auntie Ju's big sprawling hand. The contents of this unusually long letter left Juliet gasping. It was as though she had been swimming, darkly, under water, and suddenly come up into the air – through a bubble of sunlight.

Darling little Ju,

As you will see from my address I am staying here with my friend Mimi de Maureville. You may remember me telling you about her and how I first met her at our finishing school in Lausanne. She and her daughter, Simone, stayed with Bob and myself in New York.

Her husband, Lucien, belongs to one of the old French aristocratic families who survived the war and have still got a lot of money, which Lucien supplements as Director of a big olive oil manufactory – they have marvellous groves down here. They also have an apartment in Paris. This old Château is in a village named Roquemont – up above Cannes.

Mimi's seventeen-year-old daughter, Simone, by her first husband, is a spoiled brat and causing a few headaches. There is also a daughter, Sophie (Lucien's), now eight years old. Between ourselves I don't hold Mimi up as an angel. She is self-centred and leads her husband a dance (Simone takes after her), but Sophie is a cripple. The poor little thing spends her time in a wheel-chair, and is a frightful worry to Mimi who seems to have taken almost a dislike to the child. She never was a born mother, and I'm the first to admit it. And as I don't care for children myself I can't altogether condemn her. But Lucien is an idealist and pathetically devoted to his little cripple. Mimi is often away. Lucien doesn't like leaving Sophie in the care of paid nurses. I don't blame him. Mimi has been very naughty.

I suggested that YOU should come down here and look after Sophie. You are educated. You speak French better than the average English girl so you can give her lessons. You understand children's health as you've been trained and you are musical. The child worships music and would like someone to teach her the piano.

I have recommended you as being the ideal person for the job. Mimi will be only too glad to leave everything to you.

Please say that you'll give the post a trial, dearest little Ju. Here there is all the sunshine and beauty of the Côte d'Azur. The Château is too big and sometimes gloomy but Mimi has transformed one wing and it is lovely.

Get a reverse-charge call to me. If you decide to come I will pay your fare, and be here myself to introduce you to the de Maurevilles.

I showed poor little Sophie a snapshot of you and she said that she thought she would love you. She certainly hates all the mademoiselles who have kept coming and going, quarrelling first with Lucien, then Mimi.

Do say yes, darling,

Your loving
Auntie Ju.

Juliet read this letter twice. She felt slightly dazed but soon woke up to a sense of extreme excitement.

This sounded like an answer to all her prayers. She wouldn't have to go into a new job and be miserable and have to put up with it. She could go down to the South of France – to the de

Maurevilles – as soon as they wanted her. Matron had told the staff that any of them was free to leave when they chose.

Monte Carlo! Cannes! An old château in the hills! Could anything sound more attractive?

Juliet had never been to the South of France but many of her girl-friends had taken their holidays out there. If she accepted this offer it would not, of course, be just in order to enjoy the South of France but she would have a definite purpose in life; to look after a lonely crippled child; a poor little rich girl. Her father adored her but her mother preferred the other girl – Simone – who was fit and beautiful. Madame de Maureville sounded to Juliet a poor sort of mother.

Juliet was nothing if not impulsive. She gave this matter scant thought. She tumbled headlong into the golden net that had been spread for her. She would telephone Auntie Ju tomorrow and tell her that the job was 'on'. She would shake the dust of Wandsworth and London off her feet and fly by Comet to Nice airport. She would look after Sophie. She would make her life happy – teach her to play the piano – make sure that she never, *never* felt unwanted or neglected again.

It would be her new life's work.

Juliet tossed Auntie Ju's letter up in the air and watched it flutter down in four white crisp sheets on to the bed. Then she picked the pages up and kissed them.

Then she sobered down.

She remembered Luke and his offer of marriage.

What would Luke say? Ought she to go away a thousand or more miles from him instead of giving him that chance he had asked for?

Would she live to regret this thing?

She began to wonder . . .

Chapter Two

LUCIEN DE MAUREVILLE drove his black and silver Jaguar through the wrought-iron gateway, and down the long drive. Tall green trees stood in straight soldierly rows on either side, shading the road from the Mediterranean sun that was still shining brilliantly from a blue sky at five o'clock. He slackened his pace as he neared the Château noting the pleasure that he always felt when he saw the herd of small dappled roe-deer which roamed at will through the parkland. He kept these graceful animals because he liked them – not for purpose of the *chasse* to which his friends and countrymen were so partial. At no time had Lucien de Maureville ever consented to take part in a stag-hunt, even when the finest in France had been offered him. For the same reason he had refused to attend a bull fight during his many journeys to Spain either on business, or for a holiday with Mimi his wife.

He was well aware that Mimi despised him for this 'weakness' as she called it.

"I like a man to be a man!" she once had said in the cruel way that Mimi had of striking at a sensitive spot. Lucien had replied quietly:

"To detest cruelty is not to be effeminate, *ma chère* Mimi. In my opinion women more than men delight in cruelty."

She had laughed. Perhaps it was as well she could laugh frequently – although always at him, never at herself. She had a light frivolous nature which he had known little about when he first fell madly in love with her, eleven years ago.

Mimi's laughter had a pretty, silvery quality, but, for the man who had once adored her and placed her on a pedestal, it soon had a hollow echo; laughter like the tinkle of a toy piano played by a thoughtless child. That was how Mimi so often showed herself; thoughtless, childish, exacting. Yet she was older than Lucien by two years. When he first met her she was the widow of a French writer and already had a child aged six. She had seemed overcome with grief for her dead husband, and devoted to little Simone. She had also pretended to be rather helpless and in need of love and protection. Lucien had offered both, for it was in his nature to want to love and protect. He was the happier for giving. Mimi had soon proved herself to be happy only when she was receiving gifts. She was a supreme egotist.

It had been an unhappy awakening for Lucien at the very beginning of their honeymoon. But at this moment he was thinking not so much of Mimi as of Sophie, the little daughter who had been born to them three years after their marriage.

Sophie, poor little darling, Lucien thought, as he drew up in front of the Château, was too like him. She had been cursed with this desire to give too much, and had his far too sensitive nature. He felt a deep compassion for the sad and the sorry people in this world. It seemed grim that his own little daughter should have been fated to take her place among such people.

Born with one leg shorter than the other and a curvature of the spine, Sophie had never really outgrown these deformities. At eight years old, she still looked as small as a child of five. Her large dark eyes beautified an otherwise wizened little face – eyes like her father's. Mimi's were as blue as aquamarines and just as glacial. Her own child, Simone, had inherited those eyes. Once they had fascinated Lucien – appealed to him. But later on he had found them cold and without kindliness.

This morning, before leaving Roquemont for the *L'Huile d'Or* factory and the magnificent olive-groves which were only a few kilometres away, he had had one of those scenes with Mimi which had grown all too frequent. He had felt deeply depressed all day and particularly about Sophie's future.

He stepped out of his car and stood looking for a moment rather wearily at the splendid façade of the Château de Roquemont.

Long before the war the de Maurevilles had been immensely wealthy. Before Lucien had need to work or become a director of a company like *L'Huile d'Or*, the Château had been a happy as well as an historic home. Lucien had lived here years ago, with his parents and his brother. It had seemed to him the most wonderful place in the world. Now both father and mother lay buried in Roquemont in the churchyard of the Church of Saint Jean. Jacques, his elder brother by six years, had been shot down over the English Channel at the end of the war. Later, Lucien was sent by his guardians to England in order to learn the language. He returned to take up his life in France again and found himself more or less alone in the world. Alone, except for one aged uncle who fortunately, when he died, left Lucien enough money with which to purchase his directorship in the *L'Huile d'Or*. It was as well that the company rapidly thrived – achieved great success. Today his earnings, coupled with what was left of the family fortune, enabled de Maureville to live quite comfortably. He was not, of course, a wealthy man in terms of the millionaires who crowded the South of France in their fabulous yachts, or flung away small fortunes in the *Salles de jeux*. In fact it was sometimes a struggle to keep up the Château, pay Mimi's bills (she was desperately extravagant) and live as a de Maureville would wish.

Fortunately, Lucien himself had no expensive hobbies except trout fishing which he enjoyed. And when he entertained, he did it well. He had a particularly fine taste in wine. But the great proportion of Lucien's time and money went in maintaining his property. They still had to have four gardeners, for the grounds were extensive and the clipped hedges a triumph of topiary. He did not wish to let that all go. In recent years, he had also had to make extensive alterations inside the old Château. It was beautiful, full of character; of magnificent walnut panelling. Many of the rooms, including the big dining-hall, retained their Gothic magnificence. But Mimi, who felt the cold so badly, had insisted on complete modernization of the west wing; central heating, new décor. Much of it against Lucien's personal taste for he loved the antiques, the tapestries, the former atmosphere of his ancestral home. He disliked many of the expensive pieces of ultra-modern furniture chosen by Mimi. She had a passion for violent colours – bizarre design. All part of her exotic nature and that greedy kittenish quality which made her frequently stretch out her slender hands with their long varnished nails and clutch at what she wanted.

It had been a shock to Lucien to find how completely Mimi changed once she became his wife. He knew now that her whole attitude of tender devotion towards him during their engagement had been a snare and delusion – she had cheated; pretended to adore the old Château, with its original ancient beauty, and pretended to love *him*. The worst thing of all was that she had pretended to want children – sons for the de Maureville line – and Lucien had believed her. After all, she had seemed to be a good mother to the little daughter of her first marriage.

Now he knew that all she had wanted was to step out of her

impoverished widowhood and capture an aristocratic husband and home, to say nothing of a small apartment in Paris where she and Simone could spend much of their time.

Disillusionment had not only embittered Lucien but it had struck at his natural gaiety, at the depths of his integrity – his humour, his old *joie-de-vivre*.

He had changed. During the last few years he had begun to feel like a middle-aged man rather than one still only in his early thirties. If it had not been for his essential pride which nothing could destroy, he might have felt humiliated by Mimi's perpetual disparagement of him. But although he gave in to most of her whims in order to keep the peace, he would not let her turn him into the fawning complacent husband she wanted. Recently he had felt that there was little left to keep them together; but he would not permit a definite break; not only on moral grounds but because of Sophie.

To Lucien the most terrible thing of all was his wife's attitude to her younger child. During her babyhood Sophie had been left almost entirely to nurses. Now she still spent most of her time either with nurse, governess, or a domestic help. Mimi was an indifferent, moody mother. At times she indulged the child's whims – at others completely ignored her existence.

In her excitable volatile fashion she would return from Paris with expensive presents which she flung at Sophie carelessly. *For my poor unhappy child!* she would say. It annoyed Lucien when she spoke of Sophie like that. Particularly to friends outside the home. She seemed to want to drive home the fact that Sophie was disabled. She rarely tried to understand the child's condition and had no idea how to give her self-confidence. She continually compared Sophie with Simone, her half-sister – always to Sophie's detriment. Simone was so tall, so beautiful, so strong. Simone, since leaving school, was so popular; surrounded by admirers.

Simone was the lucky one, Lucien thought bitterly.

When she was at Roquemont, she filled the place with other teenagers. The constant blare of 'Pop' records, being played in her own personal sitting-room, disturbed the peace of the old Château. There was always some infatuated young man arriving to take Simone out, or ride with her, or partner her at a dance. She never seemed to care for anyone in particular for long. She seemed to Lucien incapable of sincere or lasting affection.

But Mimi adored her and enjoyed her successes. She dressed

her expensively and did all she could to further her interests. But she rarely made any sacrifices for her younger daughter. Sometimes Lucien even imagined that Mimi hated Sophie. It 'upset her' (that was the way Mimi put it) to see 'the poor little undersized skinny thing.' It gave her 'the creeps' she said, to see those huge sad eyes following her round. Yet the child adored her and hungered for the few crumbs of attention Mimi flung at her. Sophie also had a pathetic affection for her beautiful elder sister. Simone in fact showed her more consideration than their mother. In Lucien's opinion the seventeen-year-old girl had a kinder heart. She did, at times, try at least to amuse Sophie. For Sophie it was a great treat to be allowed to go into Simone's room and listen to her records.

Lucien was a worried man. All day at the office he had brooded over a conversation he had had with his wife while she break-fasted.

He thought of her – in her big blue and silver bed with the sky-blue tissue curtains spilling from a silver crown in the ceiling. Theatrical and glamorous – Mimi, in a blue chiffon jacket with her long ash-blonde hair floating over her shoulders. She looked ridiculously young like that. How, Lucien asked himself for the hundredth time, could anyone appear to be so angelic, so exquisite, yet be so unkind – so grossly centred in herself?

She had told him that she had arranged with her American friend, Juliet Ingram, for her English godchild to come over from London and look after Sophie. This girl, Miss Browning, was arriving at Nice Airport tomorrow at midday. Lucien must meet her. It was the first Lucien had heard of it. Another of Mimi's sly tricks to shelve her responsibility towards their child, he sup-posed. Generally speaking he allowed Mimi plenty of rope – but not over Sophie. He would *not* allow her to be made unhappy again. The last governess had been like her predecessors, a failure. He did not intend there should be another!

Lucien tried to give Sophie as much of his own time as pos-sible. But he had his business to attend to. He could not spare the child more than the odd hour or two. But he wished he could have handed on his physical strength to his little daughter. He rarely felt fatigue even after a hard day's riding. It was only mental worry – such as his deep concern for her – that could at times sap his strength and fret his nerves.

One day, Mimi proposed they should send Sophie to an expensive Clinic where she could be 'properly looked after'. She had regretted making that suggestion because it was the only time that Lucien had lost his temper with her and been within an inch of striking her.

"You are a devil," he had shouted, "a devil, to make any such suggestion. A monstrous unnatural mother—"

Then of course she had burst into tears and screamed for Simone. When the young girl rushed in, Mimi accused him of actually having struck her. Mimi could lie when it suited her. It had been an ugly affair and it had taken Lucien some time to get over it, but he had soon made it quite clear to his wife that he would dock her allowance and dispose of the flat in Paris which she loved so much, if she made any effort to get Sophie out of the Château.

This morning he had asked why he had not been consulted about the English girl before Mimi engaged her. Glowering at him through her fabulous lashes, Mimi had replied:

"You're always so difficult, I thought I'd make the thing a *fait accompli* before I told you."

"And I thought I made it clear that I wanted a hospital-trained nurse here this time, someone who knows how to make Sophie more comfortable. Her back has been troubling her greatly and Dr. Giraud said that what she needs is regular massage. Besides – you know what happened with Mlle Duprès."

Mimi glowered a bit harder. She had rather liked Sophie's last governess. True she had been hopeless with the child. A stupid woman but her stupidity had suited Mimi. She used to be so servile. She said *'Oui, Madame'* or *'Non, Madame'* to everything Mimi suggested.

She heard Lucien's voice adding:

"And before Mlle Duprès there was that ghastly creature you brought home from Germany who looked like a Nazi gaoler, and frightened Sophie to death with her discipline – and her lecturing. And before that, the poor old English Nannie you couldn't get on with and dismissed. I told you it had got to end, and that *I* would choose the next person for Sophie."

Now, triumphantly, Mme de Maureville played her ace.

"Well, I didn't actually choose her. Juliet Ingram did."

Lucien had stared at his wife dubiously. Admittedly he liked the American friend who, although in some ways as frivolous as Mimi, had a very kindly side. She had been extraordinarily sweet to Sophie while she stayed in the Château. She had warmed his heart by telling him frequently that she loved Sophie and found her a most engaging, sweet little girl; and that she only needed proper handling. Mrs. Ingram had tried to make excuses for Mimi, too.

"Remember, dear Lucien, that Mimi's attitude towards Sophie is psychological. It was due to her accident, no doubt, that the child was born a cripple. This makes her remorseful and remorse is a thing Mimi cannot endure. She tries to run away from it."

Yes, Lucien rather agreed with Mrs. Ingram. Mimi's attitude towards Sophie *was* psychological. Yet her very accident had been the result of selfish carelessness. She had insisted upon riding when too far advanced in pregnancy. She could not bear being deprived of her favourite sport just because she was going to bear a child. One day the mare had thrown her and for a short time they had feared she would lose the baby. Such had not been the case but unfortunately it was the unborn child, not Mimi, who suffered from the effects of that fall.

Lucien calmed down and listened to what Mimi had to say about Mrs. Ingram's choice of a new governess. The girl (also named Juliet) had apparently been working in a Home for crippled children. She was not a hospital nurse, but she did have valuable experience. *And* she could play the piano, and would teach Sophie to play, which was the child's burning ambition.

When Lucien said that he thought Miss Browning sounded suitable but that he still considered that he should have been consulted, Mimi screamed at him in her high French voice:

"Oh, I'm sick of you and what you think – always something for Sophie – never for me – never for *my* daughter whom you swore to love before we married."

He let that pass in silent bitterness. Mimi had thrown that shaft at him all too often. Yet, to begin with, he had also lavished great tenderness on Simone. He loved all children just as he loved helpless little animals. (He had put his foot down and refused to allow Mimi to keep a dog because she had kicked out at a poodle-puppy in a furious rage, and its yelps had brought Lucien rushing into the room.)

Cruel! Yes, Mimi was cruel like that handsome Siamese cat which she had once given Simone. It used to stalk the birds and bring live mice into the house and torture them in front of Sophie.

The poor child used to weep for hours over the little soft dead field-mice, until Lucien got rid of the cat.

He did not blame Simone. She modelled herself on her mother and was completely under her influence. In her way, the young girl was quite devoted to him. He felt that he occasionally received some slight return from her for all he gave her. None from Mimi!

All day he had been thinking about Sophie. Perhaps Juliet Ingram's protégée would be the right person for her; perhaps not. He could not bear to think the child would fall yet again into the wrong hands. Each fresh changeover disturbed her. It was all so unsettling for the poor little thing.

He was exasperated, too, because Mrs. Ingram — so Mimi informed him — had fully intended to be here to introduce Miss Browning to them, instead of which she had left the same day she had spoken over the phone to her god-daughter. An urgent cable from New York had recalled her.

Chapter Three

LUCIEN stood still a moment. Lighting a cigarette he watched the last bright glow of sunshine flood the façade of the Château, turning the old bricks to the colour of warm gold.

His expression of anxiety and fatigue was replaced by intense appreciation. It was beautiful, his home – with the graceful gables, great square stone-framed windows and Gothic porches overhung with purple and cerise bougainvillaea. He was never tired of admiring it. Every year, he took colour photographs of the building and gardens. He particularly loved the old wing of the Château – those spindle-shaped turrets which in France were called *tourelles*; they seemed of almost fairy-tale beauty. He had photographed them from every angle.

To the right lay a small lovely lake fringed with green alders and weeping-willows and fringed in the summer with yellow and purple iris. Lucien liked to watch wild birds. He also kept a flock of rare Chinese geese, and a pair of magnificent swans. This afternoon he could see the swans moving gracefully over the silver-bright water, followed by a new family of five cygnets.

To Lucien's left, the gardens were formally laid out, royally planned and terraced. In front of the Château there was an old fountain in the centre of which a nude stone nymph held between her hands a wide shallow basin, green with moss. As the water overflowed, it spilled incessantly a diamond cascade of water.

The Château had been built at the foot of a tree-clad hill. It looked in this light as though it were etched against the black trees of Roquemont Forest. Like this in midsummer, the house was shaded from the fierce heat of the summer sun.

It was a tragedy to Lucien that his wife-had so soon betrayed herself and admitted that she had never loved the country or cared for his old home. Sad that he had no son to carry on his name. But he had long since ceased to worry about *that*. Sophie was everything in the world to him.

Often he would take her out in his car and treat the eight-year-old crippled child with the same gallantry and attention he would have shown an elegant *femme du monde*. He would play a game with her; kissing her small wizened hand, bowing, calling her his *petite princesse*. At those times she would actually laugh – play up to him and order him about, thrilled because he took her exactly where she wished to go and bought her anything her heart desired. It seemed to him that he must spoil her in order to make up for all else that she missed in life. She could never play games with other children, nor would she be able to have boy-friends and marry, like her half-sister.

Mimi neither approved nor disapproved of Lucien's extravagant efforts to compensate the child. Only occasionally she would shrug her shoulders and say that he was turning Sophie into a spoiled difficult little brat, and made himself ridiculous.

Lucien now walked through the main door – a vast wooden affair criss-crossed with ironwork – into the big cool hall where there was a gigantic stone fireplace. There they burned colossal logs from the estate during the cold winter nights. After the heat of this May day, he was thankful for the coolness of the hall. It had an almost church-like beauty. The sunlight poured through a rose-window of stained glass. It had, too, a gallery, used in the past by musicians.

The walls were hung with Gobelin tapestries. Up the staircase, which was of magnificent carved walnut, there were gold-framed paintings of the de Maurevilles of the past.

Over the high mantelpiece hung a portrait of the present Mme de Maureville by a modern French painter. Mimi, on the black Arab mare she used to ride. Mimi, wearing an olive-green habit and a high beaver hat from which floated a veil. With her long fair hair drawn into a severe bun and her hands in yellow gauntlets, she looked both provocative and enchanting. It never failed to make Lucien's heart ache when he saw that portrait. The enchantment had gone for ever – drowned in a sea of disillusionment, quarrels, despair; all the hopeless efforts he had made to save the sinking vessel of their love. But the painting reminded him all too bitterly of her accident. It was this horse she had ridden before Sophie was born.

He passed through the medieval entrance into the west wing. At once this struck a modern note with enlarged windows, striped sun-blinds, gay Parisian furniture and décor. And this he felt to be Mimi's home rather than his.

One thing he had refused to abandon was the library in the east wing which had been started by his grandfather. It was a handsome tranquil room full of souvenirs of the past. Mimi called it 'cold and dreary'. But Lucien spent long hours there, reading or writing. And sometimes little Sophie joined him and he would show her the valuable books and paintings of the collection, which interested her.

Now he knew where he would find her. In her own little sitting-room which had a specially wide door so that her wheel-chair could pass in and out with ease.

Just before he turned the handle of that door he stopped in dismay. He could hear Sophie sobbing.

"I don't *want* a new governess. I *hate* all my governesses. They won't let me go to Papa when I want to. They make me eat when I don't want to. My back aches all the time and I wish I were *dead*!"

Lucien turned white. It was not the first time he had heard Sophie cry, or say wild things. She was a passionate dramatic little thing. Her own difficult nature made it, perhaps, even more difficult to find the right solution to the problem of her upbringing.

"Sophie!" Lucien walked into the room. "Sophie, *ma petite* you mustn't *say* such things. You must never say them. No one should wish himself dead – *no one* – do you hear? It is wicked."

The child stopped crying and turned to him. She was in her chair. She had been clinging to the hand of an old white-haired woman wearing gold-rimmed spectacles. Sophie's favourite among the staff, and former maid to Lucien's mother, old Blanche, was too old to work now. She stayed here only on Lucien's charity. He would never allow any faithful retainer to be thrown out (Mimi wanted him to – whenever he accused her of extravagance, she flung it back at him that he spent too much money on keeping useless people).

It was a pity that Blanche was, indeed, too old to look after Sophie whom she adored. But she was almost deaf and had catar-act which would shortly deprive her of sight. She could not possibly take responsibility for the little girl. In her way, too, Blanche was the cause of trouble. She was a rare old gossip, jealous and malevolently disposed towards those who came to take care of Sophie. It always seemed the same story – not only were the governesses the wrong kind but they had no chance here, for before they ever came, they were resented.

Lucien ordered Blanche to leave the room. Once alone with his daughter, he sat down beside her, took out his handkerchief and wiped the tears away from the thin little face.

"*Princesse,*" he said, "your loyal subject has come back to serve you but he is grieved to hear you say such terrible things. Please, darling, never do it again."

She put his hand against her cheek and drew a deep sigh which wrung his heart. How small she always looked against her cushions! That dark thick hair, too much of it, was bunched out wildly around the small pointed face; the huge dark, heavily-lashed eyes were *his*. There was little further resemblance, and none whatsoever to her Dresden-china mother. One of Mimi's many petty complaints was that Sophie never looked right in the clothes that were bought for her. In a short dress, the crippled leg was too obvious. Frills and bows certainly did not suit her. So for the most part her mother kept her in thin sleeveless cotton tops during the summer months, with cotton jeans; and woolly sweaters and slacks in the winter.

Bright colours did not suit her, but unfortunately she liked them. She adored dressing up, and pretending to herself (if to nobody else) that she looked like other children. Mimi had thought it absurd when a few days ago Sophie had begged for a pink frilly dress she had seen, and Lucien at once bought it for her. He and Mimi had quarrelled over that.

"She looks grotesque in pink frills. Why not leave her clothes to me? I have the taste," Mimi had screamed.

Lucien had replied:

"You have taste in clothes *ma mie*, but no understanding of other people's feelings. I don't care a damn *how* Sophie looks if she is happy, and she shall wear the pink dress when and where she wishes."

Funny, but Sophie was bringing up the point of that pink dress this very moment.

"Perhaps the new girl won't allow me to wear it or let us play the Princess game, Papa? Or she'll be like that awful Fräulein, and make me do everything by the clock, and tire me. Or she won't understand anything I say – like Mlle Duprès who was so silly. Oh, Papa, *why* must I have another governess?"

"Because, my darling, you must be educated. I, myself, haven't enough time to give you."

"But *why* must I be educated?"

"Darling, you don't want to be a dunce and you have always

27

said you enjoyed learning," Lucien reminded her gently. "When you are Simone's age you will be glad if you can write beautifully and read the classics, and be able to take part in discussions when you meet intellectual people."

Sophie drew her hand away from her father's. Suddenly she looked sullen,

"I heard that new maid, Marie-José, tell Mademoiselle that I never *would* grow up, so why bother?"

Lucien was shocked to his soul. He spoke quite sternly to the child even though he pitied her with all his heart.

"I forbid you to say that again and I'm sure that you heard wrongly. Why should you *not* grow up?"

"Because I'm not like the other children. I'm sickly – they say so, I've heard!" said Sophie, two large tears rolling down her cheeks.

The man looked at her with fresh despair in his heart. How, how could he comfort his poor little daughter? Physically she looked so tiny. Yet there was something so old about that sharp-featured elfin face. All too soon in life she had learned to suffer.

She was too much with the servants. She heard too much of their indiscreet talk. What in God's name could he do to ensure that her mind did not run on thoughts of death or suicide? Of course, they were only words that she used. She did not really understand what she said, or mean half of it.

He ground his teeth at the thought of the mother who tossed her so lightly into the care of others. Leaning forward, he gathered the sunken little body into his arms and set her on his knee.

"I'm going to be angry with my princess if she says another naughty word. My darling little Sophie, please believe that you *are* going to grow up and you will enjoy life with your books and your paintings and your music. And you will have all the riches of the mind and spirit to compensate you for the fact that you have to sit in that silly old chair. Now enough of this nonsense, and where is *Maman?*"

Sophie remained inarticulate, silently weeping. She put her arms around Lucien's neck and leaned her head against the one shoulder that was always ready. Soon she stopped crying. She stroked his hair. Papa had such nice thick dark hair with a strong wave in it. Everybody said he was very handsome and she thought so, too. He had the most gentle hands and rich beautiful voice, and he could speak beautiful English. He was teaching her English, too. But old Blanche had said that the English *Mees* would be certain to be sour-faced and difficult and never gay. Sophie told Papa this, whereupon he laughed.

"Nonsense, again. Blanche is thinking way back to her childhood. Remember, she is eighty. Seventy years ago, perhaps English governesses were dull and dreary, but today Cannes is full of beautiful English girls who are very gay. Maybe Miss Browning will be like them and make you very happy."

Sophie nodded and smiled but with reservation. She was not at all sure she would like Miss Browning. Again her father asked her where her mother was. She answered:

"Maman took Simone to Paris. Marino drove them to the Airport after lunch."

Marino was a young Italian chauffeur whom Lucien had recently engaged. Mimi had her own car – a Peugeot.

Lucien put the child back in her chair. He promised to return to her immediately. He wanted to find out what he could about Mimi's sudden decision to go back to Paris. How infuriating of her! Surely she must realize that it would be awkward for him to receive the new English girl – while the mistress of the house was away.

He rang for Maria, Mimi's personal maid, also an Italian, and, in Lucien's opinion, rather a chit. Pretty enough and an excellent needlewoman, she suited Mimi, but she was not a type Lucien cared to have about the place. She was affable enough with *him* – too much so – Lucien had no time for her provocative glances and continual allusions to *la dolce vita*. And certainly *she* paid scant attention to Sophie.

"When is *Madame* coming back?" he asked Maria coldly.

Maria produced a note for him from the pocket of her tiny frilled apron.

Lucien took it, and saw his name sprawled on it in Mimi's big handwriting. He walked away, tearing open the envelope The Italian girl looked after the tall graceful figure and wrinkled her nose. She could never get very far with this *Monsieur* (not as far as she had got with the *Monsieur* in her last job). A pity because M. de Maureville was so elegant and handsome, and it was not natural in Maria's opinion for him to waste all his charm on that poor little invalid child of his.

Lucien, back in Sophie's room, read the short note Mimi had written:

You seem intent on making trouble, whatever I do for Sophie's good, so have it your own way. You can receive Juliet's goddaughter without Simone or myself in the house. If you dislike her, send her back. I can't be bothered. Simone and I will stay in Paris until you phone for us. I, for one, will not come back unless you can be more pleasant.

Lucien tore the letter into pieces, his lips curling. It was typical of Mimi to try and turn the tables on him, to behave as though her own conduct were irreproachable and that their disputes were his fault alone.

He shrugged his shoulders wearily. He knew Mimi. She would soon get over this fit of anger. She would certainly come home if he phoned for her, because she knew which side her bread was buttered and who paid the bills. (He wondered suddenly how long it was since she had left her bedroom door unlocked or welcomed him in her bed.) So long, that he had begun to feel he was living with a difficult, unaffectionate sister rather than a loving wife.

He would not be back in Cannes until after six o'clock. Another alone and – he would certainly do as Mimi said and send her packing if he did not think Sophie was going to like her.

Suddenly he remembered that tomorrow at the time the Comet arrived from London, he would not be able to meet it. He had a business appointment which it was impossible for him to cancel. He would not be back in Cannes until after six-o'clock. Another irritation. It was so like Mimi to leave him to deal with the problems and tie up all the loose ends in this household. She was bone-lazy as well as malicious, and annoyed with him just because he had shown opposition to Juliet Ingram's choice, and Mimi's underhand methods of sending for the girl.

He was not going to let Sophie be upset about it, anyhow. He told her some story about *Maman* having business in Paris and how he, himself, would be away all day, but that Marino would go to Nice and bring Miss Browning back to Rouquemont.

"And you, Princess, must receive her in royal fashion and treat her as you would an honoured guest until I get home. You will have it all on your own shoulders. Won't that be exciting?"

"But supposing she's nasty and I hate her—?" began Sophie.

"She will be nice," broke in Lucien with small conviction, "and you will adore her."

Sophie brightened.

"Can I wear my pink frilly dress for the royal reception?"

30

"Certainly."

"Good! Then I'll make them wheel me out into the garden and I'll wait there for Marino to come back with Miss Browning and entertain her until you are here."

Lucien kissed the child and gave a sigh of relief. Sophie now began to tell him all the things she was going to say to Miss Browning. They even pretended that the moment had come: Lucien stepped out of an imaginary car and bowed to Sophie. She held out a queenly hand and said:

"*Bonjour*, Mees Browning. Welcome to the Château de Roquemont."

Lucien answered politely in a high falsetto voice.

A few minutes later, the room rang with Sophie's laughter and, instead of tears, the elfin face was wreathed in smiles.

By the time old Blanche had come back to help the child to bed, and Lucien had carried her up to her room and gone down again to pour out his first glass of wine, he felt limp and apathetic. He hoped everything would be all right. He must try and believe that Mrs. Ingram had had some judgement when she persuaded Mimi to send for this English girl. But Sophie was certainly a terrific problem – growing more so as she got older. She would be nine in September.

Lucien sat in a chair and shut his eyes. He thought of Mimi in their Paris apartment. Oh God! how lonely he was; how frightfully alone – here in Château de Roquemont – except for his child.

He wondered how long he could bear it.

Chapter Four

LUKE FARRELL insisted on seeing Juliet off at London Airport when she caught that morning plane to Nice.

She hadn't wanted him to. She knew that he was still in love with her and that it had been a bitter blow to him because she had decided not to carry on with her English job; so he would be losing her altogether.

To any girl, the love and attention of an attractive young man must be flattering; Dr. Farrell had in his way a number of attractions; it was just that he did not appeal to Juliet. She did not think it fair to encourage him even by letting him drive her to the Airport but he had insisted upon doing this. He sat drinking coffee with her in the Departure Lounge until the number of the Nice Flight was called.

Poor Luke, thought Juliet, with that inherent quality of kindliness which never failed her; he looked so sad. His blue eyes were clouded. His boyish, fresh-complexioned face was decidedly glum when he finally lifted her case and walked with her to Entrance 6 where a trim air-hostess was gathering her 'flock'.

"I'm sorry I've upset you so much, Luke," Juliet told him, holding out her hand. "Good-bye and thanks for everything."

To her surprise and embarrassment, he dropped the bag, seized her in his arms and kissed her.

"Oh, Julie – darling, you're making a mistake! I know it. You'll never like this job. This child is probably nothing but a spoilt brat and you'll soon be fed-up. Well if you are – come back and marry me."

"Luke—" she began, her cheeks hot, but there was no time to finish the sentence. She followed the rest of the queue into a long corridor and out to the bus which was waiting to take passengers over to the big Comet.

There was so much to like in Luke, she thought, why couldn't she love him? Of course he bored her – that was possibly a good enough reason for a girl not to marry a man. But even if she could visualize getting over the boredom and settling down to enjoy being a doctor's wife – she could not imagine herself on terms of real intimacy with Luke. Never at any time had he been able to rouse the passionate side of her nature. His kiss just now had left her cold. Never had she felt that strange delight – that complete transformation, which she imagined would take place if she were really in love.

She was sorry she had hurt Luke. She had not wanted to. During their last hour together he had extracted her promise to keep in touch with him; to look on him as a friend even if she didn't change her mind about marriage. Well she would be only too pleased to write to dear old Luke. (*Dear old Luke!* That certainly wasn't how a girl should feel about THE man in her life.)

This last fortnight had not been particularly happy for Juliet. She felt unusually tired although she was naturally vigorous and except for a few childish ailments she had never been really ill in her life. But she had worked strenuously to help the staff in the Home this week. She was also sleeping badly – worried about her father. Towards the end of his leave he had seemed to her unusually depressed and reluctant to return to the Middle East. At least, however, he was delighted about the job Mrs. Ingram had found for her. He thought the idea of his Juliet going to live in the South of France a fine one. He liked it. But he looked to Juliet old and worn. It upset her. He and Nick, her brother, were all she had – they were her dear ones, but even Nick was no comfort to her. She had received a disturbing letter from him a few days ago.

Nick and Juliet had always been close friends, and he had confided in her that he was in certain difficulties over a girl he had met in Hong Kong. Unfortunately, not the kind of girl Juliet wanted for a sister-in-law. Anyhow, in Juliet's opinion, Nicky was a bit young to contemplate marriage – especially as his job as a junior officer on a merchant ship took him all over the world, and he couldn't offer any girl a settled home yet. He would do better to remain free for a while. The object of his sudden and first passion appeared to be five or six years older than himself, and already married to an executive in one of the big civil air lines, who was stationed in Hong Kong.

'Love at first sight', Nicky described it.

Juliet was so upset by her brother's letter that it had completely clouded the thrill of preparation for her new job. He wrote:

I know you'll be a bit upset, Ju, but it's something bigger than I ever imagined – the real thing in fact. Lee is absolutely fascinating – half-American, half-Spanish, brought up in New York. The chap she's married happens to be English – deadly serious and immersed in his job. She hates him and I'm not surprised because he's a grim unsympathetic sort; Lee is so sensitive. She needs love and the sort of attention I pay her. I enclose a snapshot which I took of her. It's a close-up so you'll see just why I'm so crazy about her. She's stunning, Ju. She wants me to take her away. She's afraid of Bob, her husband. He has a shocking temper. I just don't know what to do.

The rest of the letter meandered on – every sentence betraying the utter hold this girl, Lee, had on Nick. Young and inexperienced Juliet might be, but she was capable of forming the opinion that her young brother was only infatuated, and that this was not at all the 'real thing'. She couldn't have felt more sorry for him, or more worried. She was sorry the girl was unhappy with her husband, but somehow she had a curious suspicion that Lee was not really unhappy – only wanted to get away from a strong-minded man who refused to let her have her own way. Nick was extremely handsome – rather too handsome – and a bit weak. He would give in to that sort of woman and let himself be ruled by her. Juliet, who was a bit of an idealist, thought it wrong that a married woman, older than Nick, should try and persuade him to take her away from her husband. For Nick – at only the beginning of life – to be involved in divorce, was a repugnant thought to Juliet.

She had sat down and written at length to Nick begging him not to do anything rash.

I'm not a prude and I know heaps of couples do get divorced these days but I just don't hold with it, and you used to agree with me. Please darling Nicky, don't run away with Lee. Think it well over, anyhow. By the time your ship sails and you get back home I'm sure you'll have got things into perspective and you wouldn't do anything so mad. I'm dreadfully sad for you, darling, if you really love Lee, but don't be carried away until you're sure about her ...'

Juliet wasn't at *all* sure why she had written like that to her brother. She surprised herself. But Nick, to be involved as a co-respondent – it just didn't seem right. She was sure Daddy would be horrified. He and Mummy had been so happy – believed so completely in honour – in keeping one's marriage-vows.

Perhaps it was the snapshot that had put Juliet off. Lee – she didn't even know her surname – was certainly pretty – more than that; quite gorgeous. The colour-photograph showed bare sun-browned shoulders (she wore a turquoise blue bikini), long dark hair with an untidy fringe across her brow; a wonderful figure. If it had been a wistful face – sad and disillusioned – it might have touched Juliet's tender heart. But the eyes were bold and the pink lips, provocatively pouting, too thick. It was really a very sensual face. It had made Juliet's heart sink when she saw it. She was disturbed to think that such a girl had taken possession of her adored Nick's heart.

It was a worried Juliet who finally left London Airport in the Comet for Nice. But all her anxieties faded once she was flying at 27,000 feet. It was all so new and exciting. For the first time, she experienced the thrill of being a passenger in a powerful jet aircraft. Mrs. Ingram had told her to take a first-class ticket. She was in a luxurious 'V.I.P.' seat, separated from the Tourist Class by a curtain. It was not long before champagne and an appetizing menu were offered her by a smart air hostess.

Juliet peered out of the window. On this fine clear day she was able to see everything. England looked strange and fascinating, she thought, made up of little green and brown squares; intersections of roads and railways; forests and winding rivers, farms and churches, and moving vehicles that looked like tiny toys. She was struck by the amazing orderliness and careful planning of all the towns as seen from such a vast height.

The brilliant sunshine poured through the windows; the sky was a marvellous blue, preparing her for the Mediterranean summer which she would soon be enjoying. It scarcely seemed possible, when such a brief while ago she had been working in a London suburb.

After she unfastened her safety-belt, she took off the short white jacket which she had bought to wear with her blue silk dress with the white polka-dots.

They had been nice to her in the Children's Home. Matron had thanked her for her services and wished her luck in her new job. The whole staff had clubbed together to give her the white leather bag with a gilt handle which had replaced her old shabby raffia one. Other than this, she carried only an overnight bag. Her suitcase was with the passengers' luggage.

She was longing to see Aunt Ju, and to meet her new employers.

She felt fairly confident about her French. She could get by. In any case Aunt Ju had told her that Monsieur spoke perfect English. He had completed his education in England. Madame, also, appeared to be bilingual. Juliet ought not to have language difficulties.

Sitting beside her was a young man. Suddenly he turned and spoke to her.

"Can I offer you a cigarette, Mademoiselle?"

A cultured voice speaking good English with a French accent. She glanced at the young man shyly. He was not unattractive, although fair and blue-eyed like Luke, and she really never *had* been partial to fair men. But this one was very different from Dr. Farrell. He was elegant – polished – immaculately dressed. Juliet judged him to be in his early twenties; with a faint thread of fair moustache over his upper lip which gave him a look of added maturity. He would have been handsome except for a rather too long nose and a faintly supercilious expression. He wore a light grey suit, a blue and white striped shirt, and blue bow tie. He held out a gold cigarette case to her.

"Thanks awfully," she said, "but I don't smoke."

"You're lucky. I wish I didn't. You don't drink, either, I gather. You refused the champagne."

"Yes, it was really a waste on my godmother's part to make me travel in this extravagant fashion."

"Your godmother—?"

Rather pink in the cheeks, Juliet hastened to explain.

"I – I'm going over to Cannes at my godmother's request to look after the child of some friends of hers."

The Frenchman raised an eyebrow, and lit his own cigarette.

"You – teach – or perhaps you are a nurse?"

"Both in a way. I believe I am going to teach this child as well as help nurse her. She is an invalid."

"You are English?"

"Yes. My name is Juliet Browning."

The young Frenchman blew a cloud of smoke up into the air and gave Juliet a sidelong glance that took in every detail of her. The slim charming figure; the attractive face, the bright brown hair and beautiful green-gold eyes.

"Br-r-r-rowning." he repeated the name rolling his r's. "Isn't that a famous English poet?"

Juliet leaned back feeling more relaxed.

"Right! Robert Browning, married to one of our great women-poets of the nineteenth century – Elizabeth Barrett Browning. No relation of mine I'm sorry to say. I wish she were my great-aunt or something! She wrote marvellous poetry, although a lot of people find her too romantic."

"But you do not. You are, perhaps, romantic?" murmured the Frenchman in an insinuating voice which made Juliet feel the conversation was going ahead a little too quickly. She answered:

"Oh, romance is okay in its proper place."

"I'm intrigued to know where in your opinion, that place should be?"

"Really—" began Juliet, pinker than before, and was glad when the discussion was interrupted by the air-hostess, who arrived with two lunch trays.

During the meal, Juliet's travelling companion continued to talk to her.

"I must present myself," he said – "Michel de Condine is my name."

"How do you do, Monsieur de Condine."

He smiled and extracted a card from his wallet (which she noted was crocodile and expensive like everything else about him). As she glanced at the card she was embarrassed to see the title – *Comte Michel de Condine*.

"Oh, I'm so sorry," she muttered. "I should have said M. le Comte."

"It is of no importance," he assured her.

A moment's silence. The Comte remarked on the perfect weather and pointed out to Juliet that they were now crossing Paris. He added that he found flying a bore.

"Oh, but it isn't!" she exclaimed. "It's absolutely *marvellous*. I can't get over the way this Comet shot off the runway. We were miles and miles up in the sky before we could think."

"Can this possibly be your first flight?"

"Yes."

"How wonderful to enjoy such things for the first time," he said intimating that he was not only experienced but bored with life in general.

His next question was to ask her the name of the family to whom she was going.

"I know most people who live in Cannes," he added.

Juliet had already come to the conclusion that she did not much care for the Comte de Condine. He was too blasé. It was also plain to her that he belonged to a wealthy set in which she could never move. She labelled him the Continental playboy type. But hardly had she told him that the name of her future employers was de Maureville than he dropped his cigarette case on to the little table with a clatter, and his air of indolence and ennui vanished. He seemed to wake up.

"*Pas possible!*" he muttered in French.

"I beg your pardon," said Juliet.

He waved a hand in the air.

"Truly the world – as you say in English – is so small. Just imagine, it is to my *own* family you are flying. Lucien de Maureville is my first cousin – his mother and mine were sisters."

Juliet was bound to admit that this was intriguing.

"What a coincidence!" she said, "sitting next to you like this."

"So – it is to the Château de Roquemont you are going. Formidable!" He pronounced it in the French way, "*Form – i – dable!*"

"Oh, do please tell me about the family," she begged, her shining eyes turned to him.

"I'd better not, I might depress you," he said with a brief laugh.

"Why do you say that?"

"I just don't envy you your future charge. My cousin's little daughter is what you would call a 'problem child'."

"I've had experience of problem children. That won't worry me."

"Woe betide you if she *doesn't* get on with you, or if her mother – Mimi – my charming cousin by marriage – doesn't take to you, either."

Juliet's pleasurable anticipation gave place to sudden doubt – a not very pleasant sensation.

"You don't make it sound attractive."

"I presume you've not yet met any of the de Maurevilles?"

"No. Everything was arranged by my godmother. She is meeting me and going to introduce me to everybody."

"I hope you will not be disappointed but I can inform you now, this moment," said the Comte in his excellent English, "that Mrs. Ingram has already left France."

"That can't be true—" began Juliet.

Michel interrupted her. He had been in London for a few

days, he said – he had his suits made by a London tailor and he had flown over for that purpose.

He lived and worked in Paris; he was in the fine arts business but was frequently in the South of France because his mother and sister had a villa in Juan-les-Pins. He was a frequent visitor at the Château de Roquemont. He was quite fond of Mimi and even more so of pretty Simone, her daughter, whom he described as being *ravissante* and an exquisite dancer – though a little young for him. He had telephoned to Cannes last night and Lucien told him that Mimi and Simone were in Paris. Michel had then phoned them, and learned that Mimi and her husband had had one of their frequent disagreements, so she had gone to her Paris apartment. Also, her American friend, Mrs. Ingram, had been forced to leave Roquemont after being called back to New York on urgent business.

Juliet's heart sank as she listened. This young man who was related to the family must *know* what he was talking about, but she found it a bit disturbing. She was bitterly disappointed that she had missed Aunt Ju. It would be an ordeal to be plunged straight into a French family none of whom she had even met, without her godmother's support. And she didn't much like what the Comte was saying about Madame – or the general situation at Roquemont. It looked rather sinister all of a sudden. Juliet half wished she hadn't come.

"Do you mean—" she broke out, "that there is nobody at the Château now except Sophie and – and – and Monsieur?"

"And a lot of lazy domestics eating their heads off," nodded Michel. "Oh yes – they have a large staff. Mimi is madly extravagant. Most people these days do with only one or two domestics but Mimi has to live in the grand manner and my cousin Lucien just pays the bills. Serve him right," Michel ended under his breath. "He's a fool, that one."

"Oh!" exclaimed Juliet, "that isn't at all what my godmother said. She told me that M. de Maureville was a very fine man indeed."

"In some respects, I agree. But he is weak with his wife and quite idiotic about that poor invalid child of his. I fear I do not understand him," said Michel.

Juliet bit her lip and lapsed into silence. Quite obviously the Comte did not care for his cousin, Lucien. As for these 'frequent disagreements' they did not sound inviting. What had Aunt

39

Juliet let her in for? It would be horrid to have to live with a husband and wife who were always quarrelling.

"Tell me more about the little girl," she said.

Michel looked bored but supplied a certain amount of information about Sophie's physical drawbacks, her wheel-chair, and how the whole thing had happened.

"Mimi looks like an angel and behaves at times like a devil," he drawled. "Fantastically selfish. The doctors say it was her fault for insisting upon riding just before Sophie was born. Of course, I adore her. I play up to her. But when she tries to get me on my knees, I do not play. I am not like Lucien."

"Is he always on his knees to her, then?" Juliet asked rather coldly.

"He used to be," said Michel with the shrug that preceded nearly all his answers. "Though I admit less so now than he was. The child is the bone of contention between them. They just do not agree about her. I only hope *you* will be able to manage Sophie; *chère* Mees Browning – in fact I hope so very much. I would like to think that you will be at Roquemont this summer," he added with a sudden glance and change of voice which insinuated to Juliet that he was interested in her. He qualified it by adding: "You are not like the other various English, French and German governesses who have tried to control *la petite* Sophie. You are very attractive, if I may be permitted to say so, Mademoiselle."

He meant it. There was something very fresh and charming about the English girl's face – the faint dusting of freckles – the wide mouth – the hazel eyes that seemed to turn gold when they gleamed. Michel was very impressionable.

Juliet blushed but not with pleasure. She really was taking quite a dislike to Michel de Condine. Nothing that he had told her had brought her any pleasure. She was depressed, and decided to ask no more questions. He seemed to think badly of M. de Maureville, was disparaging about Madame, and was interested only in her seventeen-year-old daughter Simone. None of it sounded particularly healthy to Juliet.

Michel volunteered some further information about his cousin.

"Lucien has his points, of course. He's the most cultured of us all. His head always *was* in a book; he collects paintings, he likes classical music, and sings a little. As for *la pauvre* Sophie, with

40

her short leg and twisted back, he spends most of his spare time with her."

"Then he sounds a very nice man," said Juliet. "And I cannot understand her mother not feeling the same."

Again a shrug from Michel. He passed a finger over the delicate line of his moustache.

"Oh, Mimi is not the maternal type and poor Lucien is frustrated. Mimi no longer loves him, and he is disinterested in other women. H'm – but I wonder how he will react to *you*?"

The expression in Michel's eye was so full of meaning now that Juliet felt suddenly panic-stricken.

Michel continued:

"How old are you – not yet twenty-one – h'm – only a year or two older than young Simone. But she is very sophisticated and spends her time in the Dress-salons and Beauty Parlours, trying to attract a rich husband. She amuses herself meanwhile with me . . ." he gave a laugh. "But she hasn't a hope. To Twist with Simone is angelic, but when I marry it will be somebody more subtle – somebody with more soul, shall we say? I am sure *you* have a soul, Mees Browning."

"You don't know anything about me," Juliet snapped.

"Are you cross?"

"Yes," she answered frankly.

Michel laughed.

"Delicious! You are incredibly naïve – so very English and insular. But quite charming. I hope to see a lot more of you at Roquemont."

I hope not, Juliet thought, and I pray that M. de Maureville is not at all like his cousin.

But how could he be? Michel de Condine had just called Lucien a fool because he loved his wife – or used to love her – and lived now for his child. He must have a nice character whatever Michel's opinion.

The flight to Nice had turned out to be somewhat alarming for Juliet. She wished her godmother had not been recalled to America. She wondered what lay ahead of her. The de Maurevilles sounded a most complicated family. And from one or two things Michel had said, she might even be told to pack and leave almost as soon as she got to the Château.

It was rather a subdued Juliet who finally fastened her safety-belt for the landing. They circled around Nice and over a brilliant blue sea. It all looked wonderful and exciting – and inviting – but she wished she had never sat next to the Comte de Condine and that she had not heard the things he had told her. She was not in the least flattered by his attempts to 'start something' with her, either. She was relieved when they landed.

"Who is meeting you?" he asked.

"I don't know now," said Juliet. "I had expected it to be my godmother."

"You'd better let me help you through the Customs – I'll take care of you," said Michel in his lordly way.

Barely were they through the Customs when Michel suddenly pointed through the glass barrier of the exit and exclaimed:

"*Voilà* – do you see that young man in the white coat and cap? That is Marino – my cousin's Italian chauffeur. Obviously he has been sent to meet you."

Juliet was bound to say that she was thankful for Michel's expert guidance through Nice Airport which was large and bewildering. She was even more relieved when finally he put her into the long low-built Peugeot and did not try to accompany her.

"Unfortunately," he said, "I have my own car here. I am going straight to Juan-les-Pins. My mother expects me."

While Marino attended to her luggage, Juliet held out a hand to Michel. He touched it with his lips which she knew he should not have done. The conventional thing on the Continent was for a gentleman to lift the lady's hand almost to his lips, but not *quite*, just as he would not dream of using the familiar French '*tu*' instead of '*vous*'. Those things, at least, Juliet knew.

Michel looked into her eyes soulfully.

"I will come quickly to Roquemont and see how you are getting on and make sure you are not being bullied. You are so young and beautiful," he said.

Marino drove off.

"What a conceited creature," Juliet muttered to herself, thinking of the Comte, and made up her mind to form her own opinions of the de Maureville family. She would not believe a word Michel had said. Aunt Ju would surely not have brought her down here if things were as the Comte implied.

Now Juliet was thrilled by the sight of the gay town, the municipal Casino and beautiful sea front, the broad streets, the green

42

palm-trees of Nice; the famous 'wedding cake' architecture of the Negresco Hotel.

The Italian chauffeur turned out of the crowded thoroughfares which Juliet found entertaining but extremely hot, and drove at what she thought a fast pace down the new broad arterial road leading to Cannes. Once there she caught only a glimpse of the Cannes Casino, the harbour crammed with millionaire yachts, flowers along the *Croisette*. Then they climbed the hill behind the town, and shortly afterwards came to the village of Roquemont.

Juliet was quite breathless, having to wipe her damp face with her handkerchief, by the time the Peugeot reached the wrought-iron gateway of de Maureville's house. She looked with rapture at the magnificent old Château once they reached it and the car came to a standstill.

So here she was! Whether the Comte de Condine's warning and insinuations had any real meaning or not, she was here — for better or for worse.

Marino opened the door of the car and Juliet stepped out, clutching bag, gloves and the book she had brought to read on the journey but never opened.

Chapter Five

LUCIEN DE MAUREVILLE returned home from a business conference feeling none too happy about the future. He was still smarting after his wife's unpardonable behaviour – going off with Simone and leaving him to deal alone with this English girl whom he did not know. He was also full of trepidation as to what sort of person Juliet would be, and if once again he would have to get rid of the governess and sort out Sophie's difficulties once more; follow the old, old pattern which had, to say the least of it, become miserably boring.

As he walked through the cool dim hall into the west wing, he heard a sound which made him stop and listen with astonishment; it was so far removed from the sobbing complaints of last night. Peals of childish laughter echoed through the Château. Sophie appeared to be enjoying herself in a most unusual way.

He opened the door of her room and saw his small daughter in her wheel-chair, as usual, but perched high on a pile of cushions. There was a silver crown on her head which had a medallion dangling on her forehead. Her tiny wrists and pitifully small throat were loaded with fake jewellery. She wore the famous pink dress she liked so much but over her knees there had been spread a wide silver tissue scarf, cunningly arranged to make her look as though she also had on a long evening dress. Before her knelt a young girl. Upon her brown wavy head there sat a tiara that had been cunningly shaped and cut out of silver foil. She wore a white blouse – and a long white wool skirt. She, too, was swathed in a gossamer scarf.

In extremely bad French which was obviously sending Sophie into fits of laughter, she was saying:

"I beg for mercy, oh Princess! I am but a stranger in this land. I do not wish to be sold to a cruel mistress so allow me to stay here and serve you and this crown which I wear – for I too am a Princess in my own right – I lay at your feet . . ." Whereupon solemnly she took off the silver foil tiara and placed it on the carpet before Sophie.

44

Now Sophie caught sight of her father's tall figure. She gave a cry of delight.

"Papa, Papa! *Look!* At last I am a real Princess and I have captured a slave. She was found outside our Castle and has surrendered to me. But I am not going to treat her like a slave because she is royal and I am going to be very good to her and give her lots of nice food and a nice bed and she is going to tell me all about her country and I shall tell her about ours."

"But that sounds stupendous!" exclaimed Lucien.

The man's low-pitched attractive voice made Juliet turn round sharply. She sprang up, her face hot with embarrassment and tried to unwind herself from the folds of gauze.

"Oh!" she gasped.

"Papa, Papa," Sophie went on excitedly, "Isn't she beautiful? She was captured and taken into slavery but she is really *la Princesse Juliette*. She has flown to Roquemont on a magic carpet and she is going to be my friend."

"Well now, this is excellent—" began Lucien, and was immediately interrupted by his small daughter.

"You must welcome her too, Papa, and give her her freedom and be her friend, too, Papa. Please kiss her hand because she is not a humble slave but of royal blood."

In an agony of embarrassment, as she saw M. de Maureville's serious gaze upon her, Juliet said:

"Oh, *shush*, Sophie. Honestly – what *will* your Papa think?"

"He'll think you beautiful, like I do!" cried Sophie. "Don't you, Papa?"

"But of course," said Lucien lightly.

Somehow Juliet managed to get rid of the scarf. She ran her fingers through her dishevelled hair, and smoothed her skirt. The game with Sophie had been all right while they had been alone but in front of her new employer – goodness, she thought, he would imagine she was quite crazy. He would get rid of her in the morning. To her surprise, however, Lucien advanced and held out his hand and when she shyly placed hers in it, lifted it to his lips as his daughter had suggested (only, she noticed, he did not actually kiss her hand, as Michel had done). In perfect English he said courteously:

"Welcome to Roquemont, *Princesse Juliette*."

"Speak French – speak French – I can't understand," cried Sophie.

He smiled at her.

"You must learn to speak English, mustn't she, Miss Browning
. . ." and now he was no longer involved in the game but addressed
her formally. "You are of course, Mrs. Ingram's god-daughter,
and have come to look after my little daughter?"

"Yes, Monsieur," Juliet said breathlessly.

"It's a long time since I've heard Sophie laugh like that," he
said. "You two obviously understand each other."

"I was afraid you might think I was being awfully silly," said
Juliet in a tone of relief.

"Far from it. The Princess game is one of Sophie's favourites.
I often play it with her but I have never known her to do so with
anybody else nor to allow another *Princesse* to exist. You are
honoured, Miss Browning."

"We do seem to get on very well," admitted Juliet. "We
had a gorgeous lunch together out on the terrace under the awning,
then we both rested, and after tea we dressed up. It is such a
glorious place, Monsieur – truly glorious!" She added, "Like
something out of a dream. I am so thrilled!"

He looked around Sophie's boudoir; a beautiful enough room
– madonna blue curtains; flowered wallpaper; painted cupboards
full of toys, games and books; a special alcove hung with gossamer curtains, half-concealing the bed; a radio, a gramophone,
a television. All very gay and luxurious, just as it had been arranged by Mimi when she first came to Roquemont. Lucien had
no quarrel with it, but it seemed to him like every other room that
his wife designed, to lack soul; to contain nothing of real value.
He would have preferred Sophie to grow up among pieces of his
own fine antique furniture, and famous paintings. He would
have liked her to read classical books – the sort he had been
given when he was a child, rather than the modern stuff, badly
written and illustrated, that Mimi or Simone bought for Sophie.
If he had had more time he would have played good records to
her – encouraged her to like classics rather than Simone's juke-
box music.

"In time you will be able to see and appreciate the real
Roquemont – the old part, which we no longer live in," he told
the English girl.

"Like the big hall. I thought it was quite stirring and splendid,"
she said. " So full of character."

"I'm glad you admired it."

He was altogether pleased and agreeably surprised by his first impressions of Juliet Browning. Sophie had called her 'beautiful': well, he had seen many more glamorous young women of all nationalities – in Paris, in London, down here in Cannes. But what appealed to him was the fresh youthful quality of her looks – she had such a sweet unspoilt face. Her eyes were sweet, too, and her mouth gentle. There was absolutely nothing hard or 'made up' about this girl. She was an overwhelming relief to him after that silly old Mademoiselle who had just gone: or the harsh-voiced Fräulein who had almost ruined Sophie's nerves.

He would never forget his first sight of Juliet kneeling at Sophie's feet. How splendid of her, he thought, to have thrown herself so heartily into the child's game. How good to realize that after only a few hours she had been so warmly accepted by Sophie.

He could only hope now that Juliet's scholastic ability and nursing-care would prove equally satisfactory.

"Speak French, speak French!" Sophie was begging them.

"Oh, dear," said Juliet, "I'll have to brush mine up, it's not as good as I thought!"

"You'll soon improve. You speak very well, really," smiled Lucien. He glanced at his wrist-watch.

"I must go and wash and change for dinner. Isn't it time *you* were in bed, *petite Princesse*?"

"Oh, Papa, let me stay up for dinner tonight," began Sophie.

Juliet hastily walked up to the wheel-chair and took one of Sophie's hands and pressed it between hers.

"We'll have lots of time to play games tomorrow, darling," she said in her broken French. "Tonight *la Princesse Juliette* is tired and will go to bed early, so *la Princesse Sophie* must do the same. We have adjoining bedrooms. I will knock on the wall. We will invent a language between us: so many knocks will mean so many different words. It could be fun?"

Sophie's face brightened.

"*Oui, oui*. I'll work out the French signals and you can do the English ones and then we'll change over."

Juliet began to wheel her chair across the room. Lucien watched while he lit a cigarette. He was fascinated by the ease with which this young girl seemed to be able to tackle his exacting ultra-sensitive daughter. He could see he was going to live to be grateful to Mrs. Ingram and – indirectly to Mimi, who was

47

the American's friend. It was quite apparent that Miss Browning understood Sophie's temperament and could make her happy. It was a miraculous change.

"We shall meet for dinner, Miss Browning," he said.

"Am I to have my meals with the family, then?" she asked.

"But of course!"

"Thank you, Monsieur."

"I'll come and say good night to Sophie later on."

"Yes, Monsieur."

Juliet, as she passed him, became suddenly conscious of something like an electric vibration that pierced her senses in an extraordinary way. She could not quite understand why the touch of Lucien de Maureville or the sound of his voice should affect her like that, but it was so.

He was the very opposite of his cousin, Michel, thank goodness, she thought.

His good looks were undeniable; they would have appealed to any girl. He was so tall and elegant; he moved so beautifully. She could not help admiring his finely-cut face with the deep dark eyes that he had bequeathed to his poor little daughter, the thick wavy black hair; and that proud curved mouth. He reminded her a little of a portrait she had once seen of Byron. But nothing else about Lucien de Maureville was Byronic. The poet had been self-indulgent and sensuous. There was strength in Lucien. He suggested a cool dignity, a chivalry that made him outstanding. He might look like a poet, but he was very obviously one hundred per cent a man, and a man of purpose. It made Juliet feel quite indignant to remember that his cousin had actually called him *a fool*. Perhaps that was because Lucien de Maureville possessed a sensitive quality which Michel would not understand as he himself lacked it so entirely. As for Mimi, Juliet was amazed to think that any woman would want to go away and stay away from such a husband as Lucien.

That electric current continued to spark and shiver through Juliet. Hastily she wheeled Sophie away into the dressing-room which adjoined the blue and white bathroom. The décor there was in keeping with the rest of Sophie's apartment. Old Blanche was muddling around. She started to run the bath as Sophie and her new governess came in.

"I can put Sophie to bed——" she began to mutter, fixing Juliet with a baleful eye. Juliet looked back at her rather doubtfully.

She had not seen much of the staff but she had already come up against a wall of antagonism from this old woman with which she knew she would have to contend.

"Whatever Sophie wishes—" she began.

Sophie, from the time Juliet arrived, had been enraptured with the English governess whose arrival she had so dreaded, and could not bear to let her out of her sight. And it had all begun as soon as Marino had shown Juliet on to the terrace, and Juliet had been introduced to her and said:

"*Bonjour,* Sophie, and, if I may say so, what a *beautiful* pink dress."

That had been the perfect beginning and won Sophie's heart at once. She had soon judged that Miss Browning was not going to be horrid, like Maman and Simone, about the pink dress which they despised.

"I want Miss Browning to put me to bed – go away, Blanche," she said.

Scowling, old Blanche scuttled away, muttering under her breath.

Juliet had plenty to do in her own room for she had not really got down to all her unpacking. Then there were her god-mother's clothes to sort. The long white skirt was one that had been left behind for her. Four exquisite American cotton frocks and even a midnight blue evening dress of pleated chiffon with a long blue chiffon coat to match which Juliet found enchanting. She wondered if she would *ever* have occasion to wear it – even here. Mrs. Ingram bought marvellous models – did most of her shopping on Fifth Avenue, and some when she came to France. She had bequeathed quite a small trousseau to the young Juliet. It was so singularly lucky that the middle-aged woman had the slender figure of a girl and chose young colours and designs that suited Juliet. It was exciting trying everything on. She must, she told herself, get down to writing a long letter of thanks to her godmother as soon as possible. She had so much to say 'Thank you' for.

Mrs. Ingram had obviously left in a tremendous hurry. The letter which Juliet found waiting for her was a hastily scribbled note.

Madly sorry I must desert you, darling. Do forgive me. My nephew and heir – you know – Bertie – in hospital in New York after serious car accident. Take everything you find in my blue suitcase.

49

Do hope you will be happy. Try not to form too bad an impression of Mimi. Try to get on with her. She isn't as bad as she seems, and do look after that unhappy child. She needs you.

Disappointing – but Juliet was quite sure there were many other excitements ahead of her. Life had only really just begun in the Château Roquemont.

In his own room, Lucien took off collar and tie, put on a dressing-gown and started to run his bath. The telephone bell rang. He answered it, hoping for one moment that it might be Mimi – calling from Paris – that she might want to know if Miss Browning had arrived safely and if all was well with Sophie. But that hope died as quickly as it had been born – like the others he had entertained before he began to be utterly disillusioned. He heard the voice of his cousin, Michel; never one he much cared for. He did not actively dislike his insufferably vain cousin, but he had no real use for Michel. Lately he had positively objected to the way he was hanging around Simone. He was not going to allow any nonsense between Michel and his young step-daughter. He was quite sure even Mimi would back him up in that. To his surprise, the Comte asked:

"And how is the beautiful Juliet?"

"*Juliet?* Do you mean Miss Browning?"

"I do."

"How did you know about her?"

A significant laugh from Michel. Lucien could imagine the familiar gesture of the third finger stroking that ridiculous moustache.

"I actually travelled on the Comet with the girl. You are in luck, *mon cher*. Governesses can be so lacking in personal charm or good looks. The little English girl has both. Allow me to congratulate you."

Lucien felt peculiarly annoyed. Michel nearly always managed to irritate him. The boy had a completely flippant, frivolous nature, and was a problem, Lucien knew, even to his own mother. In the past, *Tante* Cécile had had to call Lucien in to straighten out various tangles – with women, gambling, money difficulties, in which Michel had become involved. The boy seemed to have no moral stamina. Yet Lucien did not want to turn his back on him, or poor *Tante* Cécile, because of the blood-tie between them. It was a family loyalty that kept Lucien on friendly terms with Michel.

"I cannot see that you have any cause to congratulate me," Lucien said icily. "I've had nothing whatsoever to do with bringing the young English girl over here. It was arranged by Mimi and her American friend."

"Nevertheless she is charming and you must admit it."

"I've only just this moment met her."

"I want to see her again. We got on rather well during our journey."

"Splendid," said Lucien, in the same tone of voice. "But if you'll excuse me, Michel, I've just got home and I'm tired. My bath is running over."

"Give the little Juliet my regards and tell her I'll come as soon as I can to show her the *Côte d'Azur*," said Michel, laughing.

Lucien rang off.

That conversation somehow spoiled the genuine pleasure he had felt when he watched Miss Browning and Sophie together a few moments ago.

So Miss Browning and Michel 'had got on well', had they? He hoped that was not true. One could take many of the things that Michel said with a grain of salt. He was often incapable of speaking the truth. *On the other hand what do I know about this English girl*, Lucien asked himself. *I've yet to find out what she is really like. She's being very good with Sophie, but how do I know what sort of character she has, where men are concerned, for instance. She may be a terror – she may have played up to Michel – how do I know?*

How could he know anything – one could only learn from bitter experience. When first he had looked into Mimi's large aquamarine eyes he had thought them as pure and sweet as the sky. He no longer trusted any woman – no, not after *Mimi*.

He was in one of his dark moods when finally he walked downstairs to join the newly-arrived governess for the evening meal.

With a strong love of tradition, Lucien had always tried to keep up the gracious living which he knew to be rapidly dying out today. He had two sides to his character; the one that enjoyed being served at table by a trained waiter; the other that was simple and boyish; for at heart he was a man who would gladly have sat in his own kitchen and shared the work with a wife who loved him as much as he loved her.

After the heavy burden that two wars had heaped on the family fortunes – he felt it would be absurd to behave too grandly. He would never be like that arrogant and exacting old seigneur, his grandfather. That old rascal, as Lucien well knew, had enjoyed bullying the peasants who were his serfs and making humble slaves of his servants.

Lucien's father had changed all that. He had served in the Army during the war, two years of which he spent in a German prison camp. During those awful years, Lucien's mother had lived alone in this Château, and worked her fine aristocratic fingers to the bone.

Lucien as a small boy of nine or ten could well remember when the Germans had occupied Roquemont. The Château was turned into a headquarters for some of the high-up German Generals. Lucien could remember his beautiful, distinguished mother being forced to hand over most of her linen and silver, her jewellery and furs, to these men to take back to Berlin to their wives or sweethearts. She had even cooked for them. Old Blanche had suffered with her, for she had been younger then and open to the degradation of their treatment.

Lucien, himself, had learned to chop wood and light fires so as to help his mother when she was ill – which was often the case. After the Capitaine André de Maureville had returned from his prison camp and D-Day had released France from the vicious pincers of the Swastika, he had said to Lucien:

"You have done well, *mon petit*. You have been a good son to your mother, as one day I know full well you will be a good husband to the wife you choose."

With tremendous sadness, Lucien often recalled those words. Sometimes he even asked himself what good it was being too idealistic. He had tried so hard to be good to his wife; only to come up against that icy wall of indifference, sometimes of sheer hatred. Once he had cried to her:

"I would rather be a poor man in a cottage knowing that my wife loved me, than the master of this loveless house."

She had given her tinkling laugh.

"My dear Lucien, how boring you are! Don't try the love-in-a-cottage angle with me, I beg you. Roquemont to me is only bearable because you have money and my life here is luxurious. Poverty with any man would kill me!"

Tonight, after the heat of the day, it still seemed to Lucien warm and breathless. He wore a silk jacket, soft collar and bow tie.

Downstairs in the salon, he found that Hortense – a nice-looking middle-aged domestic help from the village, whom Lucien infinitely preferred to Mimi's cheeky personal maid – had already switched on the lamps. The long room was full of soft golden light. This room was another of Mimi's modern master-pieces of décor. It might have been a salon in a Paris flat instead of the Château. This irritated Lucien. His taste was for old things. This was all too new and smart – too contrived. White carpet, and ivory velvet covered chairs, taffeta curtains. The wallpaper was Japanese silk – of a pale cinnamon colour. The curtains and cushions matched.

Green malachite urns served as table-lamps with immensely tall velvet shades; there were one or two startling paintings, in ultra-modern frames, by contemporary French artists. Mimi and Simone both raved about these but to Lucien the subjects were vague and the colours too violent. The fireplace was very flat and modern – without a mantel-shelf. It had all been designed by a Paris architect whom Mimi was mad about when she first moved here. Lucien detested it all. On either side of the fireplace there were built-in glass shelves that could be flood-lit at the turn of a switch. On these shelves there was a fine collection of Meissen groups. But on the whole Mimi's salon gave Lucien a sense of coldness, of affectation. He infinitely preferred his old library, with its antiques and tapestries – the thousands of leather-bound books.

Mimi frequently changed her mind about her décor. Since their marriage she had already altered this room and her own bedroom twice. Recently, she and Simone had even been discussing getting rid of the new white and cinnamon scheme. Lucien had never dreamed any woman could be as restless or so quickly discontented as his wife. She created an atmosphere of unquiet and dissatisfaction for everybody else at Roquemont, too:

The bills were given to Lucien to pay. He had learned that if he raised objections there would be scenes. These he tried to avoid. When Mimi was in a bad mood, little Sophie invariably got the backwash of her temper. Simone didn't care. She was too used to her spoiled mother and if Mimi quarrelled with Lucien, it was of no account to Simone. But when Sophie heard her mother's high-pitched voice raised in anger, it reduced her to tears. Simone only shrugged her shoulders. If anything, she sometimes pitied her stepfather and tried to cajole him into giving her a cheque.

The hot-house flowers in a huge Ming bowl on the piano were glorious and tastefully displayed; Lucien had to admit that. Mimi was clever with flower-arrangements; it was the only job she did in the house – and she did it well.

There were times when Lucien drove over to Mougins to dine with Paul de Clermont, a friend who was a not very successful writer, and whose wife, Annette, did all the cooking and most of the housework. They were a charming pair. They had nothing of value in the place. But when Lucien was with the de Clermonts in their modest villa, watching their domestic happiness, he wished with all his heart that he could exchange places with Paul.

He looked now at his watch. It was a quarter to eight. Hortense came in to announce dinner.

"Where is Mademoiselle?" he asked her.

"I do not know, Monsieur. She is not in her room for I tapped on her door just now. *La petite* is asleep so she is not with her."

Lucien raised his brows. Perhaps unpunctuality was going to be one of the English girl's failings; not that he particularly minded. But when he entered the dining-room and stood for a moment leaning over the back of his chair, and the girl was still missing, he felt vaguely irritated.

"Hortense, didn't you let Mademoiselle know what time we dined?"

"*Oui,* Monsieur. I told her when I took up Sophie's supper tray."

Lucien frowned. What was Miss Browning doing – the first course, so Hortense said, was a cheese soufflé. it would be completely spoiled.

"By the way did Sophie *eat* her supper?" he asked the woman.

"Every morsel, Monsieur. Cook was delighted."

"I am, also," said Lucien, smiling now.

It was usually a problem to get Sophie to eat any meal; her supper she often left altogether. She had a poor appetite. Hortense was a nice woman, much sorrier for the little girl than were the rest of the staff who sided with Madame. She added, in a pleased voice:

"Mees seems very good with Sophie, Monsieur. She can do anything with her. When I first took the tray, Sophie refused her omelette and Mees went down on one knee in front of her and begged that the *petite Princesse* should accept the food from her humble slave. It was very funny, Monsieur. I laughed and

54

Sophie laughed too, for Mees had tied the serviette over her mouth as though it were a yashmak."

Lucien's stern lips softened. Well, what on earth did it matter how late Miss Browning was for her dinner if she could beguile Sophie into eating a whole omelette!

Chapter Six

LUCIEN was already seated when Juliet suddenly rushed into the room. He stood up politely. She was pink-cheeked and breathless.

"Oh, I *do* beg your pardon, Monsieur. I have only just realized what time it is."

"Please sit down," he said. "I hope your *soufflé* will not be spoiled."

Juliet took her seat, still breathing rather fast. She began to explain why she was so late. She had come downstairs half an hour ago and wandered out into the big hall and then up the stairs to the gallery. She had been so fascinated with all the portraits she had not realized that time was flying. She hoped Monsieur would be able to lend her some kind of pamphlet or book to read about the history of the de Maurevilles and who all those people were – especially those dressed as courtiers of the Court of Marie-Antoinette. She was so interested in the French Revolution. Had any of the de Maurevilles gone to the guillotine in those terrible days? Were they attached to the Court?

Explanations and questions tumbled out so rapidly and naïvely that Lucien now smiled quite broadly. What a funny little thing she was, this English god-daughter of Mrs. Ingram. She looked very young indeed this evening with that slightly freckled face all pink, and those big eyes shining. What a funny little snub nose! There was no back-combed, sleek, soignée hair style of the type Mimi and Simone displayed when they returned from a Cannes coiffure. Juliet's hair was natural – well-brushed, up-springing glossy-brown. No artifice about her at all. But the dress was chic, thought Lucien. Grey tie-silk with a pattern of huge red roses. (It happened to be one of Mrs. Ingram's expensive models which she had left for Juliet. As Mrs. Ingram was one degree thinner, it clung rather tightly to Juliet's slim but rounded body). Lucien became suddenly aware of the young girl's small exquisite breasts tilted against the silk. He looked away and continued to speak with cool courtesy.

"I have many books about my family. You shall certainly read some of them."

He was delighted that she showed this interest. He remembered how once he had started to read one of those books to Mimi and suddenly she had yawned and fallen asleep.

"I hear that Sophie ate all her supper, which is unusual," he added.

Juliet, who was now calming down and enjoying her own dinner with a healthy appetite, nodded.

"Every bit. She is a darling little girl. If one goes the right way about it, it is so easy to tackle her."

"You're the first of the many we have had to care for her who has not thought her most difficult. I congratulate you."

"Oh, maybe I'm the new broom sweeping clean," said Juliet modestly. "She may get tired of playing games with me."

Lucien smiled.

"I have not heard that English expression about the 'new broom' for years. It takes me back to my boyhood in London."

"It's really rather a good saying," laughed Juliet.

"In this case I am sure it is not applicable. I know my Sophie. You have touched her heart by playing up to her so sweetly. She will not change her mind. I can see now that Mrs. Ingram was wise in her choice. I admit I was a little worried at first about your coming."

Now he asked Hortense to pour some wine for Mademoiselle. Juliet put a hand over her glass.

"Please – I don't drink."

"Ah, but in France you must learn just to taste wine and this is very light."

"I'd really rather have just water."

"Perhaps with some fresh orange juice and ice," suggested Hortense.

"That sounds lovely," said Juliet.

Everything was lovely here, she thought, even if she found some of the decorations in the west wing a trifle too contemporary and bizarre for her liking. The furniture all seemed to have rather odd shapes. This dining-room, however, she adored. It had the kind of furnishing that she felt in keeping with the old place. The long rosewood table, the beautiful high-backed chairs with tapestry seats; the French hunting prints against panelled walls; olive-green, silver-threaded curtains.

On the table stood two silver candelabra, each holding four tall lighted candles. The centre-piece was an old French-type, ornate silver bowl on a stand laden with peaches, muscatel-grapes and pears. The crystal goblets were old, and of beautiful design; the gold and white china exquisite Limoges.

She decided that she must start to learn as much as she could about France and French antiques. She was thrilled because Monsieur had praised her and already thought that she was going to be good for Sophie. Being 'good for Sophie' would not be without its drawbacks for her; of course Juliet knew that. The poor crippled child was extremely exacting and she, Juliet, would have little time to herself, but after all that was what she had come for. She wasn't going to let it worry her.

Lucien began to discuss her position here.

"It has all been very hastily arranged. No mention was made, perhaps, of salary, or your time off. I am so very sorry, Miss Browning, that my wife had to go away so suddenly but she should be back tomorrow. All details can be settled then."

"Oh, that's quite all right, Monsieur."

"I am quite sure you will be paid a fair salary. To give you some line – Mlle Duprès, who was last with us, asked for four hundred francs a month – new francs, that is."

Juliet made a hasty mental calculation. There were thirteen-point-five new francs to the pound; about £30 a month! Goodness, she thought, marvellous pay, when one was kept into the bargain. It would mean £30 in her pocket. Three pounds a week more than she had been getting as a trainee in the Wandsworth Home.

In her frank rather direct way, she exclaimed:

"It seems rather too much, Monsieur."

He was surprised. Could there be such a thing as a woman who was not ready to snatch at every franc offered, he thought, cynically. She was really a nice little thing. He said gently:

"We shall see. We will discuss it all with Madame when she comes home, Miss Browning."

"Oh, please, c-couldn't I be c-called Juliet?" she stammered. "Miss Browning sounds so terribly formal. I've already asked Sophie to call me Juliet."

"That's very kind of you. I'm sure we should all like that," he said.

The excellent meal went on. Juliet, shyly glancing at her employer, was a little baffled by Sophie's father. He was rather a strange man – terribly reserved, she imagined. It wouldn't be easy to get to *know* him. He was not like anyone she had ever met before. He seemed to her quite a part of the old Château; with his air of dignity, of reticence, of old chivalry. He was a little scaring, perhaps, yet *very* attractive; really, wonderfully handsome. His thin fine-boned face looked tired, but his skin was bronzed by the Mediterranean sun and brown against the white silk collar. What black, *black* hair, and dark, *dark* eyes! She thought suddenly how little he resembled his cousin. Now she brought up Michel's name.

"By an extraordinary chance, I found myself sitting in the Comet next to your cousin – the Comte de Condine."

She immediately sensed that Lucien did not care much for his cousin. His voice had quite changed when he said:

"So Michel has just told me, over the telephone."

Silence. Juliet felt awkward. She cleared her voice and went on:

"He seems – very – gay."

"Very," agreed Lucien dryly.

Again silence. Juliet hoped this meant that Michel was not as frequent a visitor to the Château as he had suggested.

Suddenly Lucien looked directly at her with his dark brooding eyes.

"If it is not impertinent, I would like to know Miss B – er – Juliet – if things continue to go well that is – if you think you could settle down with us for the next year or so? I am most anxious for Sophie not to have any more changes."

"I shall want to stay. Indeed I shall," she said eagerly. "I don't like changes either, although I understood from my godmother that I was only coming on trial."

"Quite so. But I repeat, *if* all goes well, I'd like you to agree to stay. I hope you have no – er – ties."

Juliet shook her head. She told him about her father and the brother in the Merchant Navy.

"Poor Daddy and Nicky are all I have now that my mother has gone," she ended sadly. "My life is absolutely my own. Daddy is marvellous – he doesn't try to control me."

A suspicion of a smile curved Lucien's lips.

"I don't think you seem the type who needs much control, if I may say so."

She laughed. The tension, raised by the mention of the Comte de Condine's name, eased off. Then Lucien asked:

"And you are not – affianced – engaged, I think is the correct English?"

"No," she said flushing, "I just have a doctor-friend who worked with me in the Home – he wanted me to marry him, but I – well, no – not him – and I don't want to get married for a long time, anyhow."

Lucien sipped his wine. He was a little surprised that this charming simple English girl was not further involved with some man. She must be unusually dedicated to her work. She was a type he had rarely before encountered. So young, yet so different, for instance, from the nineteen- or twenty-year-olds whom his stepdaughter sometimes brought here. It was part of Simone's nature to dislike being thought immature. She chose friends older than herself. But some of her heavily made up glamour girl-friends thought of little but sex and having fun. They could not be more different from Juliet Browning.

Suddenly the thought leapt into Lucien's mind:

I wonder if Mimi will like her.

It was a thought full of anxiety, tinged with menace. He knew his wife. If for any reason Mimi took a dislike to Juliet, she would try to get the girl out of the Château in a couple of hours.

Then Lucien set his teeth.

'Not this time,' he mentally decided. 'Juliet came here at the request of Mimi and her friend and if I think it the right thing for Sophie, I shall not allow either Mimi or Simone to drive her away.'

He heard Juliet's soft voice (he was so glad it was low and soft – he liked English voices.)

"I hope my very poor French isn't too much of a drawback."

"No – you speak above average French for an English girl. Sophie will learn English quite quickly with your help. She did have an English Nannie when she was six years old. She knows a few words already."

"Yes, I noticed she understands a bit."

"My wife speaks quite good English and my stepdaughter had a year in an English school in Switzerland. We sent her there expressly to learn the language. Her accent is bad but she will be able to talk to you."

"Do tell me more about Simone," said Juliet shyly.

They were reaching the end of the meal. Some excellent cheeses had been served on a big board, then fruit. Juliet began to peel a peach. It looked luscious, she thought; and such a treat. Poor darling Mummy had been so fond of peaches. Juliet liked them, too.

Lucien leaned back in his chair and watched the young girl skinning the round golden fruit with a silver knife. Hers were not particularly pretty hands: they were a little too square and boyish. The nails were well-kept but short and unvarnished. A curious thing . . . he felt there was a warmth and kindliness about those hands that were completely missing in the hands of his own womenfolk. Once he had thought Mimi's delicately pointed fingers and long glossy nails most exciting. Simone's were a replica. He had learned to associate those polished nails and tapering hands with uselessness – and greed.

He tried to say the best he could about his stepdaughter.

"She is considered a very beautiful girl. Like her mother she has these extraordinary eyes – the colour is what I think might be described as ice-blue, with naturally black lashes and brows. Very striking!"

"It sounds terrific!" exclaimed Juliet.

"Simone is not clever but she is bright and gay, and chatters like a magpie and spends a lot of time enjoying herself," continued Lucien with a faint smile.

"I rather envy her——" began Juliet.

But he broke in abruptly:

"You needn't!"

Juliet was not quite sure what lay behind that remark. She asked no more questions about Simone.

Coffee was served in the white and cinnamon salon. Lucien lit a cigar. Standing with his back to the mantelpiece, he nodded towards the piano.

"Mrs. Ingram said that you play."

As always when she was challenged about her attributes, Juliet blushed.

"Oh, yes – but not very well."

"Well enough, according to your godmother, to teach my child."

"Yes, I think so – certainly enough to teach her primary lessons. Before my mother died – and we had a home, all of us – we went in for music. Nick, my brother, can play the violin. I used to accompany him. Mummy sang, and I played for her. Daddy adored it all although he is no musician."

"I'd like you to play for me now," said Lucien.

She got up and put down her empty coffee cup. She was frightened, but she never could bear the sort of person who when asked to play skirted around with coquettish cries of *'Oh, I couldn't!'* or *'Please don't ask me! . . .'*

"Here goes, Juliet," she said to herself, and setting her lips firmly, walked to the piano. She found that it was a Steinway. Lucien came forward and opened up the lid.

"I don't like a muffled tone," he said.

She felt her heart beat rather fast. The perspiration pearled on her forehead. Monsieur was a handsome and attractive man but there was something a little scaring about him; perhaps his old-world dignity – his grand manner; and he so rarely smiled. She couldn't believe that he was a happy man. Remembering the strong hints that the Comte had dropped while they were on the plane, about disruptions between the de Maurevilles, she felt pretty sure all was not well with their marriage.

"I'm not very good at improvising—" she began.

"There is plenty of music for you to choose from," he said quickly, opened a cupboard, and found a pile of scores and sheet-music, which he placed in front of her.

She looked through the songs and found one which her own mother used to sing. A French song. It was sentimental and belonged to a bygone age; the sort of ballad that had no meeting point whatsoever with modern music; the type that even Nicky was mad about these days. Yet Juliet loved this song, *Ninon*. It gave her quite a heartache as she played the opening bars, for it took her back to those happy evenings before Mummy's death had broken up the old family life.

As soon as she touched the keys of the magnificent piano, she gained confidence. De Maureville, standing behind her, recognized the fact that this girl might not be technically good but played quite charmingly. He looked over her shoulder and began to sing, very softly, the words of the song she had chosen.

> Ninon, Ninon, que fais-tu de la vie?
> Comment vis-tu?
> Toi qui n'as pas d'amour! . . .

Juliet was positively thrilled. Lucien had a light but pleasant baritone. He also sang with feeling.

She recalled her mother singing the English translation:

62

'*Ninon – Ninon, what are you doing with life – how can you live – you who have no love!*"

Lucien's voice gained impetus. He laid his cigar down on an ashtray and began to sing more freely. He found himself thoroughly enjoying it. He loved to sing. Because of the war, he had received no early training. But realizing that he had 'something of a voice', he had once taken lessons with an Italian teacher in Paris. But that was just before he met Mimi.

It almost shocked him to realize, in these few moments, that this was the first time since his marriage that he had bothered to ask anyone to accompany him. No – that wasn't strictly true – there had been that one unhappy evening, he now remembered, when his friends, Paul and Annette, had come over to dine and meet the newly-installed bride. Annette had asked him to sing. After they had gone home Mimi had spoiled the whole evening, which she so often did, with cruel criticism.

"I wish you wouldn't choose those stupid old songs. Anybody would imagine you had been born in the nineteenth century, Lucien. Songs after dinner. *Mon Dieu* – you're too frightfully old-fashioned at times."

"I did not know that it was old-fashioned to sing," he had said, treating her remark as a joke, but she had continued:

"A professional concert is one thing – songs in the salon another. *Mon Dieu* – you are as sentimental as that stupid Annette Clermont. It bores me; it makes me want to giggle."

After that, Lucien had shut up like a clam and never bothered to sing again.

Tonight the old urge returned. It was a harmless enough form of entertainment, and, after all, Mimi wasn't here to deride or giggle.

At the end of *Ninon*, he applauded the young English girl's accompaniment. Then he found a song in a book of Schumann's songs.

J'ai pardonné!

The French words were tense and passionate like the music. Juliet knew it although her mother had never sung it, but she followed Lucien perfectly. She managed to make a rough translation of the lyric. It was to the effect that the lover had forgiven the love that had hurt him but that his heart was still plunged in grief.

She was moved and quite troubled because she sensed beyond

63

his artistic interpretation an intolerable pain that must rise from de Maureville's very heart.

His voice rang out in the final words.

> Et ton printemps aux larmes destiné
> J'ai pardonné.

Juliet repeated to herself *larmes destiné* – 'tears of destiny – of fate'. It was typical of Schumann. He wrote the saddest of songs. What sad fate had pursued Lucien?

Suddenly the cool voice of a woman (like a shower of ice-water) cut through the golden ballad and the piano accompaniment, followed by a clapping of hands.

"*Bravo!* How absolutely charming! What a sweet reception for me, *mon très cher* Lucien."

Chapter Seven

JULIET swung round on the piano-stool. Lucien broke off in the middle of a stanza. It was as though the warm lamp-lit room turned in a split second into a frigidaire. It seemed to Juliet that they all froze. Walking across the salon came one of the most beautiful women she had ever seen. She looked a mere girl, she was so slender, so *petite,* until one got near enough to notice the small lines that pulled the perfect lips downward sulkily. But at a distance Mme de Maureville looked no older than Juliet.

She wore black and white with true Parisienne chic – a silk coat over a white dress with a pattern of huge black flowers. No hat; the thick ash-blonde hair was brushed upward into a little crown encircled with black velvet ribbon, tied into a big bow at the back.

There were water-clear aquamarines in her ears; an enormous diamond and aquamarine brooch on the lapel of her coat, and she carried short black gloves and a black velvet bag. She might, Juliet decided, have stepped straight off a *Vogue* cover.

She fastened her gaze upon Juliet who got up and stood there, feeling slightly silly and awkward.

Lucien said:

"I had no idea you were coming back tonight, Mimi."

"Well, I don't think I need have hurried back now that I see how well you are being entertained in my absence, my dear," said Mimi with her famous bell-like laugh.

Juliet flushed and glanced towards Monsieur. He had changed completely in these few minutes. His expression was wooden, his voice quite hard.

"Oh, yes, it has been a very agreeable evening. Miss Browning plays delightfully. It will be nice for Sophie to have such a teacher."

Mimi laid her bag and gloves down on the arm of the sofa, advanced to Juliet and held out a hand with a smile behind which Juliet felt lay a whole host of disagreeable things which she did not understand (nor did she wish to).

"So this is my friend Juliet's god-daughter. Welcome to Roquemont, Mademoiselle."

"Thank you, Madame," murmured Juliet.

Mimi's hand was cool and felt almost boneless. Juliet quickly dropped it. Mimi went on, still smiling, fixing her with that blue, glacial stare.

"I have heard so much about you from my friend," continued Mimi; her English grammar was good but she rolled her r's. "I'm glad you were able to come to us. I'm sure as my husband says, your gift for music will be of great benefit to my poor unhappy little child."

Lucien cut in:

"Sophie is neither poor nor unhappy. She has taken a great fancy to Juliet – they get on very well and I think in future Sophie will be very much more content than she has been in the past."

Mimi raised her brows and threw him an amused look.

"Juliet? Ah, yes – you mean Mlle Browning."

"She has asked us to call her by her christian name – it is less stiff and formal," said Lucien coldly.

Mimi turned her gaze upon Juliet again.

"I'm so sorry not to have been here to receive you. As a matter of fact, like your godmother, I was called away on urgent business, but I got through things earlier than I had imagined, so flew down to Nice by private plane this evening."

"Private plane?" echoed Lucien sharply.

Mimi gave him her sweet frozen smile.

"Yes – you know, my friend, Professor Sternburg, had to come south for a sudden consultation – a patient in the Cannes Clinic. His chauffeur met us at the Airport. I drove with Max to the Clinic since it was a matter of life and death, then his chauffeur brought me on to Roquemont."

Silence. Juliet felt that she could cut the atmosphere with a knife. All the brightness, friendliness and peace had gone. Mme de Maureville, who looked so golden and exquisite, brought with her an extraordinary aura of darkness. It could almost be called sinister.

Lucien looked at his wife intently. He was never quite sure of her and especially on occasions like this. Of course he was aware that her applauding of the song had been insincere – like the welcome she had just offered Juliet; and he was perfectly certain he knew what was in her mind. She was not in the least glad that he had spent a pleasant evening – it had been pure sarcasm when she had suggested that after all she need not have hurried home. As for Professor Max Sternburg and his private plane, for the last six months or more Mimi had been seeing far too much of that man. He was German-born. No doubt brilliant; in his early forties, and already with a huge clientele; mostly neurotic women. He specialized in nervous diseases. Mimi had met him at a party and Max, who was a bachelor, had since made it obvious, even to Lucien, that he had fallen for Mimi's charms. He was a rich and successful man. Mimi seemed to find him fascinating. But Lucien did not like Germans, nor ever would, and it worried him when Mimi indulged in one of her sudden infatuations which were growing more frequent as the years went by. She became less and less interested in her own husband. Her conduct with men, at times, disturbed and offended Lucien. Not only did she lack honour or integrity, but he thought her behaviour such a bad example for Simone.

"Where *is* Simone?" he asked.

Mimi stiffled a yawn, and, taking a black Russian cigarette from a small jewelled box, snapped on a lighter and began to smoke.

"I'm tired after that flight! It was a bit bumpy. I left Simone in Paris, dear Lucien, with one of her girl-friends whose mother asked if she might stay with them for a couple of days. She'll join us for the week-end."

"I see," said Lucien.

Mimi yawned again and turned her glittering blue eyes on Juliet who was wondering how she could best bid these two good-bye and escape from the room.

"I'm such a devoted wife, Madamoiselle – I felt I could not stay away from my husband a moment longer," she laughed.

Not a word from Lucien, but Juliet, looking at him, thought it terrible because his eyes held such an expression of cynicism. And he was thinking:

'*How like Mimi to park her daughter conveniently, then enjoy a tête-à-tête in the clouds with her latest admirer.*'

He wondered if she could ever speak the whole truth or behave as the mother of Simone and Sophie *should* do.

"Well, I'll bid you good night Mees Browning," said Mimi, "or shall I also call you *Juliet*? I'm very attached to your god-mother."

Juliet seized hold of this one link she had with Mme de Maureville.

"Aunt Ju *is* wonderful, isn't she? And she's always been so good to me."

For the third time Mimi put the tips of her fingers to her mouth and yawned. How amusing, she thought, to find dear Lucien opening up his heart in music in such a ridiculous way with the English governess. Whether she was Mrs. Ingram's goddaughter or not, Juliet must be kept in her place. She must remain a behind-the-scenes-girl. But if she got on well with Sophie, so much the better; it would be a relief. She didn't think Juliet would be much trouble; rather nice eyes and that good English skin they all had over there – but snub nose, freckles and frankness – m'm – that combination was anathema to the sophisticated Mimi.

"What a divine dress," she said suddenly, eyeing the girl up and down.

"It was Aunt Ju's. She left it here in a suitcase for me," said Juliet. "I am lucky. I can wear her lovely clothes and she is so generous to me."

Stupid, Mimi decided. Why let anybody know that your dress was second-hand?

She turned and walked towards the door.

"Do go on with your music, you two; don't let me disturb you."

As she walked out of the salon and shut the door, she left behind that frigid atmosphere and a faint perfume of Guerlain's *Shalimar*. Ever afterwards, Juliet was to associate that slightly musky, exotic, and very expensive scent with Lucien's wife.

Into her mind suddenly there filtered the memory of Mrs. Ingram's note and those words: *Try not to form too bad an impression of Mimi . . . she isn't as bad as she seems . . .*

I shall have to try very hard because my first impression is far from good, thought Juliet, rather miserably.

Lucien was closing the piano.

"Let me put away the music—" began Juliet.

"No, you can leave it to me. Good night – I hope you will find everything in your room that you need," he said. His voice was cool – his attitude of ease and friendliness – the mutual interest they had so far shared during the evening had vanished. His face had grown mask-like. Juliet felt suddenly unhappy as well as

68

embarrassed. She said : "Good night, Monsieur" and left the salon.

The de Maureville suite and guest-rooms were upstairs. A beautiful modern curved staircase with wrought-iron banisters led up to the pine-panelled corridor. Sophie's rooms were on the ground-floor. Juliet's room adjoined them. As she reached her own door, she saw Sophie's door open and the lights on. Mimi de Maureville was standing by Sophie's bed smoking. She had taken off her coat.

"You ought to be asleep at this hour, my pet," she was saying, in French, lightly but reprovingly.

The child was sitting up, hunched, gnome-like, her black untidy hair tumbled around her small face. She cried:

"Maman, Maman. I heard you drive into the courtyard. Is Simone back, too?"

"No, she isn't and please go back to sleep at once. It's nearly eleven o'clock."

"But Maman, I heard you drive in. It woke me up. That's why I called out to you."

Juliet, watching from the shadows, saw the mother bend down and kiss the child on both cheeks.

"*Bonne nuit, chérie,* and go to sleep now, do."

"Oh, Maman, you smell so heavenly. I *do* love you, Maman."

Mimi said something in French and in such a low voice, that Juliet could not hear the words, but she felt it could not be very affectionate or sympathetic because the child immediately responded with a protest.

"No, I'm not being silly. I *do* love you, Maman."

"All right, all right, and I love you if you do as you're told" Mimi said irritably, then added more sharply, "Mind – you'll burn your fingers on my cigarette, *petite imbécile.*"

Juliet was appalled. How could any woman be so unsympathetic in the face of all the adoration her crippled child lavished on her? She should, Juliet thought, be sitting on that bed, giving Sophie love and tenderness in return. Now Mimi spoke again and this time, Juliet understood.

"I'll see you tomorrow, *ma petite.* Leave go of my hand now, please, there's a good child."

"But Maman, I want to tell you something. I've got a new governess. I like her lots. She lets me be Princess Sophie and she is a Princess, too, from another land. I've captured her and—"

"Oh, *mon Dieu*," broke in Mimi, "don't let's have that Princess rubbish at this time of night, my darling, I implore you."

"It isn't rubbish—" Sophie was working herself up into a state. Juliet could recognize the signs. To be able to laugh at herself, to have a real sense of humour, did not come easily to a child who, like Sophie, had been deformed from birth. These were things the child would have to learn, like self-control, but the very worst thing for her was a lack of understanding and affection from her own mother. Mme de Maureville dislodged herself impatiently from her small daughter's clinging hands.

"Save the Princess business for your dear father or for your governess if she likes the silly game, but I really must go to bed. Now don't cry, silly. I've brought you a marvellous box of chocolates from Paris. I'll give it to you in the morning."

Sophie burst into tears.

"I don't want the chocolates! I don't want them!"

"Oh, *pour l'amour de Dieu* . . .!" began Mimi, exasperated. Then she saw Juliet outside in the corridor.

"I'll leave her to you. For goodness sake calm her down. She always gets into these moods if I won't do exactly what she wants. She's been atrociously spoiled by her father, I'm afraid."

Lucien arrived on the scene. As he was about to mount the stairs to his own room, he had heard Sophie sobbing.

"What is the matter now?" he demanded, wearily.

tween her lips, shrugged, and brushed past him.

Mimi, throwing her coat over her arm, put her cigarette be-

"It's all your fault, *mon cher*. This stupid Princess stuff which you encourage. She has to start it even at this time of night. Oh, well . . . let her new governess deal with her. I'm dead tired. Good night, Lucien."

Lucien did not even bother to answer her. He stood silently watching Juliet. She went down on one knee by the bed and offered the weeping child a glass of the fresh lemon and water which had been left beside her bed.

"If the Princess Sophie will agree to take this from my hand – it will soothe her. It is a magic potion," she said in her best French. "It will bring the Princess beautiful dreams."

And this worked like magic. Sophie's tears immediately dried. Her lips trembled into a smile. She whimpered a few words about naughty Maman, and the next moment was gulping the lemonade thirstily. Then she allowed Juliet to re-arrange her

70

pillows and make her comfortable again. The child felt hot and damp to Juliet. The Mediterranean night was very close. She sponged Sophie's face then covered her with a sheet and sat by the bed for a few moments. As soon as Sophie's heavy eyelids drooped and she slept again, Juliet turned out the lamp and tip-toed from the room.

She almost ran into Sophie's father and stepped back with an apology. He bowed his head slightly.

"*Merci* – thank you very much, Juliet. *Bonne nuit.*"

She walked into her own bedroom and shut the door.

For a moment she stood staring around her. The governess's room was not as elegant as some of the others, but it was a good deal more luxurious than anything Juliet had ever possessed. All rosy-pink and pearl-grey with French painted furniture, book-case and small desk. Charming roses on the chintz curtains and bedspread. She even had her own bathroom. Slowly she advanced to the bed and sat down on the edge. What a long, long way from the shabby Wandsworth Home, and what an astonishing end to a long exciting day.

Now there was silence in the Château – broken occasionally by the sad hoot of an owl down there somewhere in the darkness of the thickly wooded grounds.

The memory of Mme de Maureville's extraordinary coldness of heart, coupled with her equally extraordinary beauty; and of the poor little child who was almost a psychopathic case; of that interesting and delightful dinner with Lucien earlier on; all that had happened since she arrived in Roquemont crowded into Juliet's mind. But everything seemed to lead toward one focal point of remembrance ... the sight of Lucien's dark, pain-filled eyes, and his voice singing:

Ninon, Ninon, how can you live without love?

How *did* he live without it, she asked herself. Oh, poor M. de Maureville! He, who could sing like that ... be so patient and sweet with his child ... so good ... and married to such an utterly selfish person ... how *could* he exist without love?

Asking herself that question several times, Juliet found herself near to tears.

71

Chapter Eight

JULIET wondered on that night whether she would ever care for Mimi de Maureville sufficiently to stay in this job. It was not that she didn't want to; it had been made plain to her that Sophie, like many children do, had developed a kind of 'schoolgirl crush' on her. She could be of great use to the child. She was also well aware that Monsieur needed her here – again – for the child's sake. But she was so antipathetic to Madame that she doubted if she would be able to bear looking at the beautiful mask-like face, or hearing daily that high treble voice which seemed either to give orders, or ask for favours. She was the exact opposite of the type of woman Juliet admired: like the simple, frank charming mother who had died – or the Matron of the Wandsworth Home – a freckled red-haired Scotswoman with a gruff manner and a huge heart.

There were so many nice people in the world that it seeemed to Juliet a waste of time to live with or work for someone as self-seeking as Mimi de Maureville.

On the other hand, on Juliet's second day at the Château, Madame seemed delighted with Juliet. The sarcasm and veiled hostility of the night before had vanished. She sent for Juliet while she was drinking her coffee in bed that next morning, and could not have been sweeter to the girl.

"It was a marvellous plan of dear Juliet Ingram's recommending you. You're the ideal person for my poor little Sophie. I must write and tell old Juliet. Of course, I'm a hopeless correspondent . . ." Mimi trilled with laughter. "I expect I'll have to make Simone write for me."

Juliet stood at the foot of the big bed, hands locked behind her, as though she was taking orders from Matron.

There was nothing very chic about Miss Browning today, Mimi was thinking. What a badly-cut skirt (moygashel) blue like the inexpensive thin sleeveless pullover. No make-up, except a coral pink lipstick. Fresh – nice but *too ingénue*, in Mimi's opinion. Tractable – yes, she ought to be able to manage Juliet's god-daughter. And it would be most useful to have someone in the place who could control Sophie!

As in all human beings, there was something of good in Mimi. She actually apologized to Juliet this morning with sincerity. In her pretty English with its strong French accent, she said:

"I am d-r-readful with children. I am sure it shocks you. Forgive me – but I am just not one of those born mothers. Sophie requires special love and attention and I can't give them as I should. You *are* shocked, aren't you? I can see it in your eyes."

Juliet coloured.

"Not really. People can't all be the same. I've known one or two girls who don't want children at all. Of course I don't quite understand it, because I so adore them."

Mimi leaned back on her nest of pillows – big square pillows in exquisite white linen cases, the borders embroidered with deep blue flowers. Never in Juliet's life had she seen such a wonderful bed. The spread was blue and silver. The walls and ceiling were covered with a stretched material of silvery almond-green.

Green and silver curtains framed three tall windows, from which one could look towards the lake and the woods beyond. The Venetian blinds, with the slats sufficiently open to let in a drift of golden sunshine, had not yet been lifted.

Mimi wore a dark blue chiffon nightgown – a flattering contrast to the alabaster white of her still youthful throat and shoulders.

The room was permeated with that now recognizable scent of *Shalimar*. When Juliet had first come in, it had been so untidy in here that it had made her gasp. Lingerie, stockings, all Mimi's bits and pieces scattered over the floor. A long painted dressing-table, backed by silver-framed mirrors, was littered with open cosmetic pots, bottles, and all the toilette accessories that a vain woman liked to use. Mimi confessed that she had slept late this morning and her personal maid had not yet had time to clear up the debris. Juliet, ever quick to notice details, saw that there was only one photograph on view – standing next to a bowl of roses by one of the windows – a superb enlargement, silver framed, of a young girl dancing with a handsome young man. Juliet could read the sprawling signature:

For Maman from Simone.

Almost immediately, Mimi pointed to this photograph.

"This is my daughter by my first marriage – isn't she gorgeous?"

"Very beautiful indeed, Madam."

"I was just like her when I was eighteen," said Mimi languidly, " although I really think I had a better figure. Simone is too thin at the moment. But she will run to fat. She's too fond of chocolates. I keep telling her that if you want to be a success in life you've got to practise self-denial. If she doesn't, she'll never find a wealthy husband. They have their pick of glamour-girls to-day."

Juliet remained silent. Self-denial . . . yes . . . but surely if one was going to practise such a thing it should be for a worthier cause than slimming just in order to attract a monied husband!

"I hope," Mimi continued, "that darling Simone will pay attention to what I tell her. She occasionally indulges not only in chocolates but in romance. That is fatal. She's so young still. Take this boy, Paul, in that photo with her – he used to be her dancing partner in Paris. They Twisted together so divinely. Everybody talked about them. Poor Paul, poor lamb, hasn't a sou. I'm putting an end to *that!*

Then, seeing Juliet's grave interested gaze, she gave her pretty laugh and added:

"Ah, but, of course *you* are r-r-omantic, too. I suppose you think love matters more than money."

"I'm *sure* it does, Madame."

Mimi veiled her huge eyes with the long lashes – still black and sticky with last night's mascara.

"Oh, dear! You idealists! You're like my husband. I can't cure him of this belief in romance before money. After all, he has to have money to keep up the Château and pay the bills, doesn't he? And it certainly wouldn't do for Simone to marry a poor man; she hates wearing the same dress more than twice."

Juliet blinked. This was a world, these were people, hitherto unknown to her. She had only read about them or seen them in plays or films. She wasn't so stupid as to think that money didn't matter at all; of course it did. And it would be marvellous to have a husband who could give one a lovely home and, even more so, to be able to give one's children lots of lovely things. But Juliet's parents had never been more than comfortably off and there used to be a special need for economy while Nicky was going to a good school. Since Mummy died and the home broke up, Juliet had had to earn her own living; she had been forced to be money-conscious; but it never mattered as Mme de Maureville implied.

Juliet was well aware that many rich people were unhappy – and bored. Personally, Juliet preferred to be poor and happy, only never bored.

There were so many wonderful things in life, apart from spending money.

She began to wonder what kind of upbringing Simone had had. Mimi went on chatting quite amicably – treating her this morning not so much as an employee, as the daughter of her old school-friend. She spoke highly of Mrs. Ingram. She adored Americans; they had such wonderful clothes-sense, and once Mimi and Simone had gone to New York and stayed with Juliet. They had had a heavenly time. America was a paradise for smart women.

Juliet Ingram was angelic – so very kind and, as Mimi put it – (with quite charming humility) – *so much* nicer than she was! Mrs. Ingram had patience with friends and acquaintances who were not lucky in life. She could deal with the sick and the suffering; didn't mind that sort of thing. She actually worked, as her good deed, in a school for polio victims in New York. Mimi ran a mile from such things.

"You wouldn't have thought old Juliet and I could become such friends but we got on frightfully well at our Finishing School. Juliet thinks me very spoilt and naughty but I amuse her. Now your mother – Molly something-or-other her name was – she was much older than our Juliet or myself. She wasn't a pupil was she – she was an assistant-teacher of English for the French girls."

Now Juliet looked eagerly at Madame.

"Oh – Madame, didn't you ever meet my mother?"

"I only remember her vaguely," said Mimi, who at least had the grace not to tell young Juliet the truth – that she had thought the freckled, snub-nosed Molly a frightful bore. But Mrs. Ingram, Mimi admitted – typical of her, when she was young – had been especially kind and nice to the young English teacher; just because she hadn't much in the world. Darling old Juliet was such a philanthropist. Actually, of course, Mimi would not have seen much more of her had she not married Bob Ingram who was one of the wealthiest businessmen in New York, and came over so frequently to the South of France.

Then the conversation was turned back to Sophie. Mimi proceeded to give Juliet *carte-blanche* as to how she should manage the child to whom she kept referring as 'my poor unhappy

Sophie'. (Juliet could well believe how those words must irritate Sophie's adoring father.)

"Of course," Mimi ended, "you must let me know if there is anything the poor darling ever wants."

Juliet bit her lip.

"I think Madame, during the short training I have had with disabled children, that it is essential never to stress their disablement and to try and make them feel they are normal – treat them as you would other children."

"H'm – well I'll leave her to you and I'm sure you'll spoil my darling," said Mimi lazily and drank her black unsweetened coffee. That was all she had for breakfast except half a grapefruit. She was never going to relax *her* vigilance about her figure.

She was thinking about the next date she had with Max. The fascinating *Herr Doktor*, with his wonderful brain, and the power he seemed to have over neurotic women. He had once told Mimi that *she* suffered from neurosis and that he intended to give her special treatment. Mimi's lip quivered with amusement at the memory. Marvellous Max, with those brilliant blue eyes which looked down at one under heavy lids; and that massive head of thick goldenish hair. She knew that Lucien disliked Max – and his native country. She kept telling Lucien that he couldn't carry a hatred of Germany right through the ages just because his mother had had a bad time during the war in this wretched old Château.

Mimi hardly heard what Juliet was saying. She just caught occasional sentences such as:

"I don't intend to spoil Sophie, Madame. On the contrary, the sooner she is taught how to be more independent and to gain strength mentally as well as physically, the more easily she will be able to overcome her difficulties."

"Oh, yes, of course," said Mimi, hardly listening. She was dying to read this week's *Parish Match* which had been brought in with the daily papers. Juliet and her theories about disabled children were beginning to bore her. How she hated 'do-gooders', although, of course, certain people *had* to do good in the world. They couldn't all be like naughty Mimi! She had to hand it to this girl that she was an unusual character – still so young, yet so very resolute and dedicated. She oughtn't to be much trouble, unlike those other frightful governesses Sophie had had. She was definitely intelligent – all the better if Lucien got on well with her.

Lucien suddenly walked into the room. He wore a light linen

76

suit. He carried a black brief-case. Juliet thought he looked very tired in the strong morning light. By the time she had gone down to breakfast, he had already left for his factory. He was explaining now why he'd come back. A sudden crisis had arisen with the Lebanese representative whom he'd been entertaining. He had to drive to the Airport and see the man off; they needed a final conference. It was a nuisance but everybody was so short of time these days. He just thought he should let Mimi know that he wouldn't be in for lunch.

"I shan't be in, myself," said Mimi. "I'm spending the day in Monte Carlo."

As a rule this sort of news worried Lucien. Mimi was so little with their child – it greatly distressed him. But he turned his gaze with relief upon the new English girl.

"My Sophie will be in your hands today, then, Juliet."

"And such capable hands," put in Mimi in a gushing voice, "I don't think you need worry any more, *mon cher*!"

He eyed her with the suspicion he always felt when Mimi was being pleasant. What was she up to? At a guess he'd say that because she wanted to be away all day she was ready to wheedle somebody like Juliet into taking full responsibility. It would salve Mimi's conscience. (What little conscience she had.)

"Well, good-bye, then," said Lucien and turned to the door.

Mimi was about to echo the brief *adieu*, when she suddenly glanced at Juliet and was seized with one of her rather ruthless desires to be perverse. No doubt the little Browning was full of admiration for handsome Lucien *and* of pity. They had been singing together last night in such a touching way. She had better throw out of that girlish mind, with all speed, any romantic fancies she might entertain about Lucien. Mimi didn't want him, but she didn't want any other woman to have him either; she was much too possessive. She held out her arms:

"Lucien, *chéri*, aren't you going to kiss me?"

He turned back, looking quite startled. It was so long since Mimi had made a request for any kind of caress. He literally stared at her. She looked back at him with that enigmatic little smile on her beautiful sensual mouth.

"*Très cher!* . . ." she murmured, arms still extended.

He advanced slowly to the bed. He felt positively as awkward as any shy young man might be, rather than a disillusioned husband. Mimi baffled him. He had a horrible feeling that this was a bit of play-acting for Juliet Browning's benefit. He couldn't understand Mimi – who could? She was never the same. She was a creature of such stormy, unpredictable moods, and not many of them held warmth or sincerity. However, he bent to touch her cheek with his lips.

As he did so, a sudden wave of the old passion which she had once inspired caught him off-balance. She was so beautiful – so close. He said in a husky undertone:

"Why are you being nice to me all of a sudden?"

"Oh, go and attend to your business, *imbécile*!" she whispered back between her teeth, in rapid French which she knew Juliet would not understand. Her eyes derided him.

Scarlet to the roots of his hair he turned away and walked out of the room. But Juliet had neither seen nor understood this little charade. She had discreetly turned her back and, being the romantic person Mimi imagined, had hoped that she was wrong about last night and that perhaps poor Monsieur's wife *did* love him a little.

'I expect Madame's bark is worse than her bite', she thought cheerfully.

But she was to discover before long that the bite was still there all right, and the teeth were very sharp indeed.

Even now, once Lucien had gone, Mimi seemed impatient to get rid of Juliet. She had had enough of her and the talk about Sophie. Juliet was dismissed, and told to send in Mimi's maid, Maria.

Sophie now was calling from her downstairs bedroom:

"Juliet. I want Juliet!"

"I'm here, darling."

Juliet ran down the stairs. The child was still in bed. She looked fretful. Old Blanche was sitting beside her with the new box of chocolates from Paris which had been opened, trying to persuade her to eat them.

Juliet gently but firmly put an end to this.

"Chocolates are not good for little girls at this time of the morning. They will give her indigestion. We'll keep them for after lunch, shall we?"

Old Blanche, who hardly understood Juliet's French, gave her a malevolent look.

"Sophie is allowed to have as many chocolates as she wishes," she began in her high quavering voice.

"Please, Blanche, leave Sophie to me now."

"Why can't I have chocolates?" whimpered Sophie. "I like these. I wanted you to eat some with me."

"Now, first of all let's get you up and dressed, darling, and then I'll draw you a little diagram and you'll see what the digestive organs are like, and how badly you are treating them," said Juliet, smiling.

"No. I want my chocolates – Maman said I could have them," sniffed Sophie.

Old Blanche thrust the big round box forward again, glaring at Juliet, but Juliet took the box away and got Blanche out of the room.

She was determined to make various changes in the organizing of Sophie's day and general welfare. She had been given *carte-blanche* and she was going to make full use of it for the child's sake. She was quite sure that a lot of her miseries and ill-health were due to bad feeding, and poor management generally. The first thing she must do was to consult the doctor who looked after Sophie. Fortunately she need not trouble Madame for the name, for one of the first things Lucien had done was to write it down, with the telephone-number, for Juliet in case of emergency.

She asked the child a few questions while she dressed her; among them was whether she ever wore a built-up boot or used her crutches. Sophie's wizened face turned scarlet. She changed in a twinkle from the merry little playmate of the Princess game to a small virago.

"I shan't wear the beastly boot. I'll *never* wear one. I hate it. It hurts me. And I won't use crutches – they look horrible. I like my chair."

She poured out a list of other things that she didn't like. Juliet listened attentively. Oh dear, she thought, there was a bit of her mother in the child – that side of Mimi which refused to accept discipline or self-sacrifice. Fortunately, on the whole, Sophie had much more of her father in her. There was such a nice side, and one could appeal to her. She needed studying and understanding.

Juliet decided to say nothing more about boot or crutches until she had spoken to the doctor. After a few jokes she restored Sophie's good humour.

"If you scream, little Princess, your new slave will get on her magic carpet and fly back to her own country," she smiled while she brushed the black unruly hair. (*That* was very like Lucien's.)

"Oh, don't go . . . I'm sorry. Don't go!" begged Sophie, quietening down.

"Of course I won't. Just try to be a little patient, darling. I want to make a few changes but they will be for your own good, I promise you, and I'll never let anybody hurt you."

It was a hot Mediterranean morning. By midday Sophie's energies would begin to flag – hers was the physique to tire very easily; Juliet was sure of that.

She put her in her chair and wheeled her out into the sunlight. She let Sophie show her the lake, and feed the swans, and take her around the beautiful grounds. There were four gardeners. Sophie introduced Juliet to them all. They were nice genial young men, obviously sorry for Monsieur's crippled daughter, and very polite and pleasant to the new English governess.

Mimi came out on the terrace to say good-bye, looking entrancing, all in white this morning; cool and chic. She rarely wore a hat. She carried an almond green silk parasol under her arm to protect her ash-blonde head from the sun. Her Peugeot and the chauffeur awaited her.

"I don't know when I'll be back but I expect in time to say good night to you, Sophie," she said.

"When is Simone coming home?"

"Tomorrow, *ma petite*.'

"I wish she wouldn't go away so often," complained Sophie.

"Tiens – she has more to do than to hang around here amusing you, *chérie*.'

Juliet, glancing at the child, saw her underlip begin to quiver and hastily wheeled Sophie away from her mother. Sophie lamented:

"I do like Simone to be at home because she plays me her 'pop' records."

"Maybe if I could get permission to borrow them, I could play them for you."

"That would be fun," said Sophie, "I like what the English Beatles sing. Do you like the Beatles, Juliet?"

"Of course. Everybody does. They're great fun."

"They came to Paris. Simone saw them."

Now they saw a blue Citroën arriving.

"Oh, bother," said Sophie, "that's Dr. Giraud."

'Good,' thought Juliet, 'I can have my talk with him'.

"I'm sure he's a nice doctor, isn't he?" she asked the child.

80

"He hurts me sometimes when he touches my back, and I hate all doctors. I've seen dozens and dozens. Papa has had specialists for me from all over the world. We had an English one from London once, only none of them do me any good."

'Poor darling,' thought Juliet, 'no doubt her physical life has been a torment since she can remember'.

But deeply sorry though Juliet felt for Sophie, she was not going to allow her to do exactly what she wanted at all times. She felt that Sophie was the victim either of those who pandered to her every whim or of people like her mother who spent money on her but gave her none of that healing self-sacrificing love of a truly devoted mother.

"Listen, Sophie darling," she said gently, "there are lots of people in this world who get ill and suffer pain. The poor doctors try to do their best for them – just as they have done for you – so don't hate them. And cheer up – because Dr. Giraud has come to talk to me today not to upset you."

She left Sophie in her chair down by the stables, drinking iced blackcurrant juice and water. The groom was there currying Madame's new chestnut which had been sent to her from Ireland – one of Lucien's many presents which Mimi had accepted as she did all the others, as her due.

Killarney Boy was a great favourite with Sophie and took sugar from her palm nuzzling it gently with his velvet nostrils. Cou-Cou, the little undersized groom, also talked to her merrily in his Midi dialect, although Sophie only half understood it herself. But Sophie got on with him. Juliet had learnt from the start that it was quite in order to leave the little girl in his care for half an hour.

Chapter Nine

THE interview with Dr. Giraud proved satisfactory. Giraud was a youngish man, prematurely bald, wearing strong glasses and with a frank engaging manner. He was a clever young man who had studied in Paris and had put up his plate in Cannes some years ago. He specialized in children. He told Juliet that he had looked after the little Mlle de Maureville since she was five.

It was fortunate for Juliet, also, that he spoke tolerably good English, having spent a year on the staff of the Children's Hospital at Great Ormond Street. He liked to speak English and talked volubly to Juliet.

"It was a tragedy," he said, "a great tragedy that the little de Maureville girl should have been born with such defects. Poor Monsieur has spent much money bringing specialists from all over Europe and to no avail. There are calamities that attack rich and poor alike, and no amount of money could cure them. Money could only help the little victim to live with the minimum of pain or discomfort."

Fortunately, (he continued this theme), Sophie suffered only from slight backache, and not always that. The shortage in her leg was a matter of two inches and a well-made surgical boot could enable her to walk but she always set up such a storm of crying and moaning about it that Monsieur had forbidden anybody to force her to wear it. They had tried crutches with the same result. The least line of resistance was for Sophie to sit in the chair and be waited on. Besides, she enjoyed wheeling herself around and was adept at it. Monsieur had paid handsomely for the finest, lightest of chairs specially designed for her. It was all pale pink leather cushions and chromium – a masterpiece. The child rejected other help.

Juliet listened gravely.

"Does she have no special treatment?"

"A phsyiotherapist, Mlle Reviere, comes up from the town every Saturday to give her electrical treatment, vibro-massage, infra-red help – etc. Sophie quite likes it. It is a psychological thing. Mentally it does her some good. Also it keeps the muscles working – one has to build up those poor little legs. They are like a rabbit's are they not?"

"Yes, it's pathetic," said Juliet sadly.

"The back is beyond repair – she was born with this very bad curvature and the pelvis is, in consequence, tilted."

"Poor darling," said Juliet shaking her head.

"Mees Browning has had some experience of these things?" asked the young doctor.

He liked English girls and he thought Miss Browning delightful. On the other hand he was terrified of Mme de Maureville. She was exquisite to look at but her personality overawed him. As for that brat, Simone, he wondered what Miss Browning would have said if he had told her what had happened one day when he came up to see Sophie. Her parents had been out, and he had been received by the seventeen-year-old girl. He could describe the beautiful Simone in English idiom as 'quite a piece'. Or would the Americans call her 'a doll'? She had received him, and flirted with him violently until he felt hot with confusion. He could not cope with coquetry from a *jeune fille*. Of course he knew that it was rumoured not only here in Roquemont, but in Cannes, that poor Monsieur was a great gentleman who had had the misfortune to take the wrong kind of wife and be cursed equally with the wrong kind of stepdaughter.

Juliet was telling him about the time she had spent in the Disabled Home for Children in London. Yes, she did have some knowledge, although no extensive medical training. The Matron was a certified nursing sister and had taught her a lot. The poor little children at Wandsworth, who came from poverty-stricken homes had all the benefits of the English National Health Service, but none of the luxury that surrounded Sophie.

"In a way they are luckier than she," Juliet told Dr. Giraud, "because they have to learn to do many things for themselves and bear their misfortunes with patience."

"If I may say so, it is the best thing that could have happened to my little patient that *you* have come to Roquemont. You will greatly benefit her, Mees Browning."

"Thank you," she said.

"One other thing, Mees Browning, there would be great benefit for Sophie from sea-bathing. It has been recommended by one of our specialists. But when they first took her down to the sea

83

she was so afraid and begged so piteously to be taken out of the water again, it was never repeated."

Juliet nodded, but she registered a private vow to get Sophie into that healthy healing salt water just as soon as she possibly could. She was sure it was merely a question of inspiring confidence in the child. At the moment Sophie had no real faith in anybody except her father and he was far too indulgent because of his immense pitying love.

After Dr. Giraud had gone, Juliet returned to her small charge who had by this time grown tired of feeding Killarney Boy or talking to Cou-Cou. Sophie could never concentrate on anything for long – that was one of the difficulties in keeping her amused.

Juliet wheeled her into lunch. After this while the child had her customary rest (everybody in the Château seemed to take the *après midi* siesta) Juliet lay in a wicker chaise-longue piled with cushions on the terrace, under a striped awning.

Although it was far warmer than any weather she had ever experienced – she did not want to go to bed. Certainly, this Mediterranean sun made one feel a bit languid and sleepy but she had letters to write. A long letter to Daddy who would be anxiously waiting to hear about her reactions to Roquemont, and one to welcome Nicky at the next port at which his ship was due after they left Hong Kong.

She also began to scribble a note to her favourite girl-friend, Phyllis Rye, who lived in London. Phyllis was as busy as Juliet used to be. They had lunched together the day before Juliet left England. Juliet was devoted to Phyllis. They had similar tastes – particularly in music. Phyllis's father worked for a well known firm of piano-manufacturers. Her elder sister was a professional singer. Phyllis was doing a secretarial job in the Television Centre at the White City. She was not particularly glamorous but attractive and intelligent. Like Juliet – she had strong feelings about men, love and marriage. They used to discuss their affairs; and it was always the same for them both. They were not the type to experiment with sex before marriage.

A few months ago, Juliet had noticed a decided change in Phyl who was usually bubbling over with good spirits. She had become silent and preoccupied. Juliet soon heard all about *Harry*. Harry Chalmers was Phyl's boss. Juliet had met him once when she went down to the TV centre one day to pick Phyl up after work. She thought him decidedly good-looking and amusing. He was over forty – nearly twice Phyl's age. And he was already married, with a schoolboy son. He had fallen into the habit of taking Phyl out to lunch regularly. Phyl unfortunately fell madly in love with him; gave him the rather crazy, whole-hearted love that a young girl can feel for the older, much more experienced man.

A common enough situation. Phyl had suffered bitterly – she even left the TV centre and found another job. She did everything she could to keep away from Harry and preserve her belief in integrity and decency. She did not think it was decent to take a man away from his wife even if he wanted to go. And Harry was half-inclined to cut and run and take her away.

She had been terribly unhappy since leaving the office. With the supreme egotism of the conquering male, Harry had followed her, tried to get her back. Juliet had done everything she could to help Phyl during this difficult time.

She kept saying, "You'll meet someone else – someone free to marry you." But that was in the future – the present for Phyl was utterly desolate. It had upset Juliet to see her friend so badly hurt. When it was all over, and Harry had finally faded out, Juliet had said:

"I don't think I could ever have been as strong-minded as you."

"Oh, yes, you would. I know if you found yourself in the same situation, you wouldn't have gone off with him," was Phyl's response.

Now on this golden afternoon, Juliet sat writing to Phyl, and found herself mentioning Lucien's name far more often than Mimi's.

She described him for Phyl.

He's a terribly attractive man. Not at all the tough-guy type – rather artistic-looking really – pale with the most wonderful raven-black hair and big dark eyes. A bit like I seem to remember that film-star who died – Tyrone Power – only taller and very slim. And so sad-looking. I think he's had a ghastly life with this woman. One day I'll tell you more about them. I just want you to know that I am very lucky, my dear. I am in one of the most magnificent Chateaux in France – it's fabulous and I really have a mission in life, because of the little girl . . .

She filled two pages about Sophie. She ended the letter:

I wish you could save up and fly out here for your holiday. I'd try to get you a cheap room in the village and I know they wouldn't

85

mind if you spent your time with me. Monsieur wouldn't, and Madame is too busy enjoying herself to care, I am sure. Do try to come down.

After she had sealed this letter and addressed it to Miss Phyllis Rye, at her home in Purley, Juliet sat back and looked through her dark glasses at the beautiful scene before her.

The famous pair of swans with their cygnets were just moving across the lake, in sight of the terrace. The glass-like water seemed to shimmer in the heat. There was not a breath of wind. It was very quiet and all rather like a dream. How quickly one's life could change, she thought. This time a short week ago she was working like a slave at Wandsworth in that cold and damp, with a miserable vista of melancholy Common and the unending traffic. It was as though she had suddenly been transported to paradise.

Her thoughts kept reverting to last night when she had played ballads for Lucien de Maureville. She could hear his haunting voice, singing those words: *How can you live without love?*

Then she pulled herself up with a jerk. She had only been at the Château de Roquemont for twenty-four hours and already her mind was circling around her employer. This wouldn't do. She hadn't come to Roquemont to play songs to Monsieur or feel sorry for his matrimonial troubles – but to look after his daughter.

She felt rather cross with herself, put Lucien stoutly out of mind, and went into the house to get Sophie up.

The little girl was interested in going for a picnic as soon as it was cooler, which would be round about tea-time. They hadn't far to go. Juliet could wheel her a short way up to Roquemont Forest. They would take fruit juice and some biscuits with them. Juliet could see that she would have to get out of the habit of drinking English tea, much as she would miss it.

Sophie was quite thrilled by the idea of the outing. Her other governesses had always said it was too hot or too tiring to wheel her to the forest, and old Blanche and any of the other staff who had been left in charge of her were too afraid of insects or snakes up there. In fact, they treated the forest as though it was a danger-spot full of prowling wild animals. But Juliet had already discussed the matter with the head-gardener who assured her there was scarcely an animal to be found except a harmless rabbit or squirrel. There were even few birds. As in so many of the French forests, bird-life was becoming almost extinct – they had been so ruthlessly annihilated by constant poaching.

There was no nonsense about Juliet who had always been a good walker. She disregarded Blanche who hovered around, cackling about poor Mlle Sophie being bitten to death by mosquitoes. Nothing like that was going to happen, Juliet assured Blanche. She had found some strong oil of lavender and was going to cover the child's arms and legs in it. But Blanche was horrified because Juliet had also arranged to take one of the watch-dogs with them. Dogs were never allowed in the Château. Mimi did not like them and had never replaced the poodle she had treated so badly. Besides, she objected to hairs being left on her velvet cushions, or her dresses. But Juliet, with the true English mentality, believed that nothing was better for a child than to be brought up with animals.

One of the dogs they kept in the kennels was a delightful puppy – best of a litter that had recently been born to an elderly Boxer – quite a well-bred bitch of its type. They called the puppy *Tache* which, Sophie proudly explained to Juliet, meant 'a spot'. The new Boxer had large black spots on its fawn-coloured coat, and a black patch over one eye, so the name suited him.

"It is covered with fleas – it scratches all day – it will pass its fleas to my little Sophie," screamed old Blanche, tilting her chin at Juliet.

Juliet laughed and assured Blanche that she could cope with a flea if she saw one.

Tache was an adorable three-months-old creature, flopping about on big paws and slavering with joy once allowed out. It followed Juliet and Sophie, lured by biscuits and affection. Sophie who had never until now been encouraged to like dogs was a bit doubtful at first as to whether she was going to like having Tache for a pet. But Juliet's enthusiasm for Tache soon roused a similar feeling in Sophie. Having no lead, Juliet attached a cord to the collar which the groom had hastily found for Tache. They pulled him along with this. Soon he trotted beside the wheel-chair quite meekly. Tache soon became a new diversion for Sophie. The three of them had an amusing and satisfying picnic; Juliet and Tache sitting on a rug at Sophie's feet. Sophie said proudly:

"I've got a slave *and* a trained tiger too, now. We ought to call him Tiger instead of Tache."

"I don't think he snarls loudly enough for that," laughed Juliet. She was enjoying the picnic.

It was delightfully cool in the dark green forest away from the

87

dust and heat of the road. She could just see the entrance from the main road. She had not come far.

"Do you want another drink?" she asked the child.

"No, but I do wish I could get out of the chair and run with Tache," said Sophie.

Juliet after some reflection, said:

"Maybe you can't run, but you could walk, you know, Sophie."

Sophie's small face darkened. Her brows contracted in the scowl that always appeared when she felt thwarted.

"I can't. You *know* I can't."

"I don't know it at all. You have a beautiful white kid boot and if you wore it—"

"I won't. I never will. I think it's hideous and it makes me look horrible," broke in the child, her face scarlet.

"I don't agree." Juliet took one of Sophie's claw-like hands and stroked it, "Now listen to me. It is just in your mind that you think you can't wear your boot and that it is ugly. But if you persevered, with the help of your crutch and my arm, you could soon do very well and then you could take a walk with Tache, couldn't you?"

Sophie snatched her hand away. Her big dark eyes were staring with painful longing at the Boxer puppy who was chasing a squirrel, falling over himself in the effort to jump up the tree and catch it. Juliet watched, too – knowing exactly what lay in the child's mind; that intolerable longing to be as free as the squirrel – or as athletic as the dog. Full of pity, but with determination, she pursued her own theme.

"Everything is in the mind. Listen and I will translate for you some words once written by our great English Poet, Shakespeare: *Nothing is good or bad but thinking makes it so*. You understand?"

"No," said Sophie sulkily.

With patience Juliet explained.

"And so," she finished, "if you make yourself believe that you can walk, you will. And if you insist that the boot is pretty, it will become a fact."

"It won't—" began Sophie wildly.

"I'm going to tell you a story," broke in Juliet. "Listen to me – then we must go home. It is getting late . . ."

She told Sophie about a little girl named Ann in the Wandsworth Home who had exactly the same disability as Sophie, herself. Ann, too, once longed to walk. Suddenly one day the doctors designed and made for her a boot – not a pretty white one – like Sophie's which might well be used for ice-skating. Ann was poor and could not afford such a boot. Hers was ordinary brown leather and quite ugly. But after they fastened it on and laced it up, and Ann found that she was at last able to walk, she was so overjoyed that she began to treat her boot as though it was the most precious thing in the world. She would not be parted from it even when it was taken off at night, when she kept it on her little bed. She even gave it a name, *Bootiken*. Bootiken became her best friend, because it helped her more than anything else had ever done.

Sophie gradually calmed down. She became interested in the story of Ann and Bootiken. Before the picnic ended she had made a concession to Juliet. She would give her own surgical boot another trial.

"I agree – it does look like a skating boot," she admitted. "Papa took me once to the ice-rink to see a championship for children, and they all wore white boots laced up high like mine."

"There you are!" exclaimed Juliet.

On the way home, with Tache who was now hot and tired, his tongue lolling out of his mouth, Sophie actually discussed a possible name for her white boot. She also wanted to hear more about Ann.

"Why is she so poor? Hadn't she got any parents? Doesn't she get presents?"

Juliet described the sad fate of little Ann who had neither mother nor father and was an orphan. Although she had toys and books, they were as nothing compared with the beautiful things that Sophie's Maman and Papa bought for her. Now the best side of Sophie showed itself. Her heart was touched.

"Can I send some of my things to little Ann? Can we make up a parcel and send it by air over to London?" she asked eagerly.

"Of course," said Juliet, delighted.

When they reached the Château, they saw Sophie's father coming up the drive in his Jaguar. He saw them, too, waved, got out and walked to meet them.

"Where have you two been and what on earth is *this*?" He laughed and pointed to the Boxer who was tangling himself up in his cord and biting at it.

Sophie burst into explanations, talking more rapidly to her father than she did to her English governess. She had already

89

learned that she must speak slowly and concisely if she wished to be thoroughly understood by Juliet.

Lucien had never seen his small daughter in such a state of excitement, or so interested in so many things other than her own woes or wants. He heard all about Tache and the picnic and how she had been covered in lavender-oil so that she shouldn't be bitten by gnats, and wasn't Juliet *clever*! Then Sophie poured out the story of little Ann in London and her Bootiken, and how she – Sophie – was going to put *her* boot on tomorrow, so they must find a special name for it.

Lucien smiled. He had to put up a hand to stop the flow of words. He could hardly take in all that she was saying. He untangled the puppy then looked up at Juliet rather doubtingly.

"Are you sure this beast is all right for her? Her mother isn't very keen on her having the stable dogs around—"

"If you don't mind, Monsieur, I am sure it is good for Sophie to have a pet."

"Oh, yes, yes," exclaimed the child. "I want Tache to be my own dog from now on. I love him, Papa."

"Well, so long as you don't take him into the house—" began Lucien, laughing.

Sophie monopolized the conversation again with a fresh burst of enthusiasm, explaining all that she and Juliet had done today.

Lucien listened, genuinely amazed by all that this simple English girl appeared to have achieved so quickly. He was a man who noticed details. He thought that Juliet, herself, looked tired, and had lost some of her bright colour.

"You've been doing too much. You shouldn't push Sophie's chair up a hill. If you want to go for a picnic in the Forest you must take one of our boys from the estate and get him to push the chair for you. This isn't an English climate you know. The heat down here in summer can be very enervating. You must do no more today. Blanche will put Sophie to bed."

Both Juliet and Sophie started to protest against this, but Lucien insisted on sending for Blanche. Sophie went with her old nurse only after extracting a promise from Juliet to tell her a story before she dressed for dinner and to help her choose a name for the white kid boot.

After she had gone, Lucien invited Juliet to take a drink with him.

"One of your orange juices, perhaps," he smiled, "but I feel I need a glass of white wine."

She went with him and sat down with relief in a comfortable chair in the cool of the salon. She was conscious now that she *was* de-energized.

"I'll soon get used to the heat," she said. "I'm going to adore it here, Monsieur."

"You seem to be doing a lot for my child," he said and raised his glass to her. "You have a great gift for dealing with children like Sophie."

"One has to try to understand them, only I hope you won't object if I don't do everything she asks, poor lamb. It isn't good for her to be allowed to become a complete little dictator."

Lucien, balancing on the arm of the sofa, sipped his wine, and nodded.

"You're right. One shouldn't be too indulgent even with those who need so much love."

"Incidentally," said Juliet, "I'm determined to make Sophie wear her boot. The worst thing is for her to be wheeled around all the time, and Dr. Giraud assured me that it would be best for her to take exercise."

"I've known that for a long time but nobody has been able to persuade her to wear it. When she did she had a rotten fall or two, and it scared her off. Since then she hasn't worn it. She finds it too easy to wheel herself, or be wheeled around."

"She will wear that boot," said Juliet quietly. "You'll see."

"Who is this Ann she was chatting about?"

Juliet told him about the little polio victim in the Wandsworth home.

"That was a stroke of genius interesting her in another child as unfortunate as herself. Brilliant of you," said Lucien. "Both her mother and I will be eternally grateful if you can make her take some exercise and improve the general muscular condition."

"I also want to try and make her go down to the sea-baths one day and swim. I'm sure we could achieve this with the help of a professional instructor."

Lucien's eyes shone.

"That would be tremendous – a really great achievement. I begin to feel hope at last about Sophie's future."

"I am so glad, Monsieur, and I'm very happy, myself, because

I love Sophie and – I think it's all so beautiful here," she finished enthusiastically.

He found her sympathetic and refreshing. He was also impressed by the fact that she was not allowing herself to be overwhelmed by Mimi, nor was she giving way to the often wearing efforts Sophie made to get her own way. Juliet had the right sort of personality – the mixture of sweetness and authority that Sophie had always needed.

"Did you have a talk with my wife about Sophie?" he asked suddenly.

"Yes, and Madame is anxious for me to take complete charge."

Lucien nodded. He knew just how anxious Mimi was to delegate *that* responsibility.

He put down his glass. To return to the thought of Mimi was only to harass him. He had been upset all day because of the way she had stated that 'loving-wife' act this morning in order to impress Juliet. The way she had snubbed him the instant he had shown a touch of softness towards her had been a cruel blow. He felt that it would be a long time before he could make another attempt to bridge the emotional gap between Mimi and himself – if ever.

Chapter Ten

Two days later when Simone arrived from Paris she brought with her the one person whom Juliet did not particularly want to see ... Michel de Condine. His arrival was as much a surprise to Mme de Maureville as it was to Juliet. As the girl got out of the car, followed by the tall languid fair-haired Michel, Mimi, who had gone out to meet Simone, glared from him to her young daughter. She grabbed Simone by the arm and pulled her away from the Comte. He busied himself by saying "Hullo" to Juliet who had just wheeled Sophie up to the front door. It was the lunch hour – another glorious sunny day. Juliet had been sitting with Sophie under the trees giving her an English lesson.

Mimi whispered to her daughter:

"I thought I made it clear to you that you weren't to see so much of Michel."

The young girl shrugged and pouted.

"Really, Maman, you are boring about him! You know I don't take his attentions seriously and he amuses me. He's useful. He met the Caravelle and brought me here."

"You have no business to be so constantly in touch with Michel."

"*Tiens,* Maman, he is Papa's cousin, is he not?"

"That doesn't make him a relation of yours," said Mimi sharply. "Please remember that *Papa* as you call him is only your stepfather. There is no blood-tie between you and Michel. He is too old for you, anyhow."

The girl laughed.

"Not all that much. Anyhow I am no longer a child. If you don't stop nagging me, Maman, I shall run away and earn my own living."

Mimi flushed crimson with anger. The only person who ever defied her openly and blatantly was the daughter of her first marriage. Simone was like her father had been – stubborn and almost unmanageable; although physically beautiful and like herself when she was young. It irritated Mimi because she wanted complete control and Simone rejected it. Her most passionate wish was that Simone should make a splendid marriage. Mimi did not wish her to indulge even in a harmless flirtation with Lucien's good-for-nothing cousin. The de Condine title was of no importance. His lack of money damned him in Mimi's eyes.

Now Simone stared at the new English governess with some curiosity.

"How's *she* making out?" she asked her mother in an undertone.

"*Pas mal*. She seems to have a miraculous touch with Sophie which is a relief; but she is inclined to give herself airs. Already she is casting eyes at your stepfather."

Simone burst into smothered laughter.

"How frightfully amusing!"

"Maybe she'll cut you out with dear Michel, too," added Mimi. "He has already met her on the Comet. They flew over together, Lucien said he was very *épris*."

The smile that Simone had reserved for the English girl vanished. She had felt that it might be a new experience, and not an unpleasant one, to have a young girl at the Château in charge of Sophie. Like her mother, Simone enjoyed speaking English and airing her knowledge of it. She intended to have English discussions with Juliet. She could see that there must be only a couple of years difference in age between them. Maman had told her that Juliet was twenty. Simone would be eighteen in July. But she was not sure she wanted a rival even in the vaguest sense. Of course she was positive that she was more glamorous than the English girl, but if Michel had admitted that he was attracted by Juliet and the girl was 'making eyes' at Papa – *well*! That struck a warning bell for Simone. Therefore from the start, she felt slightly hostile towards Juliet.

"I'm Simone Valaise," she said, extending a languid hand towards the English girl.

Juliet answered with her usual friendly smile as she took the limp fingers. (She did so hate that sort of hand-shake ... as though the owner had no time for courtesies and was quite indifferent to the person she was greeting.) But Juliet was full of admiration for Mlle Valais. Heavens, how beautiful ... the spit of her mother – the same eyes and blonde hair, only Simone's skin was not quite so good as her mother's. And although her figure was perfect at the moment – delectably rounded – she would, as her mother had warned Juliet, run to fat unless she took care. The linen suit she was wearing had the stamp of Paris on it – palest pink, divinely cut. Her long amber hair curved down to her neck, with the merest suggestion of a curve over each cheek. She wore heavy eye make-up and pale lipstick to match her pink suit.

Sophie screamed from her chair:

"Simone! Simone! Come and kiss me!"

Simone smiled back at the little girl.

"In a minute, *mon enfant.*"

"No, now – kiss me *now*!" demanded Sophie.

Simone grimaced at Juliet.

"I expect you have already found that my half-sister likes her own way."

"I *don't* like my own way," Sophie answered before Juliet had the chance. "I like Juliet's way. She's my slave. She is a lovely Princess I've captured. We have marvellous games—"

"Oh, lord," muttered Simone, "all this comic Princess stuff she goes in for – it's such a bore."

"It's quite all right. I understand her – we get on together," said Juliet quietly. "When you're handicapped like Sophie you need a kind of 'make-believe land' where you can lose yourself and pretend you have magical powers."

"Oh, I expect so," drawled Simone, utterly indifferent to child-psychology. Like her mother, she had little patience with children and she was at times embarrassed by her stepsister's disability. Only at odd times was she willing to amuse Sophie, but speedily tired of it.

"I must go and change into shorts. See you later, Sophie. Are you going to play tennis with me later this afternoon, Michel?" she turned to the Comte.

"I haven't brought my things—" he began.

"Oh, you can borrow a racquet and some shorts from Papa."

Michel gave his perfunctory bow.

"Your wish is my command."

The young French girl looked up into his eyes, her own bold and inviting.

"Does that apply to any wish I may express?"

"But of course," he murmured. But his own eyes were slanting sideways towards Juliet. He was too sophisticated, too interested in himself to fall genuinely in love with an artificial type like Simone. He regarded her as just an attractive young thing with whom he could amuse himself. She was ready for it. And he wasn't frightened of Mimi de Maureville – not he! He knew that she detested him; what did he care? She might be unfriendly but Lucien would never close the doors of the Château de Roquemont to *him*, because of their blood-tie. Dear old Lucien who felt so passionately about family traditions, etc.!

But Michel didn't want to flirt with Simone today because it made Mimi so angry, and the atmosphere would become so unpleasant that he would be forced to make excuses and go home.

Since the flight from London, he had felt strangely drawn to the young English girl. He had rarely before met her type. She had an attraction all her own ... She was not beautiful, but her fresh charm, and touch of seriousness, combined with reserve, fascinated him. There was also something about the curve of her full warm lips and in her soft warm eyes which disturbed and invited a man, although Michel was perfectly well aware that no invitation was intended. He found her voice, her French, often ungrammatical but courageously spoken, delightful.

He made pretence of speaking to Sophie just in order to come closer to Juliet and say another word to her.

Simone pressed her pink lips together and flushed with anger. *This* she was not going to have! Michel was not to withdraw his attention from her even for a moment in favour of someone who was nothing more than an employee in this house. Yes – even if Mrs. Ingram *was* her godmother!

It was actually Sophie who provided a loophole for Simone's next move.

"Why won't you come and talk to me, Simone, you horrid thing?"

"You get Mees – er Juliet to wheel you in and I'll come down after I've changed and talk to you," she said.

She glared at Michel then turned to her mother who had been watching them all, a cynical twist to her lips.

"Maman, you will tell Hortense to lay another place for lunch, won't you?"

"Has Michel been asked to lunch?" asked Mimi with her most frozen smile.

"If there is no food, I can always share the bread that you usually throw to the swans," said Michel, his own smile freezing.

Furious, Mimi turned her back on him and walked indoors.

Michel called after Juliet:

"Sophie says you are teaching her to speak English fast. I want a lesson, too."

She called back:

"You certainly don't, M. le Comte. You speak perfectly."

"But I can't write it – you must teach me how to write English," his voice followed her.

Juliet felt embarrassed. Looking up she met Simone's resentful blue eyes. She didn't think she was being a great success with Mlle Valais. Then suddenly Simone's brow cleared and she gave a little laugh.

"The Comte is a great one for joking, pay no attention to anything he says, Mees – er—"

"Please call me Juliet."

"Yes, of course, Juliet."

No more was said between them. Sophie started to chatter about all that they had been doing while Simone was in Paris.

Juliet did not find the atmosphere during lunch, which was served at a long table under an awning on the terrace, very pleasant. Ideal conditions; dream-like beauty of scene – luxury, exquisite food, chilled lobster mayonnaise – early strawberries and cream – iced hock – the very reverse of the meals Juliet used to eat. Yet in comparison, when she thought of the old days at home when she and Daddy and Nick had lunch together (joking most of the time), then clearing away, all the washing up, the hard work, she preferred it. No luxuries – nothing that could be compared with the Château de Roquemont. But it was *fun*. This wasn't 'fun' at all. Juliet could not understand every word the de Maurevilles were saying. They spoke too fast, but her French was good enough to allow her to pick up most of it. It all seemed slightly bitter . . . acrid . . . the witty words tinged with sarcasm. Lucien, at the head of the table, hardly spoke. He looked preoccupied and was obviously disinterested in the smart repartee between his wife, his stepdaughter and his cousin. If Juliet had known, Lucien was suffering as usual from the lack of friendliness and co-operation from his wife. Just before lunch she had attacked him about Michel coming here.

"I see no harm in him having met the Caravelle and driven Simone home," he had said.

This had brought a spate of angry words from her, suggestions that Michel 'had designs' on the young girl. Lucien derided this.

"Don't be absurd. He knows perfectly well that Simone is not for him. She is barely eighteen – a mere child. He is twenty-six. He always has new girl-friends. He is just fooling around harmlessly with Simone whom he has known since you and I were married. I see no reason for you to be alarmed. Simone can take care of herself."

"You know nothing about Simone. She is *my* daughter. You have eyes and ears only for your *own*."

The old cry – the old unjust accusations. Lucien had felt too tired to argue with her. It always left such an unpleasant taste in the mouth. Then she had further worried him by saying:

"I admit that it is not Michel who is making the running this time. It is Simone. But she's headstrong and refuses to listen to me. *You* are the head of the house and could refuse to let Michel come here."

"We've had this out before," was his cold reply. "You know I will never forbid Michel the house unless he has behaved really badly."

Then Mimi cooled down.

"Maybe he will stop fooling around with my Simone and turn his attentions to the little English Mees. I saw her giving him a look, and if I know Michel, he's already planning to get her into his net. All the better if she takes him away from Simone."

It was extraordinary how that remark had annoyed Lucien. He knew his stepdaughter – even at eighteen she was not as ingenuous or inexperienced as Juliet Browning. He would not want Michel to try any of his games with the English girl; she might take him seriously. Besides Michel could neither afford to marry nor did he wish to. Perhaps, Lucien mused, it might be a good thing if he did stop his cousin from being a too-frequent visitor here.

He did not know Juliet well enough yet to be certain of her character. Some of these 'still waters' could run very deep, he knew. She was quiet and appeared to have no wiles but man-like he, as well as Michel, had noticed the warm, unconscious seduction of her mouth – in contradiction to the direct, friendly manner – that touch of immaturity which was so charming. For all that he knew, she might be impressionable. Most certainly he did not wish her to be impressed by Michel.

Mimi had asked a crowd of her smart amusing friends from Monte Carlo to go rowing on the lake about five o'clock when it began to get cooler; then, later, to have drinks on the terrace.

He was really rather relieved when he heard that Mimi had told Juliet to disappear with Sophie. Ordinarily speaking he would have been glad to include Miss Browning in any party but not when Michel was around; neither did Lucien much care for Mimi's Monte Carlo crowd. There was always the bitterness, too, of knowing that Mimi shrank from producing her disabled child on social occasions.

Michel, who would have preferred to be allowed to follow Juliet around – having made up his mind to try his best to find out what lay behind that demure mask – if it *was* only a mask – was obliged to stay at Simone's side. Soon the tranquil lovely lake became the background for a screaming, laughing crowd in two boats.

After tennis, Simone put on a white swimsuit which showed her long legs and slim thighs and the seductive curve of her breasts. Michel borrowed a pair of Lucien's trunks. They dived into the cool waters. The sound of their voices and splashing as they dived echoed from the lake.

Lucien swam with them then tried to make himself pleasant to his guests; but most of the time was wondering what Juliet and little Sophie were doing. He would far rather have been with them.

He was always the soul of courtesy. He did not let Mimi down on these occasions when she wished him to play the perfect host. He did not get away from the party till they were all drinking their aperitifs. Then he went to look for Sophie.

He found her in her own room. He was filled with joy when he saw her – actually walking. Supported by Juliet, the little girl was stumbling a little, dragging the built-up boot after her, but *she was walking*. The sight delighted the father though his heart ached because Sophie looked so small and bowed, standing up. He was not so much aware of her deformity, when she was in her chair. She turned to him as he entered the room. It was rather a red, mutinous little face but she managed a sickly smile.

"*Tu m'as vu?* You see me?"

"Bravo, I'm enchanted, my little angel!" he exclaimed. "So very, very proud of you and happy."

"I am not. I'd rather be in my chair," she muttered giving Juliet rather a resentful look.

"Now, now, Princess," Juliet laughed and shook her head, "you promised me that you'd give this a real trial and not go back to that old chair all day. Even if you only walk for one hour every morning and afternoon your muscles will improve and you'll find

99

you'll soon be able to walk without holding on to my arm. Dr. Giraud has promised."

Sophie wrinkled her nose. She eyed her father beseechingly with her big dark eyes in the effort to gain his sympathy.

"I'm not to be *made* to walk, am I, Papa?" she whined.

Juliet looked at Lucien quickly. He looked back. How flushed Juliet was . . . like a pink-cheeked child with all those freckles . . . supporting another child. His heart went out to her. He fell in with her unspoken appeal, and said to his daughter.

"Oh, but you *are* to walk, Sophie, and, as Juliet says – it will get better every day. We have made a mistake in making you stay all the time in your chair."

"Come," said Juliet, pulling the child gently towards Lucien, "move like a Royal Princess slowly across the floor towards your *chevalier*. He will, I know, bend his knee to you."

"But, *of course*," said Lucien.

Then searching his memory he added:

"And did you find a name for the boot – wasn't it *Bootikens* – the little Ann in England called hers?"

"Yes," Juliet spoke eagerly for her pupil. "We were going to call it *White Magic,* and it is under a spell which gives it special powers. Sophie has to tap it three times with her stick and then it will carry her."

"There! A magic boot for my Princess!" exclaimed Lucien. "Come along, *petite* – let's see how our White Magic works."

Spurred on by the magic of the old game, Sophie began to shuffle across to Lucien on the little white kid boots. Juliet whispered:

"The left . . . yes . . . now the right . . . come on, darling."

Sophie reached her father. Then her sulky lips curved into a delighted smile. She actually broke away from her guide, hobbled alone, and held her arms out. He caught her up in his.

"My beloved Princess, this is better than bending the knee. Now we shall waltz together," and he whirled her around, singing gaily. She screamed with pleasure. Juliet gave a sigh of contentment. It was the first lesson but she hoped it was going to be the forerunner of many. She was going to make that child mobile – or die. The screams reached a crescendo of delight.

The door flew open. Mimi de Maureville walked in, faultlessly dressed as usual, and with a cocktail glass in one hand.

"*Mon Dieu* – what goes on? As I walked through the hall I

heard you scream, *mon pauvre enfant*—" she began shrilly.

Lucien put the child down. Mimi glanced at Sophie's feet – saw the built-up boot. An expression of horror crossed her exquisite face.

"*Bon Dieu!* What madness is this?" she added. "Who made you wear that awful thing? It hurts you doesn't it, my poor darling? You hate it, don't you?"

Sophie, once more uncertain of herself, began to whimper.

"Yes, I told Papa I didn't like it, but Juliet makes me try to wear it."

Mimi turned on Juliet.

"Since when have you been asked to change Sophie's entire routine and upset her?"

"Mimi! I beg you not to interfere—" put in Lucien furiously.

She turned on him.

"You are always accusing me of not paying attention to my child. Now when I do, you take the governess's part. Perhaps, *you*, too, are responsible for this cruelty. I could hear the poor child scream – it terrified me."

Lucien began to talk to his wife in rapid French. Juliet could only half understand. She felt hot and deeply embarrassed. More than that, she was frankly angry because in one moment Mimi had undone all the good that she had been trying to do for Sophie during the last hour. She guessed that Lucien was explaining that Sophie's cries had been of pleasure not of pain, and that Dr. Giraud had ordered the new régime – that Sophie *was* to be taken out of her chair and taught to walk.

Juliet could see how angry Lucien felt. His face was white and taut; Sophie had begun to cry. Juliet took her by the arm, and led her to her chair.

"Come, darling," she whispered, "I'll wheel you through to the bathroom and give you a nice cool shower."

After they had gone, Mimi said to Lucien:

"This is quite ridiculous. I don't care whether Juliet is Mrs. Ingram's god-daughter or not – I won't have her upsetting Sophie."

He protested:

"How dare you pretend to be so solicitous about our child when nine days out of ten you hardly find time to do more than throw her a word, or the odd box of chocolates."

Mimi ignored this.

"Who does Miss Browning think she is?"

"I doubt if she thinks about herself at all. Sophie is her one concern and she is acting under Dr. Giraud's orders."

"And, since when has *he* changed his mind? He agreed that if Sophie hates to wear that ghastly boot she should not be forced to do so."

"How can you use the word *ghastly*? It is the very thing Juliet is trying to wipe out — this continual reference to the misery of Sophie's disability. As for the boot it should be taken for granted. She must be made more normal and I am in full agreement. Too much has been done to keep her a permanent invalid in that chair."

Mimi gave her high-pitched laugh. She gulped down the rest of her aperitif.

"I'm beginning to find this funny. You intimate that I do not really care what happens to Sophie and wish to keep her in her chair and it is *you* who used to forbid anybody to take her out of it."

"You are deliberately being stupid in order to put yourself in the right," Lucien said, trying but failing to keep his temper. "I am entitled to change my views and Juliet has the matter under control. We were winning the victory until you interfered."

"*We*," repeated Mimi meaningly. "Are you lining up with the little Miss Browning against me?"

"Will you stop thinking about yourself and try to think only what is best for Sophie?" he almost shouted the words.

It was rare for him to raise his voice. For years he had remained calm and controlled in the face of all her opposition and hostility, her hopeless misunderstanding of Sophie. Mimi saw now that perhaps she had gone too far. Quickly she said:

"Oh, let's drop this. Come out and attend to your guests, Lucien. I won't interfere with Miss Browning. Let her get on with it. Maybe I was mistaken in thinking that Sophie was being hurt. But you are mistaken if you imagine I have not got her welfare at heart just as much as you have. It kills me to see her suffer. It always has done, but I just cannot show it as you do."

Lucien took a cigarette from his case and lit it. His fingers were trembling. As a rule he tried to avoid this sort of fracas with his wife. It was true that he did not understand her, he thought bitterly. At times her behaviour was incomprehensible. Yet she always managed to try and justify herself and make him wonder whether it was not true that she was not deliberately cruel but just incapable of the warm mother-love that the young English girl, who had been here for such a short time, showed her pupil.

"I'll be going out in a few moments," he said. "I'll go and say good night to Sophie and try to undo some of the harm you have done. My last advice to you, Mimi, is please leave Sophie to her governess. Juliet is not like old Mademoiselle or Fräulein. She is immensely sympathetic and trained, and she has a remarkable gift for dealing with children like Sophie. I will not allow you to hamper her efforts. You understand?"

Mimi muttered something under her breath and, shrugging her shoulders, left the room.

Lucien went in search of Juliet. His eyes were so sick, so full of shame, she felt deep pity for him.

He tried to smile at her – inwardly relieved to note that Sophie no longer seemed upset.

"Juliet and I are going to try and surprise Maman – I shall wear my boot again tomorrow, Papa."

He bent and kissed her. He could have wept.

"Maman has changed her mind and wants you to try, so that will please her as well as me. *Bonne nuit, adorée,*" he said, and turning, quickly walked towards the door. Once there he turned back and gave Juliet the faintest smile. "Thank you, Juliet."

It had been the second time since she arrived at Roquemont that he had thanked her. She felt the strangest longing to drive that naked misery out of his eyes but could think of no possible way of doing it. She could see only too well how things were between Lucien and his selfish self-seeking wife. But thank goodness Madame *had* changed her mind about the boot.

Juliet, always interested in other people's points of view, tried to make up her mind as to why Mimi seemed so anxious to stick to the old unhelpful method that turned Sophie into a complete invalid. She could only suppose that Sophie in her chair, making no effort, worried the mother's conscience less than the sight of the crippled child hobbling around with a surgical appliance. What a queer complex character! What a strange household she found herself in, Juliet reflected. For all its beauty and glamour, it had a sinister side. She was going to come up against Mme de Maureville many times in the future; she could see that. It stood out a mile.

Chapter Eleven

DURING the three hot summer months that followed, Juliet worked as she had never worked before to try and bring about some physical and mental improvement in her little pupil. So far she had had no success with the bathing. She had tried only twice to get Sophie into the sea but this had met with such resistance from her – that Juliet had had to abandon it. But she did not intend to give up all hope. Anyhow, it was the walking that she felt to be the most important thing and over this she had achieved an outstanding and spectacular success. Having recovered from her former complete aversion to the boot (her *White Magic*), and with Juliet's constant drive and help, Sophie at last began to wear it – each day a little longer – until it became part of her daily life. At first she refused to walk an inch without clinging to Juliet's arm. Then she steadied herself with her little crutches. Finally she walked only with the white stick that her father had had specially made for her with a padded handle and rubber ferrule, so that she shouldn't slip.

It was a tremendous joy to Lucien to find his little daughter using her wheel-chair less and less. Finally he became quite accustomed to seeing her hobbling around on her little stick. His gratitude to Juliet knew no bounds but he never heard Mimi pay her a single compliment.

Mimi appeared more upset, when she saw Sophie walking in her slightly ungainly way, than she used to be when she was in her little pink chair.

Lucien tried to understand the psychological disturbance in his beautiful wife's mind and heart. She must, he knew, live with a guilt-complex because the whole disaster was her fault. That he could not deny. But when she chose to be awkward with Sophie or worse still to neglect her, his gorge rose; neither would he tolerate her being difficult and sarcastic with Juliet.

He had overridden her continual grumbles about the new playmate, Tache. He honoured her wish that the dog should not be allowed inside the Château, but Tache had become a regular playmate for Sophie out of doors. He had grown accustomed to seeing her hobbling along with her pet in front or behind her. Juliet was excellent with animals and was gradually training Tache to be obedient. Sophie adored him.

Now, to Lucien, Juliet could do little wrong. Only the other day, Dr. Giraud had said to him:

"The English demoiselle is a fine type, Monsieur, and Sophie is so much better, it is miraculous. Have you not noticed that she has more colour and is putting on a little weight? She is altogether less lethargic. Mees Browning has done her a world of good."

Lucien knew that. He also knew that out of Mimi's guilty conscience, there had arisen a new warped jealousy – an antagonism towards the young English girl who helped Sophie so greatly. Mimi seemed unable to resist a dig at her. When she spoke of Juliet to Lucien, she had begun to call her '*your* dear Juliet' with knife-edge sarcasm. Lucien pretended to take no notice. Only once when she had alluded to Juliet not as 'Sophie's best friend' but as a young woman who amused *him*, personally, he had turned on her.

"I know how you and most of the women in your set behave and how little you value high morality or idealism. You despise mine. I know that. Any attractive man would be a target for you or for Simone, who is rapidly growing like you. But Juliet Browning is not like that and I do not think that I am. I have no personal feeling towards this young girl except one of extreme gratitude – of relief because at last I feel that Sophie is secure and can be entirely trusted to her."

It was generally at this sort of pitch that Mimi (having made herself sufficiently disagreeable) climbed down. She patted his shoulder and pouted at him:

"Oh, you are a cross old thing! And so stupid. Can't you see that I am just as delighted as you are that Juliet has done so much for Sophie. I just think that sometimes you more or less build the world around them and their activities and that you have no interest in me or mine."

Lucien had a ready, bitter answer for that.

"It is a good many years since you wished me to show interest in you or to share with you the *dolce vita* which you adore. No – you can never accuse *me* of neglecting *you*, and get away with it, *ma chère*."

He had so much to make him bitter – to tear his nerves in shreds – for he never knew where he was with Mimi and had not done so for years. He just knew that he could not put one foot right with her. As for her friend, the German neurologist, Mimi, in Lucien's opinion, was seeing him too often and too much alone. He did not want a real show-down over Max Sternburg for the moment. For the sake of both Mimi's daughter and his – he wanted to believe the best of their mother and to preserve the unity of the home and the honour of his name. He just hoped that Mimi told the truth when she said she was interested in Max only as a friend and because of his work, as many of her friends went to him for psychiatric treatment.

Simone was more generous over the question of Sophie than her mother. She always had been. She was overjoyed to see her little stepsister walking around and when she was down in Roque-mont, she even worked with Juliet for Sophie's betterment. She used to play her 'pop' records and, taking Sophie by both hands whilst Juliet supported her from the back, pretended to make the child Twist. One day they persuaded Lucien to join in the dance. Simone had told her mother about it afterwards.

It was *formidable*, she had said, to see Papa Twisting. He looked quite handsome and amusing when he laughed like that, and his hair was untidy, and he was so relaxed. Mimi said this was ridiculous.

"Most undignified of Papa – in front of the governess, too," she had said.

Then Simone had dropped a thoughtless hint that she thought Papa seemed to find it fun dancing with Juliet.

"I've come to the conclusion that I can't stand that girl," was Mimi's snap reply.

Simone did not agree.

"Oh, I think she's quite nice really, Maman. She's been very decent to me – helping me with my English. I speak much more fluently now and Sophie can speak quite well and is beginning to write a little. Did you hear her on the piano yesterday? She started to play a scale."

"Oh, yes – I admit Juliet is excellent as a teacher and I know she is much better than the other governesses, but I just don't take to her. Juliet Ingram said she was a sweet girl but I think under the sweetness there lies a definite sting. She looks at me sometimes as though she hates me and I don't like it."

That had brought a laughing response from Simone who, un-like other people, was not afraid of her mother.

"Well, *you're* very cool and distant with *her*, *chère* Maman."

"Nevertheless, I will not have her casting eyes at your step-father," said Mimi suddenly in a venomous voice.

"I didn't think you'd mind if she did—" began Simone. But even Simone was not allowed to say things like that, and her mother, scarlet in the face, hissed at her:

"You're being impertinent. Please leave my room."

Simone walked off, shrugging. Mimi, who had been dressing for dinner when this conversation took place, sat down at her telephone and called Max's number. She needed soothing. Wonderful, understanding Max always said the right things to her. Once he had said: "You are a sweet cat with claws. You need petting and caressing. No man can expect such a divine creature to be interested only in being a wife or mother. Poor de Maureville is no psychologist."

Mimi knew that. Max was the man she needed. Max had more money, too. Much more. His brother was one of the biggest industrialists in West Germany. But for the moment he valued his reputation as a doctor and did not intend to have a divorce, so Mimi dared not show Lucien what she really felt about the future. And she certainly was not going to have a young girl like Juliet trying to take her place as Sophie's mother, (which was what she was doing when it boiled down to it), or thinking that she could make herself indispensable to Lucien. She, Mimi, would be a laughing stock with all her friends if they thought that her husband preferred to dance with his child's governess than with his own wife.

Out of sheer perversity she decided to arrange a dinner-dance with Lucien.

She had some difficulty in persuading him to accept the arrangement. Cunningly, she invited the friends he liked – the de Clermonts.

"I thought we'd all go and have dinner and dance afterwards at the Carlton," she told Lucien.

She had wandered into his dressing-room while he was changing for dinner; only half-dressed, herself, she wore a transparent negligée, her long amber hair tumbling around her shoulders.

The husband who had once been so passionately in love with her, barely glanced in her direction. Once, if Mimi had come in like this, looking so alluring, he would have felt his pulses stir. This evening he was impervious to her feminine seductions. He knew her too well. He was surprised by what she told him and immediately suspected that she had some hidden motive although he said nothing about this, having no wish to start a row. But he did point out that he wasn't fond of dancing, which she knew. Then she pounced:

"Oh, but I've been hearing wonderful reports from Simone that you are learning to Twist, *chéri*. Perhaps the little Juliet's freckled nose is leading you into bad ways—" Mimi trilled with laughter.

Lucien, his lips grim, went on brushing his hair. So that was it! She didn't particularly want to dance with him, herself, but she couldn't bear the thought that he had danced with Juliet Browning. What a little dog in the manger! And how Mimi hated any other woman having anything that she couldn't get herself. If *he* had suggested a dinner-dance with her she would have made a dozen excuses not to accompany him.

He said quietly:

"My dancing as you call it with Juliet was a question of just a few steps in order to amuse Sophie. Juliet is trying to interest her in new ways of using her muscles by moving to music."

"I am delighted," purred Mimi. "Long may your British paragon of virtue last."

He turned now and gave his wife a long searching glance.

"Anybody would think, my dear, that you were displeased rather than delighted that your child is being so well looked after and has made such progress."

"Oh, don't let's start all that," she pouted. "You are so obsessed with this subject. I *am* delighted but I can't keep making a terrific issue of it, day and night."

"No, you can't," he said ironically.

"Well, are you going to agree to the foursome at the Carlton?"

"If you wish," he said wearily. "Although I didn't think Paul and Annette were keen dancers."

"I told them you wished them to be our guests."

"Well, since you have arranged the party in my name, of course I will go," said Lucien coldly.

She looked at him through her lashes. She had no real interest in this handsome aristocratic husband of hers. He and his ideals bored her, but a sudden desire to practise her wiles seized her. She liked to think she could drive that cold hostility from his face.

Suddenly she gave a merry laugh and, coming close to him, flung her arms around his neck.

"*Mon petit Corbeau* ... must we always quarrel? Don't you love your Mimi any more?"

He stood stiff and unbending in that rare and unexpected embrace. She had not called him *Corbeau* for years. In the passionate warmth of their early love she had given him that as a nickname. *Corbeau – Raven –* on account of his black hair. It was strange but the sound of that name no longer moved him. On the contrary it increased his feeling of bitterness because she had destroyed his boyish absolute love for her. *Even more terrible than losing love through death is to have it destroyed in life.*

He unclasped her fingers from his neck and gently drew back from her.

"My dear, it was agreed between us long long ago that love no longer has any real meaning for us, and we only live together because of the children *and* because of my name which you bear. If I thought your sudden interest in me was genuine, I would act differently, but I don't intend to repeat the experience of the other morning, and be rejected the instant I make an advance. We will go to The Carlton and dine and dance with the de Clermonts, but please let there be no hypocrisy between us."

She very quickly proved that he was justified in what he said, because she swung in an instant from seduction to rage. She looked for a moment as though she could have hit him, then gave a rasping laugh.

"Charming! Very gentlemanly indeed – trying to humiliate me."

"Oh, don't be absurd, Mimi."

She marched to the door and flung a passing gibe at him over her shoulder.

"I was absurd even to remember that I once cared a fig about you, and if I don't love you any more it's your fault. Because Sophie was born as she is – you've always blamed me and—"

"Please be quiet. I will not be drawn into one of these senseless discussions about the past. You know perfectly well how sympathetic I was with you at the time Sophie was born. It has been your attitude to her since, as well as to me, that disgusts me."

She screamed at him:

"Oh, go to the devil and spend the rest of your time with dear little Juliet Browning whom I am sure does not disgust you. She is a 'yes' girl. She does exactly what you tell her. But I will not have you fooling around with her in front of Simone or the staff. It will cause a scandal."

If Lucien hadn't been so infuriated he would have laughed. That was rich, he thought ... Mimi, complaining about scandalous behaviour. But he was not going to have Juliet's name tarnished by this cruel and egotistical woman and he said so.

"If you think you are going to worry or influence me into getting rid of Juliet, you are wrong. She is here to stay for as long as Sophie needs her and as long as *she* will stay. But I warn you, not for the first time, Mimi, that you had better not upset her and try to drive her away. Sophie *needs* her. Do you understand?"

He heard Mimi's high-pitched voice from the next room:

"So do you, don't you, *mon cher*?"

She did not wait to hear his angry reply.

Dinner that night was rather strained. Mimi had lapsed into sulks. Simone, herself, was in a poor mood because she had been prevented from dining out with a new boy-friend whom she had recently met at a party in Mougins. He belonged to the fast-driving, fast-living playboy set that Lucien particularly abhorred. Even her own mother had told her that young Jean–Paul was not a suitable escort for her, for although he came of a wealthy family he was not yet twenty-one and certainly not yet contemplating marriage. It was a brilliant match that Mimi wanted for Simone.

Simone was bored because even Michel's attentions had fallen off and lately when he had come up to the Château he had rather brazenly shown a preference for trailing around after Juliet and Sophie. Juliet had made it quite clear to Simone that she had no interest at all in the Comte de Condine, but Michel's attitude hit at Simone's vanity. She thought Juliet a nice girl but she couldn't quite see why she seemed to charm men with so little effort. Maybe, as Simone had told her mother on one occasion, men *liked* freckles and wind-blown hair and a complete lack of artifice. But Maman was rather nasty about Juliet and accused her, behind her back, of angling for favours, even from Papa. Simone wasn't altogether in agreement about that. She really had a sneaking regard for Mees Browning.

Juliet, during the meal this evening, was conscious of an atmosphere and, as usual, felt desperately sorry for Lucien. He tried in his courteous way to keep up some kind of discussion during dinner – he did so dislike an undignified row in front of Hortense.

Just before they rose to go into the salon for coffee, Mimi suddenly came out of her sulk and flashed a brilliant smile at Juliet.

"I was *so* glad to hear that you have been encouraging my husband to dance, Juliet. It's done him so much good, and I owe you a favour. For the first time for a long while he is taking me out to dance. I shall be able to test your powers of teaching."

Juliet cleared her throat. The swift colour came into her cheeks which Mimi noted with malicious pleasure. Lucien flung his wife a warning glance, but she went on:

"Do you think he has any real talent for Twisting?"

"R-really, M-madame," stammered Juliet, "it was Sophie I was teaching. W-with Monsieur I tried j-just a brief step or two."

"And I do *not* intend to Twist in public," put in Lucien curtly. "If we dance, we *dance* at the Carlton, Mimi."

Mimi got up, trilling with laughter.

Juliet felt uneasy. She didn't quite know what lay behind all this but it wasn't the first time she had sensed the enemy in Mme de Maureville. Juliet coud not cope with her rapid changes of mood, her petty jealousies and digs. Juliet had decided that within herself, Mimi must feel thwarted in some way. Surely only a frustrated woman could behave as she did.

As for Lucien ... Juliet followed the tall graceful figure of her employer as he moved out of the dining-room with his wife and stepdaughter, and decided to avoid the family this evening. She would skip the coffee and go to her own room. She disliked Mimi in a bad mood and she could hardly bear to see Lucien being taunted – quite apart from being the butt herself of Mimi's gibes. What did Mimi know about that Twist lesson? Presumably that silly girl Simone had made mischief. (Juliet had come to the conclusion that Simone was silly rather than deliberately malevolent like her mother.) It had all been so innocent – just a game, really, with Sophie, and she had been so pleased because Lucien was happy and gay as a boy, laughing – following her steps for a brief second, then interesting Sophie in the rhythm. They had been playing one of Sophie's Beatle records:

> She loves you, yeh, yeh, yeh,
> Because she loves you and you know that can't be bad.
> Yes she loves you and you know you should be glad.

There was a lot of truth in those silly popular words, *A Love Like That* . . .

Like what? Juliet for one blinding moment had looked at Lucien de Maureville and realized that he and love were synonymous in her heart.

This was the man she could have loved. This was the one for whom she had been waiting ever since she learned the meaning of the word love. Lucien was the most marvellous man in the world . . . the *beau idéal* as the French would call it . . . the *preux cheva-lier*. For surely Lucien was the most valiant of creatures. The gallant type who in the Middle Ages would have been some girl's hero and lover – for whom she would have embroidered her hand-kerchief so that he might wear it on his sleeve during the Tourna-ments.

All rather ridiculous and romantic and impossible. Juliet had trodden on this flash of emotional awakening, trying to stamp it out at birth. Lucien de Maureville was Mimi's husband. No mat-ter what Mimi was like, he was her husband and he of all men was the first to recognize that fact. Never once in the months she had lived at Roquemont had he given her a single look or touch to suggest that he thought of her *as a woman* as well as Sophie's governess. She knew that he respected and liked her for he said so. He never stopped showing his appreciation of the progress little Sophie had made under her care. When she wrote to Aunt Ju, she had told her many times that the job had proved a great success and that she was eternally grateful. She was so happy at Roquemont. It was a wonderful life as well as a wonderful job – taking part in the rehabilitation of the little girl.

Whatever happened, Juliet told herself not to allow a senti-mental note to creep into her regard for Sophie's fascinating papa.

She settled herself down to do some letter-writing. Hortense, looking rather sour, came in with a cup of coffee and said rather pointedly that Monsieur had sent it.

Juliet thanked her, embarrassed. She adored this French coffee but she had no wish to make the staff wait especially on her. She knew that they resented it. In particular old Blanche was horrid. Unco-operative and always trying to make mischief with Sophie, out of pure jealousy, of course. Juliet could forgive the old peasant woman, but she found it hard to forgive Mimi for some of the things she did or said.

Then there was Maria, Mimi's personal maid, who in her sly

fashion had once tried to gossip with Juliet; first of all praising Madame for her beauty and elegance, then discussing her behaviour, and her affairs.

"M. de Maureville is so 'andsome. I lika him. But she lika the Herr Doktor. He very 'andsome and blond but I no lika him, but Madame always on telephone and one day I hear her say '*Io t'amo*', which mean she love him . . ." The Italian girl had ended with a giggle. Juliet, with fiery cheeks, had ordered her out of the room.

"Don't dare come here and talk about Madame behind her back," she had said, thereby making a future enemy of Maria.

It left a nasty taste in Juliet's mouth. It seemed terrible if it were true that Mme de Maureville had a boy-friend behind Lucien's back. *Simply terrible!*

Am I a prig, she asked herself? Just a pompous prig? Ought I to be more tolerant about married people who get divorced?

To Juliet, marriage was a sacrament: if not why take vows in church? Why even sign a contract in a civil office? What was the value of these vows and contracts if they were so easily to be broken? What was the value of love if it was only to end in hatred? Why have morals? Why didn't all men and women behave like savages and give way to lust? Surely after all these thousands of years of civilization people should *be* civilized and stick to the rules laid down for them.

Juliet thought over these problems with misgiving. The letter from her brother had upset her. Nicky wrote that he was still in love with *his* married woman, and had admitted, frankly, sleeping with her, yet he had told Juliet he knew she was right and that he ought to break with Lee. He just couldn't bring himself to do so. He was thinking of sending for her as soon as his ship reached the next port, he said.

Juliet had written back, frantically begging him not to do this.

Tonight was her night for writing to her father but she only got a quarter way through her letter and stopped. She couldn't tell Daddy about Nicky's love-affair. She couldn't write a completely happy uninhibited letter such as she had done these last few months. Tonight she felt certain reservations, tendencies within herself to feel a strange but definite distress whenever she mentioned Lucien de Maureville's name – or Mimi's.

She was still wondering whether to tell Daddy about the

113

unhappy state of affairs between her employers when Lucien knocked on her door. She heard his voice:

"Are you there, Juliet?"

Immediately she ran to the door, opened it, and joined him in the corridor, attractive with its graceful archways, walls and ceiling hung with a charming paper patterned with roses. A rose-pink carpet covered the floor. Little gilt wall-lights with crystal drops diffused soft, golden light. All very French and delicately beautiful – like Mme de Maureville Juliet always thought. She never failed to admire her taste and to wonder how any woman with such an eye for beauty could have such an ugly character.

Juliet looked up at Lucien with her usual frank friendly smile. She thought she had never seen him look more tired. Was it her imagination or was he losing weight? His face seemed thinner and there were deeper lines carved on either side the fine mouth. He held a half-smoked cigar in one hand. Suddenly as she looked up into the dark deep eyes, despite all her efforts not to let it happen, her truant heart jerked with unbearable emotion. He spoke to her as he usually did, in English:

"I have been wondering, Juliet, whether it would do Sophie good to get away from the extreme heat on the coast for the last two weeks of this month. Whether I would send you both to Leques-les-Bain."

She flashed a look of inquiry. He continued:

"Leques is a health resort, not very gay but they have an outside band in the summer and a Casino, although I know these things do not really attract you. It is on Monte Coldes-Leques, high up above Cannes, and the air is very beneficial, and the hotel excellent. I will send you up in the car. I can come up during the week-end with Mimi and Simone, or by myself – to see Sophie. It is a wonderful place and you get these restorative baths and drink the waters. The treatment would be good for the child's limbs. It is also deliciously cool compared with the Midi during August. I've never before considered sending Sophie away from home because I have never known anyone I would trust her with, but *you*! . . ." he broke off, signifying his absolute confidence in her. She felt her cheeks grow warm. She said:

"Of course, Monsieur, I will take Sophie to this place, if that is what you would like."

He was silent a moment. Even though he had formed the plan, he had known that he would not like it for *himself*. The Château de Toquemont would seem a sad place once his adored little Sophie – and Juliet – had gone. He had no wish whatsoever to be left alone with his wife and stepdaughter. But that wonderful mountain air would be better for the child, and he also had a definite wish to get Juliet away from Mimi's continual taunts and unkindnesses for a bit. He was sure they did not go unnoticed by Juliet although the young girl never retaliated or complained. Suddenly, involuntarily, he said:

"I shall miss both Sophie and you, *mon enfant*, but if you are willing to take her, I will make the arrangements."

She lowered her gaze. He had never called her '*mon enfant*' before. It made him seem older – yet to her, he was still a young man – what was he – thirty?

"When are we to go, Monsieur?" she asked.

"I will telephone the hotel and see if they can give you communicating rooms at once. The day after tomorrow is Saturday, isn't it? I will send you up then, or drive you there myself."

"Very well," said Juliet, "I'll tell Sophie. We'll have a wonderful time together, I am sure, and I shall adore to see the mountains."

"You adore everything," he smiled.

He found himself looking at her with a yearning which he could barely conceal. How sweet she was – docile, co-operative, reasonable; and yet self-possessed and independent, too. He could certainly trust her with Sophie – anywhere in the world.

For a split second, a wildness that was rare in a man of Lucien's strong nature, compelled him to look at her not merely as Sophie's governess, but as a woman with a sweet ardent body to be loved – caressed – *possessed*. She was made for love, he thought, and so deserving of it. Oh God, what a fortunate fellow the man would be who would eventually marry her. She was all that any man could desire; born to be wife, mother, lover and friend.

Tonight, for the first time, de Maureville saw Juliet as all these things in wonderful, thrilling combination. In particular, he saw her as a lover to be taken physically, and adored. He was amazed to find how tremendously she appealed to him.

She was very attractive. Almost as petite as Mimi whose head barely touched his shoulder – she gave the appearance of being stronger than Mimi. But she had nothing brittle or artificial about her. She was more truly feminine than Mimi and much more lovable in the nicest sense. Of course she was younger – only two years older than Simone. The glorious bloom of youth was upon her. In the dewy freshness of the freckled face that was richly tanned now like the slim arms, the brown legs with faint golden down upon them and rounded knees, and rather chubby childish feet in their white sandals. She looked like a wood-brown nymph this evening, he thought – all that glowing colour accentuated by the pale cream of the short silky dress, which was drawn into the small waist by a suède belt. Her hair had a new tinge of gold at the tips bleached by the Mediterranean sun.

Lucien for some time had been aware of the young English girl's physical development. She had definitely blossomed since she exchanged the old hard life in London for the more luxurious one at Roquemont. She was almost beautiful tonight, he thought. Mimi attempted to belittle her; to sneer at the blunt freckled nose, the unruly hair, the occasional *gaucherie*. But to Lucien, Juliet was a lovely person in every way and he loved her. She had done more than enough to make him love her by changing Sophie from a whining chair-bound invalid into a happy little girl who could walk around in her *White Magic* boot.

He could so easily have lost his head, pulled her into his arms and kissed that tender generous mouth quite madly. Instead he swung round, and without even saying good night walked away from her.

Juliet looked after him. Her heart raced and her thoughts were chaotic. What was the matter with Lucien? Had she annoyed him in some way? Why had he stared down at her in that queer, almost wild way? She could not bear to think that he was displeased with her. Neither did she wish to read more into that look – that abrupt departure – than had been meant. She hardly dare think about Lucien de Maureville any more at all. She only knew that the letter to Daddy would not be finished tonight.

Half-confessed, half-understood emotions, confused and troubled her, long after she was in bed. Lying there, sleepless, gazing at the brilliant moonlight that poured through the half-open shutters, she tossed and turned. Her limbs seemed to tingle. Her head was hot – aching. She began to wonder if she had a fever. She longed for sleep – wanted to stop remembering Lucien, and that deep crazy look that had suddenly flamed in his eyes. She pressed her flushed face into the pillow and tried not to let her feelings run riot. But she discovered that she was frantically in love and that love was something she had never known before. She was up against emotions stronger than herself.

This was not like a moment with a man like Luke Farrell – or a light romantic skirmish with any other boy-friend she had made.

Lucien de Maureville was different. His was a powerful personality. He had a disturbing influence over her. Perhaps it was his loneliness. He was such a tragic figure somehow, in his vast magnificent Château with all his wealth, his possessions and the beautiful wife who seemed to hate him; a man in hell. It haunted Juliet. She felt so desperately sorry for him. Such compassion might lead her into dangerous waters. She could well believe that.

She put both her hands over her ears as though to shut out the sound of her own mad heart-beats. It was as though that heart was betraying her – forcing a wedge between her and her old principles.

"You can't fall in love with him, you can't, you can't – he's married. It's all wrong. You mustn't love him!"

She found herself saying those words aloud. She sat up, her body drenched with perspiration. The very sight of the romantic exotic moonlight became a torment. Angrily she closed the slats of the shutters and returned to her bed. In total darkness she tried once more to sleep – to shut herself and her stupidity up in a dark silent void.

Oh, it was a good thing she was going away; that *he* was sending her and Sophie out of the Château even for a short while. It would give her time to recover herself – to sort things out; and when she came back here she would let nothing that Lucien did or said affect her in this terrifying way.

Chapter Twelve

ON the night when the de Maurevilles went to the Gala dinner in Cannes, they took Simone with them. Annette de Clermont had telephoned Mimi earlier to say that a cousin – a young student – had suddenly descended upon them. Mimi wasn't going to have her plans upset and told Annette to bring the nephew to the Carlton with them. He would be a suitable *vis-à-vis* for Simone as he was charming and, according to Annette, good-looking. The party would be six now instead of four; a little more gay.

Simone grumbled to Juliet who had become the recipient of her confidences.

"He sounds *too* dull – only nineteen. I hate very young boys. Besides I had hoped to meet Michel this evening. I was going to meet him surreptitiously at the Casino. I'm really very attracted by him, you know."

"Are you?" Juliet asked the question a trifle dryly.

"Yes, he has such sophistication. He amuses me."

"But you know your parents do not want you to see so much of him."

"Forbidden fruit is always the sweetest," said Simone languidly, then giggled.

Juliet shook her head. She was really rather sorry for this young girl who received such hopeless advice and training from her mother. But she thought it more tactful not to let Simone know what *she* thought of the Comte.

Juliet stood a moment in the salon with the de Maurevilles while they drank sherry, waiting for Marino to come with the car and drive them down to the town.

Madame, thought Juliet, was breathtakingly beautiful tonight, in a long tight dress glittering with light blue sequins that matched her eyes. Her amber hair was dressed high on her head with an aquamarine velvet bow at the back. Juliet wondered how any man could look at her without desire.

Simone wore a long dress, too – a pleated chiffon – caramel-coloured – moulded to her figure. Mother and daughter made a striking pair; but Lucien did not seem very impressed. Juliet noticed how he stood by the fireplace sipping his sherry, unsmiling, unbending. He certainly did not look as though he wanted to dance. He, himself, wore a white dinner-jacket tonight, with a black satin cummerbund. He looked remarkably smooth and attractive, Juliet decided.

Her heart flowed over with the deepest feeling for him but only once did she catch his eye; that was when Hortense announced that the car was at the door; Lucien put down his glass and turned towards her. Those dark sad eyes were unfathomable but they seemed to pierce her very soul. She suddenly lost her colour. She hoped nobody would notice. Mimi and Simone were busy with their own conversation, but Lucien saw the young girl's sudden pallor. As his wife and stepdaughter left the salon Lucien turned back to Juliet:

"Are you all right?"

She laughed nervously.

"Of course, why not?"

"You look – unusually fatigued."

Her teeth closed over her lower lip but she laughed again.

"I'm fine, thank you, Monsieur."

"I'm sorry you must be left behind," he said. "I assure you I'd rather you than I went to the Gala Night—"

He got no further. Mimi had come back. She now wore a billowing taffeta evening coat the same colour as her dress. Whether or not she had heard these few words spoken between her husband and Juliet, neither of them knew, but she gave Juliet one of those dazzling smiles that had such a knife-edge, and said:

"*Bonne nuit*, dear Juliet. It's sad you won't see your distinguished pupil twisting with his devoted wife."

Juliet felt her cheeks go hot. She saw Lucien's mouth tighten. Without a word he walked out of the salon.

Juliet smiled wryly once she was alone.

'*Tiens, tiens*, as they say over here,' she reflected, 'how catty can Madame be? Sometimes I feel I want to pack up and go home.'

When she thought about Sophie, she put that idea right into the background. Yet she was beginning to find things a little awkward at the Château de Roquemont. She looked forward to her fortnight away even though it meant leaving *him*. It would be almost a relief.

She wanted to write and tell Phyl all about the present state of affairs here, began the letter, then stopped. How could she possibly tell her friend that she had fallen in love with her employer? How could she reconcile it with all the good advice she used to give Phyl?

The Château seemed silent and deserted after the others had gone. The staff did not come near Juliet. They were fully occupied in watching television in their own quarters. Juliet made sure that Sophie was fast asleep then retired to her own room. She decided to wash her hair, then get down to some dress-making. Last time that she was in Nice, on her off-duty day, she had bought a length of most attractive terylene. She intended to make a straight sheath dress for these summer evenings which were still so warm.

She was just about to change into a dressing-gown when she heard old Blanche's cackling voice outside her door.

"A visitor for you, Mademoiselle."

"Who is it—?" began Juliet.

But Blanche had shuffled off. Juliet could only presume that Hortense and the others were so busy enjoying themselves that they had let the old nurse open the front door.

Without the least idea who she might be going to see, Juliet ran a comb quickly through her thick unruly hair and walked into the hall. She was dismayed to find the tall elegant figure of the Comte de Condine standing by the staircase. He bowed low, passing his finger over his moustache.

"Ah, Mlle Juliet, *comment ça va?*"

Juliet's eyes were unwelcoming.

"I'm sorry, M. le Comte, nobody is at home."

"All the better – I only came to see you. I knew you would be alone. I happened to telephone Simone this morning and she told me they were all going to the Gala Night at the Carlton. How remiss of them to leave you out of it!"

"I'm not here to go out dining and dancing, but to look after Sophie," said Juliet, with as much dignity as she could manage. She never had been the haughty, dignified type. She was naturally friendly, but Michel de Condine irritated her. She disliked everything he stood for. He was so worthless that she was surprised that he was of the same blood as a man like Lucien de Maureville.

"You must excuse me, M. le Comte," she said abruptly, "but I am going to be busy this evening. I have no time for entertaining."

"Oh, come," he protested. He gave her a deep intense look from his heavy-lidded eyes and came nearer her. She wrinkled her small nose; she could smell the perfumed brilliantine he used.

"You must forgive me—" she began again.

He interrupted:

"Surely you're not going to be so discourteous? In the absence of my relatives will you not offer me a glass of wine?" Then as she remained silent, he went on: "You know how Lucien dislikes to refuse hospitality to any of his family or friends."

Yes, she knew that; but she also knew that Lucien had little time for Michel. Nobody really, but that silly girl Simone, was at all keen on him.

She did not see, however, that in her capacity of employee here, she could order the Comte from the Château. She said in a cool voice:

"If M. le Comte would like a glass of wine, I will, of course, give him one."

"Ah!" he exclaimed, "you are speaking delicious French to-night. Congratulations! Even your accent has improved vastly since that flight we shared in the Comet."

Juliet made no answer. As she turned, she noticed old Blanche still standing in the background near the entrance to the kitchen wing. She was peering at them out of the shadows. She looked like an old witch. In Juliet's opinion she was rather a nasty old character – a sort of spy, always making mischief with everybody. In a more peremptory voice, Juliet asked:

"Where is Hortense?"

"Off duty," muttered Blanche. "They are all off duty."

"Then will you please bring a tray and a glass, and I will find the wine for M. le Comte."

"I am not a servant—" began Blanche rudely, but this time it was Michel who crossed swords with her. In her own language he informed her that she was a rude old so-and-so and that she was to obey the English Mees immediately, or he would report her to Monsieur.

Blanche eyed Monsieur's cousin as though she could kill him, but went off to do as instructed.

Juliet did not like the whole set-up. Reluctantly she joined Michel in the salon and gave him his glass of white wine from a bottle that remained over from luncheon.

"I must apologize if it isn't properly chilled," she said.

Michel seated himself on the edge of the sofa, raised his glass, and smiled at the girl ironically.

"The expression on your face, my dear Juliet, will chill my wine as surely as a block of ice."

She said nothing.

He went on:

"By the way, don't let that wretched old woman be rude to you. She's often rude to me. Mimi hates her. She lives here only because Lucien has the notion that he owes her bed and board because she is eighty and has been in the service of the de Maurevilles for so long. Lucien, as you know, has such a high standard of behaviour."

"Which is in his favour, Monsieur."

Michel grinned.

"You, too, have high standards. You amuse me."

"You are easily amused, Monsieur."

"But not so easily attracted."

She pressed her lips together, declining to make any comment.

"Oh, I know what you are thinking," continued Michel. "Everybody has told you I am chasing Simone, but I assure you that is only *pour passer le temps*. She looks divine but she has neither your intelligence nor your peculiar charm. You are very out of the common and very provocative in your quiet reserved English fashion."

Juliet deliberately glanced at her wrist watch.

"You must excuse me if I ask you to finish your wine and let me go, M. le Comte."

He set his empty glass down. Now he made a sudden movement towards her. Before she could prevent it, he caught her hands in his.

"For heaven's sake stop being so prim and formal. You are only flesh and blood, my dear, don't pretend! This attitude of the prude which you strike is all very well for a few moments, but it becomes boring."

"If you are bored, all the more reason why you should leave," she snapped, and tried to drag her fingers out of his which she found hot and unpleasant to the touch.

Deliberately he drew her closer, still smiling.

"Sweet cold maddening creature! I'm quite mad about you, you know. Don't ask me why. You aren't really beautiful except for your eyes and that divine English complexion, but you have a *je ne sais quoi* – what we French call *allure* – and it makes you irresistible."

Her heart began to beat disagreeably fast.

"Monsieur le Comte—"

"You have known me now for three months. Call me Michel."

"I will not and I would like you to let go my hands."

"Dar-r-r-l-eeng," . . . he used the English endearment, rolling the r's succulently, "your resistance fires me. You know they say that when one dies, one regrets only one's lost opportunities. Let us consider ours here tonight – alone with the family away. Let us take the chance the gods offer us. I assure you that you will not regret it. I don't believe you have ever had a lover, have you – you little cold thing? Why not let me teach you the delights of passionate love?"

"Because," said Juliet, her eyes blazing, "if I had any wish for sex-instruction I'd buy a book about it. I wouldn't consult you."

Her voice was biting.

Michel flung back his head and laughed.

"You are absolutely *delightful*. But when I look at the shape of your mouth, that full curved underlip, I cannot believe you so devoid of feeling. Now stop struggling. Resign yourself to this wonderful moment. And do you know, I find you so charming (and you are wonderful in every way – not only with poor Sophie), I might even ask you to marry me. My mother wishes me to settle down; so does Lucien. Of course I have no money, but if he thought I was going to make *you* the Comtesse de Condine, he might offer me an allowance. They are all so anxious for me to pay my bills and be a good boy. Would you not like to do some good for me as well as for Sophie? You *like* doing good. Sweet, sweet Juliet, you would be so *very* good for me – *hein*?"

After this long speech Juliet felt ready to scream. It was not that she couldn't take care of herself and she was not in the least afraid of Michel, but she felt infuriated by every word he said, and not in the least impressed by his tentative proposal of marriage. She said through her teeth:

"If you were the last man left alive, I wouldn't marry you."

"Then kiss me," he said.

And now, like a flash, he pulled her into his arms and smothered her protesting "no"; his lips hard against hers, one hand against her breast.

The familiarity infuriated her. She tried to hit out at him. He

123

took her hands, laughed and covered her soft crimson face and throat with kisses.

Outside the salon, old Blanche had been hovering, spying. The salon door was half open. Her eyes, still bright and hawk-like under her bushy brows, saw the young couple; the passionate embrace. Before Juliet tore herself free, the old woman turned away and hobbled back to the kitchen.

She had seen enough. She was cackling with malicious laughter. She wondered whether after this she would not be able to get her own back on the English Mees. Juliet had completely parted her from her little Sophie, and in her stupid, bigoted mind, Mees performed many acts of cruelty, such as making Sophie walk, giving her a cold bath, letting that flea-ridden dog play with her; a dozen other acts that Blanche called criminal.

Once free from Michel, Juliet blazed at him, protesting violently against his attempt to assault her. She told him to get out of the Château and stay out. Then she ran out of the salon and locked herself in her own room.

She was trembling from head to foot. Her lips felt bruised. No man before had ever kissed her like that. It was so very different from Luke's gentle love-making.

It was a relief beyond words to Juliet when she heard Michel's car start up and knew that he was leaving the Château. How dared he! *How dared he!* And she had meant it when she had told him that if he were the last man on earth she wouldn't marry him.

For a long time she felt thoroughly upset, unable to settle down to doing anything except walk up and down her room and brush away her angry tears. Of course she must tell Lucien – she must refuse to be left again in a position where Michel could repeat such behaviour. On the other hand, once she cooled down, she decided that it would not be nice of her to add to Lucien's burden by telling tales – letting Lucien know what a cur his cousin really was. She could imagine how furious he would be if he thought she had been insulted. Of course Blanche knew that Michel had called. Juliet could not conceal that fact. She would have to admit so much, but she wouldn't tell them about the kissing. And she was quite sure that Michel, himself, would keep quiet about it. By now he was probably regretting his idiocy.

All this increased Juliet's longing to get away to the mountains with Sophie. But everything considered, she had never felt more like going back to England. She had had a letter from Luke only yesterday telling her that he never stopped missing her, and that there was a place for her in the new Home in Bristol where he was now Medical Officer, if she wanted it.

But Luke was not the man for her and she knew it; much as she appreciated his friendship and fidelity.

She was at this precise moment, she told herself, what the French called *bouleversée*. Upside-down in her mind – confused – hardly knowing what to think, what to do for the best, mainly because of this sudden cyclone that had torn her by the roots from her usual tranquillity and reserve.

She was in love. She could not even *think* about Lucien de Maureville without feeling weak at the knees – shaking – feverish – almost as though she had been suddenly bewitched.

She knew that she mustn't give way to such feelings. Eventually she managed to calm down and go to sleep. She did not even hear the de Maurevilles return from their dinner-dance, so she had no idea of the miserable scene to which Lucien was subjected once they were back.

Mimi, divested of her gorgeous sequin dress, came into his room in a chiffon negligée and started a vicious attack on him.

To begin with, she was furious because he had only danced with her twice, then coldly, courteously declined to dance again except with Annette, or Simone. Mimi was well aware that it was her fault. She had not been pleasant to him even during their first dance. He had said:

"It's a farce, putting an arm around you, pretending to enjoy music and this rhythm. Please let us remain at our table for the rest of the evening."

She had nagged him to try once more, then unfortunately he missed his step and made her stumble. She had sneered: "You want a better teacher, *mon cher*. The snub-nosed Juliet is not so efficient after all."

That decided him. He would not dance with her again.

In the early hours at home she had something more with which to torment him. Almost triumphantly she broke into a tirade against Juliet.

"What do you *think*? Poor dear loyal old Blanche waited up to tell me; once we had left and your precious Juliet thought the staff was busy watching television, she let Michel into the house. Blanche was told to fetch them white wine, then to vanish, but she came back and saw the two of them in a clinch – passionately kissing *and* a bit more! A nice thing! Poor conduct on the part of the one who is supposed to be looking after our innocent child—"

Once Mimi drew breath Lucien spoke. He was dead-white. The muscles in his cheeks were working.

"I don't believe one word of this."

"You are so infatuated with Juliet, you call Blanche a liar?"

"Blanche dislikes Juliet. She has been jealous of her ever since she came and took Sophie out of her charge. She has trumped up this ugly story."

"You would make any excuse for that English girl!" said Mimi between her teeth. "You are ridiculous!"

"And you – what are you trying to do?" he demanded. "Do you *wish* to destroy Sophie's happiness and welfare and force Juliet out of our house?"

"You insist on glorifying her and stay blind to her faults. Well, ask her about Michel. I bet she won't deny it."

"Maybe Michel did come; what of it? Knowing him, he might well have kissed her – but I am sure not with *her* approval."

"How can you be so sure?" Mimi asked, scarlet in the face. "Since when have you become so intimate with Juliet that you know her character thoroughly? How can you be sure she is as innocent as her freckles? It strikes me that you have fallen in love with this English Mees. The sooner she leaves Roquemont the better."

He felt a freezing dislike of this woman whom he had once loved to distraction and made his wife. She was trying to destroy not only Juliet but *him*. Honour meant everything to Lucien de Maureville. Even in the year 1964, he was a man who detested promiscuity, uncontrolled sex and all the things that people laughed at and treated so lightly. For years he had lived without love and longed for it. But he had refused to take a mistress – to break the vows he had made to Mimi even though she, for all he knew, might long ago have broken hers. In the early hours of this morning, she was bringing him face to face with facts. He was in love with Juliet Browning. It had taken the thought of Michel embracing Juliet to alert him to it; to make him conscious that he loved Juliet.

At first she had not appealed to him in the physical sense, but lately he confessed to himself – he had been charmed by that young, eager, freckled face with the clear honest shining eyes.

Many a time he stopped outside the door of the salon and listened to her playing the piano for Sophie, or heard her laughter, her gay voice, in Sophie's room. Many a time he watched from his window while she and Sophie walked through the grounds followed by Tache the dog. He had seen her change from a pale, too-thin London girl into a strong, rounded, tanned young woman, deliciously full of health and vigour and the joy of life. He had thought what a sweet wife she would make for any man, what a wonderful, wonderful mother.

Silently he listened to Mimi's accusations. What she was saying about Juliet and Michel became more than destructive to his peace of mind. He could not tolerate the thought of Juliet in Michel's arms. 'More than a kiss' Mimi had said. Damn Michel. *Damn him*. He was not fit to touch her. There had been too many women in Michel's life. He had no respect for them.

Lucien heard Mimi repeat that it was high time Juliet returned to London, and that she would write and tell her friend, Juliet Ingram, how mistaken she had been in her god-daughter. Lucien turned on her. He said:

"I've heard enough. I don't care whether what Blanche has said is true or not; Juliet Browning is free to kiss whom she pleases. But Michel is a rat and always has been one, whether he is my cousin or not. However – he, too, is free and if they wish to kiss each other that is their affair. I shall not allow Blanche – or you – to turn this episode into a crime necessitating Juliet's dismissal. Only one thing counts with me – Sophie's happiness, and for every possible reason I intend to keep Juliet here with Sophie."

"Then I shall leave the Château—" began Mimi hysterically.

"You'll do nothing of the kind. As a rule, Mimi, I give you your head – but not this time. Quite apart from wishing to be fair to Juliet, I refuse to allow Sophie to be upset. And you will only leave the Château and go off to Paris during the fortnight that Juliet is up at Leques with Sophie. As you know I intend to send her and Sophie there to get some mountain air."

"And pray when will that be?"

"I had hoped this week-end, but they cannot take them at the Grand Hôtel de Leques until next Saturday."

Mimi made no response. She was tearing at the satin ribbons on her chiffon coat. He added:

"If you attempt to leave the Château for a night and try to trump up one of your vicious stories about Juliet and implicate me as you have done Michel, I shall do something I have never done before."

He broke off, clenching his fist.

"And what is that?" asked Mimi sullenly.

"I shall stop your allowance and cancel the lease of our Paris flat."

Mimi cooled down. She knew Lucien. She could drive him so far and no further. She was not really jealous of Juliet Browning; such an idea to her vain mind was laughable. It was just that she was annoyed because Lucien made such a thing over the English girl. His respect for the way Juliet handled Sophie always had the effect of doubling Mimi's sense of guilt. If darling Max would have taken her away, she might have gone to him tomorrow, but she knew he was not ready for her yet; neither had she any other man in view. She knew perfectly well that she must have money and luxury, and she was mad about Max. But until he was ready, she would stick to Lucien. He was rich. When she chose to be nice, he was also very generous. Besides, Simone was at an age when she needed money and security – and Lucien's authority. Bad as she was, Mimi was not prepared to wreck her elder daughter's life at this very moment. And certainly she was dismayed by the possibility that Lucien might cut off her allowance and take the Paris flat away from her.

She climbed down.

"I'm sorry. I know I've blown my top but I was so upset at the thought that that girl behaved so badly while we were out."

"I refuse to believe that she has behaved badly until I have questioned her about it. Then if she admits it, I shall merely warn her against Michel. After that, it is her business and not ours if she goes on seeing him."

Mimi controlled her wish to be nasty again. She put a hand on her husband's arm.

"It's stupid, fighting like this. Let's call a truce. I admit Juliet is wonderful with Sophie. I don't really want her to leave us."

"Then you had better start behaving as though you don't."

Again Mimi had to control herself.

"I'll do my best – but she annoys me."

"If she was a girl you liked – someone you could admire – she would not really be much good for our child," said Lucien cynically.

"Oh, good night," muttered Mimi and turned away, but as

she went she flung a final remark at him over her shoulder. "You don't mean that about my allowance or the flat, do you?"

"No – not if you stay at home for the summer and behave reasonably. I hate to use threats but you drive me too far, sometimes, Mimi."

She shrugged and left his room, shutting the door behind her. Lucien turned out his light and opened his shutters.

Dawn was breaking. A faint white vapour hung over the palm trees in the garden. The man's face was as grey as the morning light, and in his heart was the bitterness of death – of a pain almost too great to be endured.

He thought of that young girl sleeping in her room beside Sophie's – of all the kindness and patience which she showed to Sophie. He thought of her, kissing Michel; and of his own impossible position. He had no right to resent that picture of Juliet with a lover.

But he was in love with her. That was the ghastly part of it. He loved her as he had never loved Mimi whose attraction had been wholly sensual; nor as he had ever loved any other woman in his life and there had been one or two before Mimi. He was no saint.

He threw himself down on his bed and buried his face in the pillow.

For Sophie's sake he would try to keep Juliet at Roquemont, no matter what Mimi did or said; but he was beginning to realize that it might be much more difficult for him to live under the same roof with Juliet than to say good-bye to her.

Chapter Thirteen

JULIET sat on the veranda of the Grand Hôtel de Leques writing to her brother. She had just had a letter from Nicky re-directed from Roquemont. It had been a relief to her because he told her that soon after leaving Hong Kong he had decided not to break up Lee's marriage. He had realized that it would be foolish apart from the morality of the thing. He had no money and was committed to his career in the navy. He could not give Lee a proper home. It would never work out and at last he had admitted it.

Juliet's relief was tempered by her pity for Nick. His letter was unhappy. The Juliet of today was herself beginning to realize to the full what it meant to say good-bye to anybody you loved. She felt at a loss as to what to write to Nicky now.

It seemed to her a year instead of a week since she and Sophie came up to *Monte Coldes-Leques*.

It was a wonderful place. She had been able to write a glowing account of it to Daddy and her friend, Phyl.

The Grand Hôtel de Leques had been built close to a glorious mountain torrent which cascaded thousands of feet down towards the Leques Gorge.

The place had an almost Tibetan atmosphere – the village behind the hotel had been built out of reddish-coloured rocks which were almost vertical. Juliet had explored every inch of it; the tiny shops in a maze of narrow lanes and old galleried houses rising one above the other.

Even the hotel, itself, seemed to be fashioned from the rock-side although it was of modern structure with long glass-paned windows looking over the pines and fir-trees down towards the coast.

In mid-winter it was a ski-sports hotel. Now it was perfect for mid-summer – hot in the sun but exquisitely cool at night. The fresh mountain air had already made Sophie sleep better and brought some pink colour into that small face. She seemed to enjoy walking around Leques with Juliet although she said that she missed her frisking, gambolling pet, Tache; and, of course, she spoke continually of Papa.

Juliet was pleased with the progress in health and spirits of her little pupil, and she, herself, found it most relaxing and restful up here. But although she should, like Sophie, have slept soundly at night, she found it impossible to do so. She was so haunted by the thought of Lucien. She could not hear Sophie mention the word Papa without feeling that a knife was being twisted in her heart.

She gave up her letter-writing this afternoon and began to walk through the grounds. The gardens were terraced and she could go down hundreds of little steps, on either side of which the most beautiful coloured mountain flowers were cultivated. The rocks were deeply red. On one side she could see the waterfall, cascading like tumbled diamonds that glittered in the sunlight, making a pleasant hissing sound. On the other side she could see the little church of St. Pierre, and the chestnut groves which were famous up in this mountain resort.

At least once a day she and Sophie walked to the small medieval bridge which stretched across the torrent and looked down into the frothing, creaming water, which fascinated Sophie. It was truly a paradise. There was none of the artificial elegance of Cannes up here. The hotel itself was furnished simply with picturesque mats on polished bare boards; and the minimum of furniture; but it appealed to Juliet after Mimi's over-exotic Parisian décor. She knew that Mimi would have been bored to tears here – so would Simone, but Lucien would have loved it. He *did* love it; he had told her so, and she hoped to see him this week-end. Tomorrow, Sunday, he was driving up. Alone? She did not know. Half guiltily she hoped so. With all her heart and soul she wanted to see him because she had missed him so much – yet she dreaded him coming because of her new dangerously emotional attitude toward him.

While she wandered towards the pretty rustic bridge – she had still twenty minutes to spare before she need get Sophie up from her rest – her mind reverted to the week before they had left Roquemont. It had not been a pleasant one. True, she had grown accustomed to an atmosphere between husband and wife, but they had seemed on the worst possible terms after the night at the Carlton. They rarely spoke. Even Simone had started to grumble to Juliet about Maman and Step-papa's disagreements, but Juliet refused to discuss this with her. Then there had been that extremely unpleasant moment when Lucien questioned her about Michel.

He had asked her to speak to him in his library. She had had no idea why; then to her perturbation he had told her what old Blanche had said:

"I do not like servants' gossip and although Blanche is privileged as an old nurse of eighty years – I am not excusing her for spying. But what she said to my wife has disturbed me, Juliet, and Mimi, herself, does not wish to be involved, so *I* am going to ask you about it."

"About what, Monsieur?"

Lucien, standing by his desk with a book in his hand, stared at it, refusing to meet the clear shining eyes of the young girl.

"You and Michel . . ." he stammered a little, "my cousin, the Comte de Condine . . . Blanche seems to have seen you two together and . . . it isn't really my business what you do. You are not a child. But I would not care to think that Michel came here late at night when we were out and—"

"Oh! I see," Juliet had interrupted in a whisper, and drew a long breath.

"Is it true . . . what Blanche saw?"

Crimson to the roots of her hair, Juliet answered:

"I don't know what she told Madame, but she could well have seen me struggling with your cousin, Monsieur. He was kissing me against my will. Do you understand? I told him to leave the house."

How could she know what a throb of joy entered Lucien's guilty heart as he heard those words. Guilty, because he loved her and should not, must not do so. Joyful, because he had been so afraid that she might admit that she had *enjoyed* Michel's embrace and wished to repeat it. (Let her love and marry any man – *any man* but Michel!)

Still stammering, Lucien apologized to her.

"From the bottom of my heart I deplore this gossip. I am sure . . ." he had to add the lie, "Mimi would agree. We neither of us for a moment imagined that you would wish for my cousin's attentions. He is not to be taken seriously. But I assure you that he will not repeat his stupidity for while you are in my house, I shall forbid him to enter it."

In the end, Juliet had recovered her equilibrium and Lucien had seemed to recover his. They had even smiled over the incident. In quite a casual voice he had ended by telling her he would be delighted if she found a suitable boy-friend while she was in

France and that she must realize that he had only her good at heart. She had eventually left him, gone to her own bedroom and struggled to regain a composure which she was far from feeling. It was not that she minded that unpleasant incident with Michel being repeated by Blanche but she could hardly bear the thought that Lucien *expected* her to have a boy-friend and had said he would welcome it so long as it wasn't a man of Michel's reputation.

He would *like* her to fall in love and get married. *Why not?* What was she to him except somebody whom he liked and trusted with Sophie?

Oh God, she had said to herself with her face in her hands, *Oh, God, how can I bear it?*

For the rest of the week she had hardly seen Lucien except when he spent his usual hour every evening with Sophie, and then she made herself scarce.

Mimi seemed to be completely detached. She was neither pleasant nor unpleasant, but she seemed to ignore Juliet as much as possible, and when she was sweet it was with that freezing sweetness that had a disagreeable tang to it.

Juliet had begun to look forward to her fortnight away from the Château, but if she had been unhappy to discover her sentiments for Lucien in the first place, she was a good deal more unhappy by the time that week ended. He used to be so friendly and full of praise and to show her a certain warmth and sympathy which she had found most satisfying. Now he deliberately ignored her unless she was mistaken.

One evening she had felt particularly hurt. She had been in the salon alone after Sophie went to bed, playing the piano, and he had come in. Mimi and Simone were at a cocktail party. Lucien advanced to the piano and for a few moments she was delighted because he was his old self – relaxed and ready to talk about music.

"What were you playing? That was charming," he motioned her to sit down again when she half-rose from the music stool. With pink flushed cheeks, she answered:

"The old Londonderry Air."

"Of course. I must have heard it several times. I love it."

He had asked for an encore and stood quietly smoking a cigar while she played the sad haunting Irish tune again. He even remembered the words: "*Oh, Danny Boy!* . . ."

Her heart beat fast with an almost painful pleasure as she heard that tender, pleasant baritone. She had not heard Lucien sing again since the night of her arrival.

As she finished, she swung round and spoke impulsively:

"Oh, please do sing some more and let me try to accompany you."

"Yes, *bravo!*" came the chilling voice from the door – the same voice which on that other occasion had frozen them both as it did now.

Mimi and Simone had come back from their party. Mimi, very chic as usual, drew off her long gloves and took off her hat, pushing her hair into place.

"Such a crowd at the Duchesse's party. Too hot for words. *Don't* let us interrupt you two."

"Yes, please sing some more, Papa," said Simone with sincerity.

Juliet glanced shyly at her employer, but he had no answering smile. He turned from her and walked towards the fireplace.

"No thanks," he said harshly. "It was just that old English tune that attracted me."

Mimi gave him a malicious smile through her long lashes and sank into a chair.

"Darling Lucien, when you sing it reminds me of our early days together," she murmured. "I wish you would continue. It makes me feel quite sentimental."

He clenched his teeth. Her hypocrisy sickened him. As if he did not remember how she had always sneered at his love of singing. Then Mimi turned to Juliet.

"Play us something, *ma chère.*"

"We must not keep Juliet. She has other things to do," interrupted Lucien sharply.

Without looking at either of them, Juliet shut the piano and left the room.

She had felt snubbed; by Lucien more than Mimi. She did not know what she had done to make him speak with such sudden coldness and even hostility. He did not seem to want her in the salon.

All night she was in tears.

Then had come the moment of good-bye. Lucien had at first suggested driving up to Leques with them, she remembered that, but had now found an excuse for not doing so. So Mimi had gone

134

with them. Mimi was amused to act the devoted parent; placed Juliet in the seat beside the chauffeur and herself sat in the back of the car with her arm around Sophie, who was enchanted by her beautiful mother's sudden wish to caress and pet her. Sophie cried as she kissed Lucien good-bye, whining that she didn't wish to leave her dearest Papa. Juliet had watched him take the child in his arms and smooth the dark hair back from her forehead.

"*Mon petit ange*, Papa wants you to get some more colour into those cheeks and come back full of energy and it will only be for a short while."

"I don't want to leave my Papa."

"Of course not, and I don't wish you to go but you will have your – your Princess Juliet with you."

The child turned to her English governess.

"Kiss Juliet good-bye, too, Papa. She will miss you."

"*Tiens!* How amusing," said Mimi who was witnessing this little episode and gave her bell-like trill of laughter.

Juliet, scarlet, had not dared look in Lucien's direction, but heard his voice harder than usual.

"I will spare her that embarrassment. Good-bye, both of you. Enjoy yourselves. Maman or I will telephone every night."

Juliet had left the Château without so much as shaking Lucien's hand. She had felt quite miserable all during that drive which should have been so wonderful – through olive-groves, past fields of magnificent carnations, or plantations of lemon trees and olives; up, up, thousands of feet, the white road spiralling into hairpin bends until gradually they lost sight of the brilliant blue sea and the Côte d'Azur, and were on the lonely magnificent heights. She had seen it all through a mist of tears. Uneasily she decided that Lucien had thought that she had led Michel on that night and he disapproved of her. She could not bear it.

Mimi had been maddening. Having wooed her little daughter all through the drive, she reduced Sophie to frantic tears once they reached the Grand Hôtel de Leques.

She became tactlessly emotional with her.

"I don't think I can bear to leave you here, sweetie," she had said when it came to the final farewell after tea. This had resulted in Sophie clinging to her mother's neck and howling:

"Oh, don't leave me, Maman!"

Juliet had looked on in helpless anger. Why must this woman

always tear the child to pieces either with neglect or senseless behaviour of this kind? There were actually tears in the aquamarine eyes as though Mimi really felt some deep tenderness for her poor little crippled daughter; even perhaps a deep disgust for herself. But it was all so superficial and she seemed unable ever to put the child's feelings first.

Juliet knew that the moment that Mimi returned to Cannes she would scarcely give Sophie a thought.

It was Lucien who telephoned most nights – not Mimi. Juliet had to speak to him because he wished to hear about Sophie from her lips. Their conversations were brief and formal.

"Yes, Monsieur, Sophie is much better."

"Yes, Monsieur, she is eating well."

"Yes, Monsieur, the food is excellent. Simple but what Sophie likes and can digest."

"Yes, thank you, Monsieur, I am well and it is a wonderful place to be in."

That sort of thing; never once any indication from Lucien as to how he was feeling or what was taking place at Roquemont.

Every time Juliet put down the receiver she felt more out in the cold – disassociated in a queer terrifying way from this fascinating man who had unconsciously taken complete charge of her mind and her heart.

At least she felt she need not be troubled by the detestable Michel again. She had been told by Simone that there had been a ghastly row between Lucien and his cousin and for the first time in history the Château de Roquemont had been forbidden to a blood-relative.

This had had the rather unhappy effect of straining the relationship between Simone and Juliet. The young French girl had even been nasty to Juliet about it.

"I'll never be able to see Michel again, now. It's all your fault – I'm sure you led him on."

When Juliet had tried to point out that this was not so, Simone had tossed her head and walked away. She was now entirely on her mother's side. She was jealous of Juliet and could not forgive the fact that Michel had tried to make love to her.

It seemed so extraordinary to Juliet that these two selfish people – mother and daughter – practically always put themselves first and the little girl's happiness second, but it was certainly only on account of Sophie now that Juliet stayed on in her job. Things were too awkward to please her. As for glamour and luxury – such things meant little in comparison with peace of mind.

There were even moments when she weakly asked herself whether she would not be wise to try and think more about Luke. But at the very memory of the young doctor holding her in his arms, she shrank away. She was far too deeply in love with Lucien now.

Once Sophie was up, the two of them took their usual stroll in the warm sunshine.

"I do miss Tache. I want to go home and see him," Sophie said, not for the first time.

"We'll tell Papa tomorrow and see what he says," Juliet answered. "But you really are looking so well, I am sure he'll want you to stick it out for the fortnight, darling."

They were talking English. These few months together had worked magic for the little French girl. Her accent was poor but she really could speak English with comparative ease and only when she was excited broke into French. Alternatively, Juliet's French had become fluent. She could cope with any situation now in shops or restaurants or with any native of this country who came her way.

Sophie was walking so well with the *White Magic* boot that it delighted Juliet to see her. The chair had been completely abandoned. Sophie, herself, found it infinitely preferable to walk around. It gave her a new sensation of independence which she had never had before. Dr. Giraud and the physiotherapist were both delighted with the improvement in her limbs. Her muscles had strengthened and she had put on some weight.

It had only recently been discovered that Juliet and Sophie practically shared a birthday. Juliet was coming of age on the 15th of September. On the 16th, Sophie would be nine. They had made plans for a wonderful joint birthday party. Cook was going to make a monster cake, with thirty candles. Nine pink ones in the centre for Sophie – and the rest around the edge for her governess.

Recently Sophie had made some new friends at Roquemont. An American family had bought one of the big villas close by. They had three children, two of whom were in Sophie's age-group. They showed immense tact and kindness towards the little girl with the boot and the humped back, and they were certainly coming to the party along with some children of French families in or near Cannes, who had known the de Maurevilles all their lives.

Today as Sophie walked with Juliet towards her favourite bridge, she discussed the birthday party which was to be one of the great events of her life.

"How funny it is to 'come of age', as you say it in England, Juliette—" (she always pronounced that name in the French way).

"Yes, it does sound funny," laughed Juliet.

The child walking down the steps from the terrace, her arm through Juliet's, went on:

"Will you be quite different when you are twenty-one?"

"Not at all."

"But Papa says that coming-of-age means that you stop being an infant."

Juliet laughed again.

"I'm afraid I stopped being one a very long long time ago, darling," she said rather sadly. "It's just a sort of legal expression. You are responsible for paying all your bills, and for whatever you do, as soon as you are twenty-one."

"But you won't change, will you? I don't want you to," said Sophie fervently.

Juliet put an arm around the small bowed figure.

"I never shall about *you*."

"You love me, don't you, Juliette? You aren't my slave any more. You're my bestest friend."

"I am!"

"And you love my Papa, too?"

Juliet's whole body tensed but she made a calm reply.

"I have the deepest admiration and respect for your Papa."

"Doesn't that mean you love him?"

Juliet closed her eyes against the glare of the sun which suddenly hurt in spite of her dark glasses.

Oh, how that childish question wounded the depths of her heart!

"There are all kinds of love, Sophie. It would not be respectful for me to say that I *loved* your papa. He is my employer and my friend, of course . . ." she had to clear her throat because it felt so dry, and hastily put an end to the questioning. She began to point out a new little flower growing among the warm sunlit stones.

"You must pick one of those for me, Sophie, and we'll take it back and ask monsieur the director of the hotel what it is called."

"I want to go to the bridge and see the torrent," said Sophie.

They made their slow progress to the wooden bridge. Juliet leaned over one side and stared down at the frothing, creaming water that ran beneath it; water so limpid that you could see every stone on the pebbled bed, every green weed that swayed and moved under the rushing steam.

It always seemed cool and beautiful here. As she gazed into the water it became a mirror. She fancied she could see the face of Sophie's papa . . . that pale haunting face with the large dark eyes that held such melancholy, yet could still sparkle with merriment. How handsome he was! What a wonderful head, with that broad brow, and that black upspringing hair!

"Oh, Lucien, Lucien," Juliet whispered his name very softly to herself as though it might bring some comfort, and ease the aching in her heart.

It was then that the terrible thing happened. She had only time to hear a crack, to turn, and see the other side of the bridge giving way. The wood was rotten. Nobody had dreamed it, nor ever repaired it. Sophie must have lifted herself up on her good leg and been peering over. Before Juliet's horrified gaze, the structure disappeared into the torrent, taking the little girl with it. Her wild scream broke the stillness of the summer afternoon. Juliet's very heart seemed to stop beating. Then she tore down the bank and, thanking God that she wore linen slacks which would not impede her progress, jumped into the water.

It might have been an absolute disaster and at that time she had no idea to what extent Sophie had been hurt. She only knew that the dreadful thing had happened and although it had not been her fault, she was responsible.

Fortunately at the point where the torrent rushed under the bridge it was fairly shallow. She could wade in it, breast-high. There was also an enormous clump of weeds – forming a miniature island – against which Sophie, still screaming, was washed and caught. Juliet reached out, grabbed hold of Sophie and dragged her on to the river bank. The child had lost consciousness.

It was a drenched, dripping trembling Juliet who finally staggered up the steps and through the terraced garden on to the porch, carrying the light childish body in her arms. She kept praying: *"God, let her be all right. God, let her be all right. Oh, God, hear me!"*

An elderly French couple who were sitting on the terrace, saw Juliet with her burden and ran to meet her. The next half-hour was chaotic. The director of the hotel ran out with several of the staff. Juliet's main terror was that the child's heart might cease to function, although Dr. Giraud had always assured her that Sophie's health was not really affected other than structurally, and that she might live as long as anybody else. But Juliet, who was bitterly frightened and temporarily losing her control, began to weep as she gasped out her story.

"It happened in a split second – I turned and saw her fall. Oh, if I had never turned away only for the *moment!*"

Everybody tried to comfort her.

It was not her fault. Who was to know that the bridge was rotten? M. le Directeur would send immediately for some men to put up a barrier until it could be rebuilt.

Juliet soon knew that she need no longer fear the worst, for Sophie opened her eyes whilst still downstairs in the vestibule, and began to scream shrilly. She was suffering mainly from shock. Never had Juliet been better pleased to hear those cries for they were strong, and did not suggest that little Sophie was in any way near dying. They carried her up to her bedroom.

Then came a moment of exquisite relief when an English doctor, who was staying up in the hotel with his wife for a health-cure, examined Sophie.

He was a man who had recently retired from a practice in Yorkshire. A bluff but kindly Northcountryman. He made a rapid examination of the child and could find nothing sinister.

He told Juliet to wrap her in blankets, keep her warm and give her a drink of glucose or sugar to counteract the shock. Her pulse was rapid but her heartbeats were more or less normal. So far as he could see there were no bones broken, and scarcely a bruise, except on the left cheek which had been grazed by a stone.

"It's a merciful thing, the water broke her fall and getting tangled up in those weeds helped," Dr. Ambler told Juliet.

Looking at the young English girl now – she was extremely pale and shaking – he added: *"You're* the one who looks as though she needs help. I think you ought to go and lie down, my dear, and let me give you a sedative."

She shook her head vehemently.

A *femme de chambre* came in with a cup of strong black coffee for Juliet. She drank it, but refused to leave Sophie's bedroom. Then Dr. Ambler volunteered to sit by the little girl and talk to her while Juliet in her own room telephoned to Roquemont. She had nothing too bad to tell the family, thank God, but she knew that it was her duty to inform them what had happened.

Unfortunately Mimi answered the call. When she heard what Juliet had to say she had hysterics, which did not surprise Juliet although her heart sank as she heard the shrill cries. Mimi behaved as though she worshipped every hair of Sophie's head and this thing had shaken her to the marrow. She hurled abuse at Juliet.

"*Imbécile* to have taken her on that bridge and not kept hold of her. *Insensée* to do such a thing! You are not fit to have charge of my poor baby. I will come at once and remove her from you . . ."

She continued to scream, not allowing Juliet to say one word – without listening to her reassurances that Dr. Ambler said there was nothing wrong with Sophie that a good night's sleep would not put right. Also, that Sophie, with all the resilience of extreme youth, had so far recovered already as to giggle when the doctor complimented her on being able to dive and swim. To treat the whole thing lightly was the best thing in his and Juliet's opinion. Juliet shrank from the mere idea of Mimi de Maureville coming up to Leques to make a scene.

When Mimi rang off Juliet returned to Sophie's bedroom, pale and shaken. What would Lucien think when he heard Mimi's version of the accident? She would certainly make the case against her black as pitch. It might result in her being told to go back to England.

She concealed her feelings as best she could for Sophie's sake, and smiled and joked with the little girl who was sipping her drink – still giggling.

"Give her half an aspirin and let her go to sleep," Dr. Ambler whispered to Juliet as he left the room.

This done, Juliet sat beside Sophie's bed and talked and talked until Sophie seemed to be completely normal again.

Sophie laughed:

"I can swim now. The English doctor said so. Wasn't I clever – I *swam*, Juliette!"

"Indeed you did. It was wonderful. I saw you. I am proud of you."

"I didn't like the choking, though, when I went under the water for a moment."

"Of course you didn't. Some people feel a bit like that when they first learn to dive. You've just got to shut your mouth and learn to be a real little fish."

"But fish *open* their mouths all the time. I've watched my gold-fish."

"So they do!" said Juliet and laughed with the child, trying not to tremble so badly.

"I'm a heroine – Dr. Ambler said so – and so did *Monsieur le Directeur*."

"Of course you are – you are my brave little Sophie."

"I want to see Papa. I want to tell him and Maman about me being able to swim."

"They'll be coming up to see you this afternoon."

"*Ah! C'est bon!*" exclaimed the child in her own language.

Then, suddenly, after all the fright, exhaustion and excitement, and aided by the aspirin and hot drink – she fell asleep.

Chapter Fourteen

"I INSIST upon you dismissing this girl," said Mimi not for the first time.

"And I insist on waiting for her explanation of what really happened," was Lucien's reply.

They were driving up the mountains towards Leques, in the Jaguar. Simone sat in the back of the car. She looked as sulky as she felt. She couldn't think what all the fuss was. Maman had been told that Sophie was neither dead nor badly injured. They wouldn't leave *her* behind, either. So afraid she would get in touch with Michel; she thought, furious and discontented. She listened in silence while her mother and stepfather wrangled. Although she was on her mother's side as a rule, she sometimes pitied Papa. Maman did keep on and on – and she was so hysterical once she lost control.

Lucien drove fast, eyes grim, lips set. He only half listened to the spate of angry words that flowed from Mimi. He had telephoned to Leques as soon as he returned to the Château from his walk. He did not speak to Juliet, but to M. Guillivin, the director, who gave him a fair picture of the accident. Lucien was told that one side of the bridge had been rotten and had given way. What he did not quite understand was where Juliet had been at the time. It seemed so unlike her to neglect her duty for a single moment. She was always so careful of the child.

If, as Mimi suggested, Juliet was really responsible for this thing happening to poor Sophie, he might have to consider dismissing her. But that was such a dismal thought that he refused to allow himself to entertain it for more than a moment. Poor little Juliet – she would be half-demented, he felt sure. M. Guillivin had tried to put Lucien through to her on the telephone but told Lucien that she was in the child's bedroom where no calls were being accepted. So Lucien, without wasting more time, got hold of Mimi and Simone and drove off to the mountains.

He had intended to drive up to Leques tomorrow, in any case. Mimi now insisted on playing the frantic mother. He always tried to believe the best of her – to feel she could show some real feeling for Sophie. But he felt weary of her dramatics before that long drive ended. Mimi would not relax – or stop vilifying Juliet. As he stepped out of the car he spoke to her in an undertone:

"*Tu parles! tu parles … Pour lamour de Dieu, tais-toi!*"

But Mimi stepped out of the Jaguar with a handkerchief pressed delicately to her nose, and when M. Guillivin stepped out to meet them, she played the distressed mother dramatically, huge tears in her blue eyes. Simone looked on a trifle cynically. Maman should have been on the stage, she decided.

Now that Simone knew that her little half-sister had suffered no injury, save for the odd scratch and bruise, she lost interest. Through her long lashes she had just seen on the veranda a good-looking boy, wearing white shorts and singlet – holding a tennis-racquet. She was glad now Papa had made them bring up overnight bags. Maybe later on or tomorrow morning, she would get a game with this boy. He really was quite handsome, and as she walked up on to the veranda to the hotel entrance, she caught his gaze. They exchanged exploratory glances and tentative smiles. Simone read in his eyes all the admiration to which she was accustomed. Thank goodness, she thought, she had had time to put on that pretty shocking pink cotton dress with the wide skirt and very low back that showed her golden tan. It was an ill-wind that blew no good. Maybe this trip, which she hadn't wanted to take, would end rather more cheerfully for her.

The director led them all upstairs, lamenting the poor state of the bridge and the accident and full of profound apologies. He thanked *le bon Dieu* that the *pauvre petite enfant* had come to no real harm. As for the English Mees, she had been splendid, and saved the child's life by jumping in so promptly to pull her to safety. The entangling weeds on that little island had been helpful to the child too. Monsieur would show them everything in a moment. Without the weeds breaking the fall, Mees Browning might have had a more formidable task to fight the strong current. The child could even have been carried farther down stream.

All this was poured into Lucien's ear. He listened, conscious of deep thankfulness that his small daughter was all right; and that M. le Directeur attached no blame to Juliet.

"I told you she was not to blame," he turned to Mimi. "It was not her fault that the fencing gave way."

Mimi ignored this and sobbed into her handkerchief.

"For God's sake, do not make a scene in front of Sophie. It will be bad for her," Lucien whispered fiercely.

She turned on him.

"How can you be so heartless about our poor little one?"

He shut his eyes and prayed for patience.

Then Juliet came out on the landing. She shut Sophie's door behind her. She faced the parents with courage. She knew she would need it. She could hardly bear to meet Lucien's inquiring gaze but she put a finger to her lips.

"Please, Monsieur . . . Madame . . . Sophie is fast asleep."

"I wish to see my poor child——" began Mimi hysterically.

"You heard what Juliet said, Mimi," broke in Lucien sternly. "If Sophie is asleep we must not disturb her."

"She has been asleep for several hours," said Juliet. "Dr. Ambler says it is for the best. He gave her a tablet. There is nothing wrong with her, Monsieur – Madame – it is just exhaustion. I assure you she was laughing and joking with me before she slept. She wanted you to know that she could s-s-swim . . ." Juliet stumbled over the last word because she was now in tears.

Mimi glared at her.

"How *dared* you leave her alone for a single moment on that dangerous bridge?"

"Madame," said Juliet more calmly although her heart jerked and the tears were still rolling down her cheeks: "from the bottom of my heart I apologize if you think that I neglected Sophie even for a few seconds. But we have gone to that bridge every day and it has always seemed safe. The sides looked perfect. The wooden rails suddenly cracked and gave way."

"I'm quite sure it was not your fault," said Lucien loudly, and added to his wife in an undertone: "Please say no more, Mimi, for heaven's sake, and let Sophie sleep."

"Madame might like to look at her," suggested Juliet. She was flushed and trembling nervously. She stood aside. Mimi walked past her, tight-lipped, and tiptoed to Sophie's bedside. Once in the corridor again she spoke to Juliet in a short, acid voice:

"Well, she looks all right and seems to be sleeping peacefully enough, but I still think you were neglecting your duty shamefully by allowing her to climb up on the bridge, and *you* with your back turned!"

Lucien answered for Juliet.

"It is absolutely wrong, Mimi, to accuse Juliet in this way.

145

According to Guillivin the bridge side was so rotten that it was just that one bit of pressure when Sophie leaned over caused the collapse. Besides, Sophie is not a baby. We cannot expect Juliet or anybody else to watch her like a lynx – never to turn a back for a few seconds. The child will soon be nine, remember."

Mimi threw him a furious look, ignored Juliet's tear-filled eyes, and marched away.

Left alone with Juliet, Lucien looked at her with deep compassion. He was shocked by the change in her. She looked ghastly in spite of her sun-tan. Her eyelids were swollen and pink with weeping. She hadn't even bothered to make up, poor child, he thought. The small snub-nose shone – the nut-brown hair was untidy – she hadn't combed it. Poor distraught little thing – how terrible it must all have been for her! What a strain! And how deeply she seemed to love his child. His whole heart went out to her. He suddenly caught both her hands in his, and raised them each in turn to his lips.

"Thank you for what you did – for jumping into that torrent – for being so quick and resourceful. For everything, in fact."

Juliet lost control and began to cry helplessly. Her trembling fingers clung to his. His kindness and understanding upset her even more than Mimi's venom.

"It was so awful! A nightmare I shall never forget. Oh, my God, what a fright I had! Monsieur, Monsieur, forgive me. If I am to blame, *forgive me!*"

"You are *not* to blame. You are completely exonerated. My wife is terribly upset, otherwise I am sure she would never have said such things to you."

Juliet shook her head. She began to sob uncontrollably.

Lucien had tried to excuse Mimi but he suffered for and with Juliet. He had no more qualms about his little daughter. He was completely satisfied about her condition. The English doctor had said there were no injuries. The child had admitted she felt no pain. But Lucien could see and feel that for this young girl what had happened had been a calamity and she still felt it.

He put an arm around her.

"Go into your own room, *mon pauvre enfant*," he said with great tenderness. "Lie down and sleep – forget this thing. I will sit with Sophie until she wakes."

"She ... she ... will l-like that," stammered Juliet, gulping, and wiped her tears away with the back of her hand – a gesture so young, so lacking in any attempt to impress or beguile, that Lucien's whole being glowed with fresh tenderness – and love for her. He knew in this moment that he loved Juliet Browning so much that it was difficult for him not to pick her up in his arms and carry her into her bedroom and cover the freckled tear-wet face with kisses.

"Please, please don't worry about Sophie any more. Forget the whole affair," he said.

She nodded. She was too unnerved to say another word. It was only after she was alone in her own bedroom, lying on her bed, her face buried in the cool pillow that the fresh tears came; and with them the memory of his hands on hers and the homage of his kisses.

Lucien ... Lucien ... she thought in an agony of emotion, *dearest and most dear ... darling, marvellous Lucien!*

But what was the use? What was the use of anything? Mimi loathed her. Her position at Roquemont would soon become untenable. She could only be grateful that *he* had absolved her from guilt, and did not believe that the child's accident had been *her* fault.

A difficult evening followed for Juliet.

Sophie showed amazing resilience, for she was so much stronger these days than she had ever been. She insisted upon getting up and going down to dinner. When she first woke up and found her beloved Papa sitting beside her, she went wild with delight. Then when Mimi joined them, dutifully sent for by Lucien, Sophie, starry-eyed, gave her parents her version of the accident. Quite obviously she was proud to be the heroine of the occasion. She kept telling them how Dr. Ambler had said that she could swim.

"I'm not frightened of the water any more. I shall swim in the sea soon! Isn't it super?"

Mimi raised her brows. She did not understand Sophie. She never would. Lucien was amazed and pleased that the child suffered so little from reaction, less in fact than poor Juliet. But he knew that children and animals could tumble around, fall into water, pass through every kind of crisis and bob up again with remarkable elasticity.

He realized that both the English doctor and Juliet had been clever to treat the whole thing with a sense of humour and talk

Sophie into thinking she had actually dived into the torrent and started to swim. Although it wrung his heart to think of that little misshapen body tumbling into the water, he managed to laugh with her. She chattered on excitedly ... telling them how the water had stung when she hit it; how cold it had felt, how nasty it was when her mouth and nostrils filled; and how her darling 'Princesse Juliette' had saved her life.

"She's terribly brave. She rescued me. You've got to decorate her, Papa. *Hasn't* he, Maman?"

Mimi flung her husband a cynical look.

"Oh, of course," she said and she laughed unpleasantly. "With a diamond star!"

"I'm going down to dinner with you – Dr. Ambler said I could because I've slept all afternoon," continued Sophie.

"Of course, darling," repeated Mimi, and for a moment that wicked selfish heart of hers was touched by the light in Sophie's big brown eyes and her gaiety. Poor little devil, what had *she* got facing her in life? Nothing but being a cripple and wearing a boot for the rest of time! Let her enjoy herself while she could. As for the 'darling Princess' – Mimi secretly decided to deal with *her* once they returned to the Château.

A proud Sophie, dressed in her favourite pink frock which set Mimi's teeth on edge went down to the *salle à manger* and sat propped up high on cushions at the table. Some of the guests came over to talk to her and compliment her on her escape; and to commiserate with her mother who flung them such charming smiles, with an expression of motherly concern in her huge black-lashed eyes. Then the guests turned politely to Juliet and complimented her on her prompt action in getting the child out of the water. This was less popular with Mimi.

Juliet had few answering smiles for her admirers. Quiet and subdued she sat beside Sophie, her eyes downcast. She would have preferred not to have appeared at this dinner party at all but Sophie insisted when she tried to excuse herself. Only once did she glance in Lucien's direction, then her heart gave a frantic leap. He was looking straight at her. For a second she told herself that she was insane to imagine it – but his eyes seemed to express something more than ordinary appreciation. The look in his eyes was so deep, so sad, so *hungry* it almost robbed her of breath. She was thankful, once the sweet had been served, that Simone broke up the party.

"I'm skipping coffee. I have got a date – playing table-tennis with Yves. Come and watch us, Maman."

"Who on earth is Yves—?" began Lucien.

"Yves Maillard – that good-looking boy over there," said his stepdaughter in a low tone and nodded in the direction of the tall attractive young man who was just walking out of the restaurant with his mother.

Mimi, drawing a cigarette from her gold case, gave a short laugh.

"Darling Simone has found a new admirer."

"Then she'd better make the most of it," said Lucien shortly. "We shall be driving back to Roquemont first thing in the morning."

Simone started a complaint.

"*Non, non,* Papa! I like it here. If I get on well with Yves, why drag me home? He's a sweet boy and his father is very wealthy – he has a large silk factory in Lilles. You know ... Maillard's Silks – they're the best in Europe."

"Excellent," purred Mimi. "Cultivate him, dearest. Don't drag us back to Roquemont, please, Lucien."

Juliet now had to listen to the usual wrangle between husband and wife. Poor, tired Lucien. He must be so maddened by his wife's continual changes of mood.

"I thought you didn't want to come up to Leques—" he began.

"Well, now I'm here, we'll stay a day or two," Mimi said. "I agree with Simone. If she's found an attractive boy-friend, and with a millionaire like Henri Maillard behind him, why spoil her chances? We've had enough trouble over your dear cousin, haven't we?"

Juliet raised her eyes just in time to catch a nasty look from Madame. Flushing, she lowered her gaze again.

Lucien was chewing at his lip. He drew a cigar out of his case and pierced it with a gold puncher. How well Juliet knew that little instrument. She was familiar with so many of the things that he had or wore; like the signet ring on the small finger of his left hand, with the de Maureville crest on the onyx stone. Once again her whole being thrilled with the memory of those slim fingers holding hers outside Sophie's door – and of the touch of his lips against her hands.

Lucien struggled with himself. He wanted to get back to Roquemont for many reasons. Sophie still had another week left up here with her governess. Lucien needed that week without Juliet in the house, in order to regain his sense of proportion – to stamp out the temptation that was becoming more and more difficult to control ... a temptation to tell Juliet what he really felt about her.

But Mimi left him no alternative. He was defeated. He could not reasonably refuse her request to stay up here over Sunday, anyhow. If she and Simone liked it in Leques how could he insist upon taking them back? Sophie was making things twice as hard by pulling at his hand and saying:

"You promised to spend tomorrow with me, Papa. You can't go home – you *promised*."

He had to give way.

Juliet said:

"Come along, Sophie darling, bed-time. Do you realize it is half past nine?"

After she had got the child to bed, and all was peaceful again, she was unwilling to go downstairs and rejoin the family. In any case she was sure they would not want her. Mimi and Simone had gone into the Games Room where Mimi was flashing her sweetest smiles at young Maillard's mother and chatting to her while Simone and Yves started their table-tennis. Lucien had announced his intention of going into the bar to have a coffee and brandy with Dr. Ambler.

The nights up in Leques were not cold but cooler than in Cannes. Juliet put a white cardigan over her shoulders and went out into the garden. The sight of the enormous stars – the freshness of the air soothed her. Her head ached violently. She felt in no condition to stay in her bedroom alone with her thoughts, or even attempt to go to bed. But she reproached herself as she moved down the steps towards the scene of Sophie's accident.

Better take hold on yourself, my girl. You're letting things get out of proportion and if you're not careful you'll really be in a fix. You've got to stop thinking about Sophie's Papa – and how!

Easier said than done. Bitterly she faced the fact.

But she just didn't think she could stand much more of these innuendoes and jibes that Mimi de Maureville flung so continually in her direction. No, not even for Sophie's sake. There must be a limit to the sacrifices one made in this world. What she ought to do was to hand in her notice as soon as they got back to Roquemont. Her heart sank at the prospect; England ... London (friends who wrote to her said it was, so far, a ghastly cold summer with perpetual rain) ... a new unglamorous job. Or she might even go to Bristol and work there – with Luke Farrell once more in attendance.

Oh, no, no! she said the words aloud. *I couldn't bear it!*

Somebody called her name.

"Juliet!"

She swung round. In the clear luminous light from the moon, she saw the tall figure of Lucien, a half-smoked cigar between his fingers.

She gave a nervous laugh.

"Oh, hullo!"

"Hullo! Lovely out here, isn't it? I needed some fresh air. It was stuffy in the bar. Nice chap, your English doctor. He assures me that all is well with our Sophie."

"I'm so glad ..." Juliet's voice was still nervous and her eyelashes flickered as Lucien came closer to her. "I wanted fresh air, too."

"I thought I'd go and have a look at that wretched bridge."

She nodded. He stood still, staring down at her. All through dinner he had been staring, and he knew it and despised himself for his own weakness just as he despised himself now because his heart beat so damnably fast as he looked down into the shining beauty of her eyes – the unconscious seduction of her slim young figure. She wore a white dress tonight. In the moonlight her youthful sun-tanned arms and neck looked like polished bronze – like her hair. She was a sweet brown girl. It was fatal to be alone with her out here in this beautiful mountain garden.

"It's very peaceful, isn't it, Juliet?" he said. His voice was hoarse. "Glorious! The stars are so bright and so pure. It makes one feel that there should be nothing but beauty and purity and peace in this world. But it isn't so. It's full of cruelty and darkness and despair."

She tried to laugh.

"Oh, you do sound gloomy, Monsieur."

"Don't call me that."

"What must I call you?"

"Lucien. I've never heard you say it. *Lucien.*"

"I ... oughtn't to. You are my employer, Monsieur."

"And does the fact that you are my employee and my child's governess prevent me from calling you *Juliet?*"

"That's – different."

"It doesn't have to be."

"Oh, it does!" she exclaimed suddenly in a voice of distress. "It does have to be!"

He flung his cigar into the bushes. The muscles in his cheeks were working. His breath came fast. Somehow the sight of her standing there looking so lost and lonely and small (yet she was so strong and wise) moved him dangerously.

"Juliet, Juliet," he said under his breath.

"I must go in," she said.

"Not till I've thanked you again and again for all that you've done for my child. For all the health and brightness you've brought into my home and, incidentally, for all you've done for me."

She tried to answer. No words came. She felt that she was standing there before him in mortal peril – as though suspended over the edge of a chasm. That she must soon fall over it – to her doom. Her eyes, large with fright, with emotion, looked wildly up into his, and they, too, were large and wild, and she knew that if she went on looking into them she would be lost.

"Oh, Lucien!" she began and spoke the name as though in terror of him and herself.

"That's what I wanted to hear – my name spoken by you."

"I *must* go in . . ." she repeated desperately.

But it was too late. She was drowning in the dark and passionate gaze of those wonderful eyes that for so long had haunted her thoughts and dreams. And he was lost, for he caught hold of her, pulled her against him, and they exchanged that kiss so long forbidden to them – the kiss they had both wanted – the embrace they had both so ardently and hopelessly imagined and desired. They kissed as though life and death itself depended on it; with only the stars and moon to witness it. They clung feverishly, their arms around each other, as they kissed and kissed again.

In all her life, Juliet had never imagined such kisses, nor such intensity of feeling. If it was wrong, she was not yet strong enough to face the fact and draw back. She surrendered to his arms and his lips. They whispered to each other feverishly, almost incoherently.

"I love you, I love you, Juliet."

"I love you, Lucien."

"Oh, *bon Dieu, bon Dieu,* what can we do?" he groaned.

"Nothing, nothing," was her gasping reply.

"Kiss me again, Juliet. Again – again. With every bit of me – body, heart and soul, I love you, *ma très chère* Juliet. *Amour de ma vie!* . . ."

"Love of my life," she gasped, translating the words.

"Yes, love of my life. You always will be that, always, always, *always.*"

"And you will be mine always, too."

"Do you remember that song on your first night in the Château? *How Can I Live Without Love?* – I have often thought about it. I know that I can no longer live without it, *or* without you."

It was then that she drew back, her eyes huge in her flushed face. Her body shuddered with a mixture of pain and ecstasy.

"But it can't be! You know that it can't. I know it. You're not free to love me. I had no right to tell you how I feel about you."

"But you did. Rightly or wrongly, we both know now that we love each other."

She pressed her palms against his shoulders, trying to move back from him.

"It's all wrong."

"Rightly or wrongly, we know that we love each other," he repeated, stubbornly.

"But you're married. Married to Mimi."

The very name of his wife seemed to sober Lucien, bring him down to earth as though somebody had thrown ice-cold water over him. Cold as the blue of Mimi's eyes and the whip-lash of her tongue.

"*Mon Dieu,* what a frightful tangle," he said. "How am I going to stand it now that I know you love me as much as I love you? I give you my word I never imagined you felt this way, Juliet."

"I never imagined I'd fall in love with a married man."

He put out a hand to her.

"That sounds so sinister! Come and walk with me a little way, darling. We can't go back just yet feeling like this. Let's talk to each other."

She hesitated but only for a moment. She wanted to do the right thing but she felt weak and unusually helpless in the face of sudden overwhelming passion. With her fingers locked in Lucien's she walked beside him down the terraced garden out on to the mountain-side. There it was wilder and most beautiful, flooded with white moonlight.

After a few moments Lucien stopped. Without speaking they turned to each other. The next moment they were locked in each other's arms in an embrace that left no room for doubt in the minds of either one how they felt about each other. Honour, good sense, reserve, no longer had any part in that fierce shared hunger. It was a long time since Lucien had held and kissed a girl like this, and for Juliet, it was a first experience of all the madness and danger that could accompany passionate love.

She felt his hot kisses, first against her mouth, then her throat and finally the warmth of his hand pressed against her breast. She felt him shaking. Her now vibrant young body responded. She would never have recognized herself in the crazy girl she had become. She only knew that she loved Lucien so much that she felt half mad. They talked to each other breathlessly in between the hot kisses. From his lips there came disjointed sentences in his own language, and in hers.

"*Tu es merveilleuse!* Juliet! Juliet! I love you. I want you. *Mon âme . . . mon coeur . . . bien aimée . . .* you are sweet . . . too sweet. *Je suis fou de toi.*"

"Lucien, I love and want you, too."

"I'm crazy with love."

"I'm crazy, too."

"Darling, darling, let me kiss you again. Your mouth is as sweet as honey and much more intoxicating."

"I never thought anything could be like this, Lucien."

"That's part of your sweetness – your extraordinary innocence. Simone is always telling me that young girls are no longer innocent and that I'm old-fashioned. But you are different."

"Everybody's different. A lot of girls experience love when they are very young. I've just never wanted to before because I've never been in love till I met you."

"You mean you've never kissed anybody or let any man make love to you this way?"

"Never," she said and thought almost with pity of Luke Farrell and his tepid love-making.

"I can't believe it."

"You can – you can – *you must.* I want you to believe that you are the very first man to make me feel like this."

He lifted her arm, bent and kissed the blue veins inside the delicate inner curve of the elbow. Then he let his lips slide along her bare shoulder. He was lost and perilously close to asking Juliet for more than a kiss. It was the hardest fight he had ever had to make in the name of honour. But after a few moments Juliet seemed to become aware of the peril, and of her own part in it. What was it that her friend Phyl had once told her, she thought wildly.

'My boy-friend always says that it is the girl who has the last word and that if she stands firm there can never be any trouble.'

Juliet had shrugged her shoulders about it at the time because the fierce flame of desire had never swept *her* until tonight. But in this moment she realized the wisdom that lay in Phyl's carelessly uttered words. As for her brother – when Juliet remembered how shocked she had been because he fell for a married woman, it made her feel very small. She was every bit as bad as Nicky.

She drew herself out of Lucien's arms.

"Oh Lucien, we must be more sensible," she said in a low voice.

"Juliet – my little Juliet—"

But Lucien got no further than that. He pulled a handkerchief from his pocket and wiped his forehead and face. She could sense the effort that he was making to regain control. She was desperately sorry for herself and for *him* – but she knew perfectly well they must not carry this affair one step further. Tonight, already, it had gone far enough. She was perfectly certain that he would never ask her to live with him, and he, to whom honour meant more, perhaps, than to some men, could not contemplate dishonouring his marriage. Never like poor old Nicky, would *he* suggest divorce.

"It's all hopeless, Lucien," she said. "There's no future in it for us. The sooner I go back to England the better."

"My dear, there are other issues at stake besides ourselves. Obviously it will be difficult – more than that – for us. An appalling strain – but there is Sophie to consider. Try to imagine what she would say if you told her you wanted to go home."

Juliet looked desperate.

"I know! That is one of the real problems. It defeats me. Yet how can I stay on at Roquemont? We should never have done this," she added to herself. But he caught the words, took her hand and held it tightly between his own, hurting the fine bones of her fingers by the strength of his.

"You mean we should never have acknowledged our love for each other? Maybe not. But now it's done we've got to be strong for Sophie's sake."

Juliet gave a half-hearted laugh.

"That sort of strength isn't easy to come by. We see each other every day; it will be so difficult."

"And I love you more than my life," he said under his breath.

"Lucien, Lucien, you'll have to let me go away."

He set his teeth.

"It would be weakness on both our parts if I agreed. For *Sophie* we must be strong. She really would break her heart if you left her now; besides Dr. Giraud has continually told me that it is somebody like you she has needed so badly all these years. We could never replace you, Juliet – never!"

"Nobody is indispensable."

He shook his head.

"Unfortunately – if I may put it that way – *you* are!"

She looked up at him wildly.

"But Lucien, think of life at the Château with both of us feeling the way we do and knowing that the other *knows* about it! We'll be bound to give ourselves away some time. Something awful will happen – Mimi will find out, and then—"

"Oh, *mon Dieu*!" he broke in and closed his eyes as though to wipe out the memory of his wife's icy indifference coupled with her fearful malice. In time it would all react upon Juliet. That was what he could not tolerate. Mimi could do what she liked to *him* but he wasn't going to have Juliet hurt.

"Oh, *mon Dieu*!" he repeated.

She trembled violently.

"It's getting late. I think we ought to go back to the hotel separately. We don't want them to talk . . ."

"And that is how it will always be—" he said harshly. "Going our separate ways – trying to avoid suspicion. It doesn't sound too good, does it?"

"It doesn't, and I doubt if we can face it," she said with a brief laugh. "In the long run I'll have to leave you, and poor darling little Sophie must learn to do without me."

He looked down at her with his hungry tormented eyes.

"So you condemn me, too, to live without you."

"Lucien, don't make it harder for me," she said in a voice of such pain that it wrenched his heart. He caught both her hands, kissed them, then pulled her back into his arms, and laid his cheek against her hair.

"Oh, how desperately I love you, Juliet! It is just about the cruellest thing that has ever happened. If I thought Mimi deserved my loyalty it would perhaps be easier, but she doesn't. Still there is nothing I can do about it. There can never be a divorce."

Juliet was crying now but she tried to laugh.

"That's right, my darling. There must never be a slur on the name of the de Maurevilles. And look at me – I've done nothing all my life but moralize about people who run out on their marriages. When a special girl-friend of mine fell in love with a married man, I told her it would be shocking of her to influence him to leave his wife for her. Not that I ever *could* take you away from Sophie, even if I tried. Sophie remains the crux of the situation. She mustn't be hurt. It doesn't matter about us."

He brushed her wet eye-lashes with his lips. He dared not touch her mouth again, then roughly he pushed her away from him.

"This is more than flesh and blood can stand. You'd better go in, my darling. Try to forget everything that has been said between us. No, *don't* ... never forget," he hastily corrected himself. "Always remember that I love you. I shall be proud to remember that you love me. But for the child's sake we must what you English call 'snap out of it'."

Juliet was laughing and crying together, fumbling for her handkerchief, emotionally spent. She felt as though she had been flung from the heights to the depths and that she would never be able to get up again. She could see nothing ahead but pain and grief and renunciation.

Whether she meant to stay at Roquemont or go could not be decided in this moment; but that she must run away from the temptation of his arms and his kisses tonight was a more immediate necessity.

Without another word she turned and ran up the steps, up, up, to the hotel, leaving him standing there alone under the white light of the stars which seemed suddenly to have grown cold and cynical and as cruel as the hopelessness of their love.

Chapter Fifteen

Now there followed long days and nights in Juliet's life when she might well wish that she had never known the mad happiness of being held in Lucien de Maureville's arms, and of hearing him say that he loved her.

The price she paid was a bitter one.

It had been easier to carry on with life when nobody shared the knowledge of how she felt about Lucien. Then it was just a marvellous secret to be treasured and dreamed about, even though it gave her pain. But once that secret was out – shared with him, and she, in turn, knew how *he* felt, it became as terrible as it was beautiful. It was something that must be smothered – choked back at any price. She dared not betray what she felt. After a few weeks of indecision, she felt so exhausted in body and mind that she hardly knew how to carry on.

In one way she had gained the world when Lucien told her he loved her. In another, she had lost everything, for now she no longer even enjoyed his friendship.

He avoided her. Once she and Sophie returned to the Château, life seemed to be the same on the surface but under it lay sheer misery for Juliet. He was abrupt with her ... spoke to her only formally in front of the family, and never allowed himself to be alone with her. When he was with Sophie, and Juliet was also present, he addressed himself almost exclusively to the child.

At first Juliet felt that she understood, because she, too, had to 'put on a face'; to behave as though he meant nothing more to her than her employer – a man whom she respected, but who was of no personal importance to her. At first, she accepted, meekly, his new, studied, cool treatment of her.

Then things began to take on a new shape. His behaviour became the source of sharp suffering for her. She even began to wonder whether that coldness was altogether assumed – or if he had regretted that episode up at Leques. She wondered if he wished her to understand this, and forget it.

It was not an attractive idea. She was shaken by it when she allowed it to formalize.

Yet it seemed incredible that Lucien could be like that. He was surely not the type to enjoy a few moments of fun and games with a girl, then want to forget it and make sure she didn't take him seriously.

At these moments Juliet bolstered up her pride by reassuring herself that this was not the case. He had been quite serious but because of his principles and their invidious position he did not intend to give way to his feelings again. He knew how dangerous it was. He was wise – strong-minded – and with his particularly acute sense of honour, he was unwilling to betray what he felt when he saw her here at Roquemont. He was strong, she thought bitterly. *She* was the weak one. She was a fool to think so much about him, to worry so much. If he wanted a complete breach, she must be proud on her side and accept the situation.

It didn't mean he no longer loved her. It meant that he loved her too much to want a promiscuous affair.

But she would have been less than human if she hadn't longed to be reassured by one tiny sign or word that he did still feel deeply for her.

It was a case of having to battle against her every emotion every single day – and battle so furiously that nobody would see what she felt – least of all, Lucien, himself.

She made a desperate effort to appear as cold, as distant as Lucien. She threw herself with renewed devotion into the sometimes difficult task of helping and training Sophie.

The little girl returned from the mountains looking brown and well. Their birthday party – the great double event – was looming up on the horizon. Lucien, of course, would be present. It would need so much effort on Juliet's part to appear as gay and as carefree as the child would expect. She dreaded it really. She didn't care a damn she told herself, about her coming of age. Everything was spoiled. Life and love was proving too bitter.

During the last few days, Mimi was unusually pleasant to Juliet, though they did not often meet. Madame was engrossed in her own personal life – a feverish search for admiration and pleasure outside her own home. She seemed quite to have forgotten the personal attack she had made on Juliet at Leques after Sophie's accident.

Juliet sometimes wondered what Mimi was up to – and worried on Lucien's account.

Once a week, on Hortense's day off, Maria served the 'school-room tea'. The Italian passed on titbits of gossip to Mees, about *Madama* – although Juliet tried to stop this. When Juliet told her to be quiet, Maria was irrepressible, she only laughed and snapped her fingers.

"Oh, but it ees-a so funnee, the way Madama make-a the tele-phone call to her boy-frienda. I hear her call him 'Max – dar-leeng,' ... *mein lieba Max* ... she arranga the meeting, and tella me to getta out her new dress. *Amore! Amore! Eban!*" And Maria would roll her eyes and go into a peal of laughter, un-ashamed.

Juliet turned her back on the girl but without success. Maria went on chattering. She had no loyalty and wished to make it plain to Mees that Madama was carrying on a clandestine affair with the Herr Doktor behind Monsieur's back.

In one way this made Juliet feel less guilty because she knew that she loved Mimi's own husband. But in another, she hated knowing about Max. The affair disgusted her. She felt it deeply because she knew how much Lucien would hate it. Lucien had put an end to his own brief surrender to passionate love. Mimi seemed to be unable to understand his kind of honour.

Yesterday Juliet was sent for by Mimi and invited to talk in a friendly way while Mimi was sipping her coffee. She seemed in very good spirits. She lay back on her pillows in the beautiful bed smiling at Juliet through her lashes.

"You are looking tired, *pauvre enfant*," she said in her own language. "Is my exacting little daughter wearing you out?"

Juliet coloured.

"No, thank you, Madame. I am perfectly all right."

"Really," Mimi purred, leaning back against her embroidered pillows and linking slender fingers behind her fair head. "We ought to drop this *Madame*. After all, you *are* Juliet Ingram's god-daughter and she is my friend. Why not call me Mimi?"

Juliet was alarmed by the sudden show of friendliness. What did it mean? What lay behind it? She didn't trust Mimi. She felt that the beautiful heartless creature never did anything with-out an ulterior motive.

Mimi continued to be charming.

"I think you have rather a dull time, really, and you are such a good girl. You work so hard on Sophie's behalf. I was nasty to you up at Leques, and I apologize. I am ashamed of myself. It was just that I was in such a terrible state about my darling – I wasn't responsible for what I said. Simone told me I behaved frightfully to you and I am sure I did."

Juliet stared. This was a Mimi she certainly did not know; Mimi, of all women, to humble herself like this ... what had got into her? As for that business about 'my poor darling' it was hypocrisy. Juliet had lived long enough in this house now to know something about Madame's queer twisted character. It no longer surprised her when Mimi swung from complete lack of maternal concern to sickening sentimentality over the child. Her unpredictable behaviour certainly did not make her an easy person to understand or to work for.

Juliet's fascinated gaze noted the extraordinary beauty and fragility of the woman, sitting there in her sumptuous bed; her fine bones, her strange slanting blue eyes and smooth waves of ash-blonde hair. Juliet could see so plainly her great attraction for men – understand why Lucien had once been so madly in love with her. She found it difficult to understand how he could care for *her* – Juliet. She felt plain and dull in comparison with Madame de Maureville. But Mimi was actually paying her a compliment at this moment.

"That cotton frock you are wearing is very chic – it's one of Juliet Ingram's, isn't it? – yes I thought so. It has the Paris touch. It's beautifully moulded to your figure and you know, Juliet, you have a lovely shape. You're lucky to be so young, too, *chérie*. As for that attractive schoolgirl face of yours – all wide-eyed innocence – it really *is* quite charming. I'm surprised some man hasn't fallen for you long ago."

Juliet stiffened.

Mimi was *getting at her*, she felt sure. She suspected that some malice lay behind the amiability. She said:

"Schoolgirl innocence sounds too deadly, Madame. I can't feel flattered."

"Mimi – not Madame – *They call me Mimi!*" the older woman sang the famous line from *La Bohême,* then gave her tinkling laugh. "Don't be cross with me, Juliet. I didn't mean to annoy you. Would you prefer me to tell you how sophisticated you look? No – surely not! Lucien thinks your chief charm lies in your simplicity. He says you are as fresh and charming as an English rose. He doesn't really care for sophisticated girls. Of course he *used to* – when he first knew me. But times change –

so do men. I think Lucien's tastes have definitely changed and you, *ma chère,* today, are more his type than I."

Juliet gasped. She felt her cheeks change from crimson to white. Now she was tense with suspicion, right on the defensive – quite certain that all that Mimi was saying had a definite significance. It was designed to hurt rather than please. Juliet began to wonder in horror if Mimi had guessed at the truth . . .

Mimi knows . . . Somehow or other she has found out about Lucien and me, Juliet thought, feeling utterly confused.

Then, in a flash, Mimi changed back to the friendly person she had seemed when Juliet first entered the room.

"You're very good for Lucien. You cheer him up. He's terribly inclined to get depressed. It's one of his failings. Gloomy natures are so difficult to cope with, aren't they?" And without waiting for Juliet to answer, continued: "Oh, well, I'm very happy to know that while I am out, you can make my two dear ones happy . . ."

Mon Dieu, thought Juliet, heaven preserve me from this woman. She is the most appalling hypocrite I've ever met.

"I've got a dress for you, by the way," Mimi rattled on. "That white two-piece which you liked so much. You've only got to let Maria put the hem of the skirt down for you, as you're taller than I am. It will suit you. I would have given it to Simone but she's much too tall. Would you like it?"

Still in a state of confusion, mixed with guilt Juliet mumbled a *'merci, Madame,'* which she hastily turned into *'merci, Mimi,'* before she could be corrected again.

When she left the room it was with two dresses, a white bag, and a box of new nylons, all pressed upon her by Mimi. It was most embarrassing for Juliet. The last thing she wanted was to have to accept presents from Lucien's wife.

In her own room, she flung the things on to the bed and stood staring at them hot-cheeked and angry. The whole situation was becoming too involved. *Did* Mimi know how Lucien felt about her? *Did she?* That was the sixty-four-thousand-dollar question, Juliet told herself with an unhappy laugh. But it was certain that Mimi was playing both with her, and Lucien; like a cat with mice.

What was such a woman worth? Why should she feel any sense of honour towards Mimi? Why should Lucien remain faithful to his wife? But the answer gradually became clear. One must do these things if one wished to keep one's self-respect.

Juliet suddenly made up her mind that Sophie or no Sophie, she must leave Roquemont. If she stayed she would be driven quite crazy. Cheeks aflame, she recalled the words that Mimi had thrown at her: *'Schoolgirl innocence'*. To the devil with that; *'Au diable,'* Juliet repeated to herself furiously – both in English and French.

She was no schoolgirl and she didn't feel particularly innocent when she remembered how madly she had clung to Lucien and kissed him. Honourable she might be and in a way, perhaps, still innocent. But her whole heart cried out for this man who was Mimi's husband. Her whole body clamoured for him. This she could not deny.

She felt terribly alone and friendless at the moment. Even Simone was disinterested in her these days. She was busy with her new boy-friend whom she had found in Leques – young Yves Maillard. His parents had already called on the de Maure-villes, and Mimi and Lucien later returned the call in Paris.

A week before the birthday party, Simone went to stay with Yves and his parents in their Paris apartment; but she was due back home for the birthday party. She had promised Sophie she would come, so long as she could bring her boy-friend with her – and nobody objected to that.

One September morning, for the first time since her return to the Château, Juliet was summoned to Lucien's library. The message was brought to her by Sophie, herself.

"Papa wants to talk to you – and I know what it is about – it is a big secret for me, for tomorrow," said Sophie excitedly.

She had been talking non-stop about the party during the past fortnight.

Juliet smiled and joked with the child, but it was with scant pleasure that she went to that interview with her employer. She had almost reached the state when she really did doubt Lucien's true feeling for her. He was far too strong and cool, and apparently indifferent. She felt bitterly unhappy. The joy had been drained out of her life. The last thing she wanted was to be made to feel ashamed of having loved Lucien and it was rapidly approaching that pitch. She was beginning to feel cheated and humiliated and it was not pleasant.

In the library, she found Lucien sitting on the edge of his desk examining a small box which he held in one hand. As she drew nearer she could see that this was a painted and gilded musical box. It had one of those exquisite little jewelled birds on the lid, that Fabergé had made so famous. When the lid opened, the bird moved and sang. It was a miraculous piece of mechanism.

Lucien lifted his head. He gave Juliet a brief glance.

Her heart jerked uncontrollably as she looked into his eyes, but she read nothing in them. They seemed surprisingly blank. He held the box out for her to see and said:

"I had to order this. They had run out of them at that shop in the St. Honoré. It is a copy of the original, of course, but the bird sings an especially beautiful song, and I thought Sophie would like it. It's a pretty toy. What do you think?"

"I think it's lovely and she will adore it," said Juliet and added the word Monsieur in a voice meant to be as cold and as hard as his. But the fingers, which she clasped behind her back, twined together so tightly that they hurt.

He opened the lid. The little jewelled bird began to trill with the sweetness of a thrush. Its tiny beak opened and shut. Its head moved from side to side. It was so charming that Juliet would ordinarily have been enchanted, but she stood there now feeling unhappy and with nothing to say. Then Lucien snapped the lid down. The song abruptly ceased. He said:

"I wanted to let you know that I have made plans for going away for a month at the end of September – to Majorca. Mimi has a cousin there with a rather beautiful Villa. She and Simone and I will probably stay there for about three weeks and young Yves will go with us. That seems quite an affair – between Simone and Yves," he added with a short laugh. "Well – I am encouraging it. He is the best choice of a boy-friend that Simone has yet made."

Juliet forced herself to reply.

"Yes, I thought he was charming, up at Leques."

"I just wanted to find out," Lucien went on coolly, "whether you will be quite content to stay on alone with Sophie at Roquemont; or you could invite one of your friends from England to stay with you. You did once mention one friend whose company you particularly enjoy."

"Oh, yes. Phyl . . . Phyllis Rye. I could ask her if she could get away, for part of the time anyhow. It would be nice."

"Mimi doesn't particularly wish to take Sophie with us to Majorca and I think perhaps she is better here with you."

"Yes," Juliet agreed.

She felt sunk. Three weeks alone – well – even if Phyl couldn't come, that didn't matter. Perhaps three weeks without having to see him, hear his voice, or note the cruel change in his attitude towards her – might be a relief. Never until this moment had she felt more dreadfully aware of Lucien's new indifference to her. She could hardly believe that those dark expressionless eyes had ever glowed with ardour, or that those slim strong hands now fingering the musical-box, had once held her so passionately.

She must have *dreamed* that night at Leques, she thought bitterly. It could never have been a fact.

Lucien got on to his feet, and turning his back to Juliet, placed the musical box on a table.

There was quite a pile of parcels there awaiting Sophie.

One of them, which had been unpacked, displayed a doll beautifully dressed in violet and gold brocade as a seventeenth-century lady of the French court. This, Juliet knew, would be especially dear to Sophie because it had been made by her little opposite number, Ann, in England, the crippled child from the Wandsworth Home. A regular correspondence now took place between the two little girls. Every month, Sophie insisted upon wrapping up a parcel of games or books and sending them to Ann. With the help of the nurses, Ann had dressed this period doll for her little French friend's birthday present.

Rather sadly, Juliet eyed the doll. After that morning in Mimi's bedroom, she had felt determined to quit this place – get away from the awful undercurrent of feeling. Yet so far she had been too weak to go – too weak, she told herself wryly, to leave either Sophie *or* Lucien.

There had been a discussion recently about Ann and a suggestion from Lucien that at his expense the English child should be flown out to Cannes to spend Christmas in the Château with Sophie. It was quite obvious that everybody expected Juliet to be here this winter!

Suddenly Lucien turned round to her.

"About your birthday – you are coming of age, aren't you, Juliet?"

"Yes, Monsieur."

"Oh, for God's sake, call me Lucien."

She said nothing but her heart gave a violent leap. It was the first kind of intimate communication she had had with him for a long, long time. So, she thought, with guilty joy, he was not altogether impervious to her.

"Well — why are you standing there like a little dumb thing — not speaking?" he demanded harshly.

She felt stupidly tongue-tied. She raised her eyes to his. He was looking directly at her, and once more she saw in them all the feverish desperate passion that had lain in those big dark eyes that night at Leques. She pressed her hands against her breast. She had never fainted and was never likely to, she told herself, dryly, but she felt decidedly dizzy. She made an effort to speak in an ordinary way.

"I don't — really want much attention — paid to *my* birthday."

"Why not?"

"I just *don't*. I — I'm not in the mood for it."

"I'm afraid you'll have to take your orders from Sophie," said Lucien with a dry laugh. "She expects you to celebrate in a big way with her. Aren't you sharing a cake?"

She nodded.

"I just want to tell you," he went on, "that I can't give you the sort of birthday present that I would *like* to have given."

She gave him a slightly bewildered look.

He added:

"Oh, dammit, I mean that I would like to have chosen something especially beautiful for you but I have had to leave it to Mimi. She said she would choose a gift, to come from all of us. God knows we owe you enough after all you have done for the child."

"I don't want to be continually reminded of what I have done for the child," Juliet flared up.

"Oh, don't be difficult," he raised his own voice and looked suddenly so angry that she drew back. She was used to dealing with calm prosaic people like her father — laconic men, like Luke Farrell. She really did not feel equipped to cope with a temperamental Frenchman, she told herself. Ironically, and because she was so confused and upset, she began to laugh. This seemed further to annoy Lucien.

"What's the joke?"

"I don't know," she said, helplessly, gasping.

"Did I say anything particularly funny?"

"No, nothing. Oh — I'd better go. You have told me what you wanted to — about the holiday in Majorca, I mean. I'll write at

166

once to my friend Phyllis Rye and ask her to try and join me here."

"I insist on knowing what you were laughing at."

"Oh, nothing ... really nothing ... oh, leave me alone, *please*. I do wish everybody would leave me alone! ..."

Then to his utter consternation, she broke off, and covering her face with her hands, burst into tears.

The sight of that young dejected figure swept away all Lucien's resolve to be strong and to keep his emotions in check. He could see that Juliet was mortally hurt. It was more than he could bear. He made a movement towards her and swept her into his arms.

"Juliet, Juliet ... oh, my darling, I've made you cry ... forgive me!"

She hadn't the strength to resist. She wouldn't have cared at that moment if somebody had opened the door and walked in.

Here they were in the old library, so full of past splendour and traditions. Tapestries; a tattered silk banner that one of the de Maurevilles had carried in battle ... thousands of leather-bound books by the great French writers ... old faded, still magnificent, curtains, sweeping on either side of the long narrow windows that belonged to the old wing of the Château. Above the great carved stone fireplace a painting of Lucien's great-great-grandfather; a haughty gentleman of the French Court of the seventeenth-century – with one delicate hand on the hilt of his sword, smiling at them a trifle superciliously.

Honour ... antiquity ... decay ... gloom. Yet the present was here, too. The sharp poignant present. She, herself, was in the arms of the man who should have been her lover and to whom she knew she must say good-bye for ever because things were getting beyond their control. It was unbearable.

Just for a moment longer she lived in this golden electric present ... her arms wrapped around his neck; feeling the burning ardour of his kisses on her lips and throat. She listened to him telling her again and again that he loved her to the pitch of madness. For him, she was not just a young English governess full of what Mimi called schoolgirl innocence – for him, she was all woman and the woman whom he desired.

She sobbed against his lips:

"I thought you didn't love me any more. I thought you were sorry about what happened that night in Leques. I've been so dreadfully unhappy."

"Oh, you little fool, I haven't forgotten for a single moment. The memory of it – of you – has been driving me mad. Don't you understand that *I love you?*"

She shook her head dumbly. The scalding tears poured down her cheeks. What he said made her wildly happy but it was a happiness that she knew could only end in grief, and the longer she allowed herself to enjoy it, the worse it would be afterwards. She gasped:

"We can't go on, Lucien. I think we seem to love each other too much. I've *got* to get away."

For one insane moment he toyed with the idea of begging her to go with him this very moment to Mimi, tell her how they both felt, and ask her to set him free. But it was only a temporary insanity. He shut his eyes because it broke his heart to see Juliet's tears. Then with a heavy sigh, he pushed her gently away from him. Turning he fumbled for a cigarette.

"You're quite right. We can't go on. We're defeated. You've been marvellous and I've tried – God knows I've kept away from you. Hardly spoken to you. But it's only hurt you and it hasn't helped me. Poor little Sophie will have to learn to live without you, my beloved Juliet."

She stood very still, wiping away her tears, blowing her nose forlornly like a sad child.

I bet I look a sight now, she thought, grimacing. *I bet I do! I just don't know why he loves me!*

But he did. With all his heart, Lucien loved this young, beloved girl with her snub nose and freckles and tears. Behind it all lay that extraordinary strength and judgement that he admired so much, and those fine principles that matched his own. He could not have loved or respected her more deeply – or regretted the whole situation with a greater sense of despair.

He wanted so much to pull her back into his arms, but instead, stood apart, smoking, staring at her helplessly. Now she gave him a small tired smile and said:

"You don't know how much better I feel."

"Better!" he repeated, staring.

"Yes. You see I thought you were avoiding me and being very cold to me, having regretted what happened at Leques."

"Oh, my dear! What *did* happen?" he exclaimed. "We did little harm. We kissed each other. We made love a little, but *that* was not as I would have liked to have made love to you, my heart's darling. You can't believe how much I wanted you."

She blushed crimson. He loved to see that red colour rush under the fine skin and the way her eyelashes flickered with nerves and embarrassment. She was too young and too sweet, he thought, to be involved in *this* sort of affair. She should be in love with a nice boy who could marry her and make her happy. *This* wasn't fair on her.

"I've loved you madly ever since then. Night and day, I've wanted you," he said in a low voice, "but it was agreed that we had to forget what we felt about each other."

"I expect I was just an idiot – longing to be sure that you hadn't forgotten, and that you did still love me."

"Well, I did and do, and it will never be otherwise. I shall always love you, *petite* Juliet, but I admit we cannot go on living under the same roof."

"Then Sophie must be hurt."

"Sophie must be hurt," he repeated the words.

"Oh, it's so *miserable!*" she exclaimed.

"That's putting it mildly."

"And I'm not sure Mimi doesn't guess. She said all sorts of odd things this morning – suggesting that I was your type and so on."

"I'm afraid I'm past caring whether she guesses or not," said Lucien harshly, "except so far as it reflects upon you. No doubt she has suspicions, but she has absolutely no right to be jealous or mind anything that I do. It is just that her vanity would be enormously hurt if she really thought you attracted me. I think she'd like to believe that I shall spend the rest of my life grieving because *she* no longer loves me!"

Juliet put her face in her hands. The tears trickled through her fingers. She felt she had nothing more to say. The idea of leaving Roquemont – little Sophie – and this beloved man who had become her whole world, shattered her completely. The worst part was the knowledge that it would react so badly upon Sophie. She would have to think up a very good reason for leaving – try to make the parting easy for the child.

"One thing is certain," she heard Lucien say, "you can't leave us before the birthday party. That *would upset Sophie!*" . . .

Juliet lifted her face and looked at him with her wet anguished eyes.

"What can we do to make it easier for her? If only I could think of something."

"The hell of it is, you can't be replaced. However, we have *some* breathing space. You need not pack up and go in the morning," he said with a twist of the lips. "Don't forget I am supposed to be taking my dear wife and stepdaughter to Majorca, which gives us three weeks for you to stay here with my poor little girl. Then, by the time we come back, you can have told her something; perhaps that you have had a letter from home to say that your father wants you to go back to London and keep house for him."

"It might even be true," sighed Juliet. "My last letter from Daddy was very gloomy. He seems so fed up with the Middle-East, and his health isn't what it used to be. I think he might like to try and get a job in England and have a home with me. It's only the need for money that keeps us away from each other at work. We're both really a home-loving pair."

Lucien looked at her hungrily.

"What a fine person you are! I shall always be glad that I've known you."

She felt as though he had stabbed her in the heart with a sharp knife.

"Oh, don't. It sounds so final – as though you have already put me in the past."

"I've got to put you there, my darling. I have no choice."

Once before – up at Leques – madness had seized Juliet, and she had faced realism as well as romance. Now again today she was filled with an overwhelming physical need of Lucien – recognized to the full the urgency of the feelings they shared. Once again she remembered what Phyl had said about the girl having the last word. Now Juliet was utterly feminine, she felt neither smug, good, nor sensible. She just flung herself into his arms.

"Lucien, I can't bear this. Take me – take me, please."

Down went his own defences. He held her tightly – horrified by the pain in her eyes and the misery on that young sensitive face.

"*Mon Dieu,* Juliet, you don't mean that, darling. Do you think *I'm* finding things easy? You mean so much to me that I would like to pick you up in my arms at this moment, carry you out there into the woods, and give way to every primitive feeling a man can have. I'm no angel, my darling, believe me. I try to do the right thing, but I'm only human."

"I want you to be," she was sobbing, out of control, her arms straining him against her with desperate strength.

"No, you don't—" he pressed her face against his shoulder. His own face was strained and sad and full of bitter irony. What a life, he thought . . . what a damned awful life . . . for this perfectly good sweet child (for that was all she sometimes seemed to him) – to be virtually offering herself up on the altar of love. Only she didn't know what she was doing or where it would all lead; but he, older than she and married, *he knew*. And he had seen plenty of this sort of thing going on among his friends. Married men taking advantage of young girls who were madly in love with them. Taking what they offered. Ruining their lives. What sort of man would he be if he did this to Juliet? Some might say he would be justified in the face of what Mimi had done to him and if Juliet was willing. But nothing (and he knew it) could justify him taking advantage of a wholesome adorable girl like Juliet Browning.

"Lucien, Lucien! . . ."

He heard her broken voice. When she lifted her face and he saw the tears pouring down her cheeks he was half inclined to take her at her word. But soon he was in control again. Very gently he wiped the tears away with his pocket handkerchief. He shook his head.

"This won't do, my darling. It just won't!"

Suddenly she felt as though she was coming up above the surface of rough water, and was able to breathe normally – see clearly – and swim for shore. She had nearly drowned, she thought grimly. She felt thoroughly ashamed of herself. She resorted to laughter. Helpless, hysterical laughter.

"Oh, God . . . how f-funny . . . me behaving like this and after all my lectures to Phyl! I'm as weak as water. Oh, Lucien, Lucien I'll never lecture anyone again. Now I know what it means to lose my own head absolutely and completely."

"It's a very beautiful little head and you've only lost it for a few seconds," he said and kissed both her hands. "I understand. Believe me! And I thank you for what you have just said. I thank you for your sweet generosity."

Scarlet and miserable she covered her face with her hand.

"I'm sorry."

"If you dare to start apologizing, I'll lose my own head and rush you into the woods – as threatened."

She tried to laugh again but could only cry. For a moment she stayed close to him her face pressed against his breast. Then she moved away. She stood staring blindly out at the garden.

"You must think me an absolute idiot."

"Juliet, will you *please* stop apologizing. This thing is mutual, my dear child. We're both very much in love and we've both got to be strong about it. And you've got to help *me*. If you go on being so utterly charming and generous, I won't be able to stand up to it, I assure you! All we *can* do is to try, and to laugh, my darling. And what we must both do is to be proud and glad we've loved and known each other."

She turned to him; no longer beautiful, eyelids swollen, face blotchy with grief, hair untidy; his handkerchief pressed against her quivering lips. But to Lucien she still seemed very lovely – the most wonderful person he had ever known. He gave her a long, long look.

"I'll love you till I die, Juliet," he said.

She ran out of the room, through the hall and into the garden. She cut through to a small clearing where one of the de Maurevilles of the past had built a Regency 'Folly' backed by ilex trees. It was a small, attractive circular building with a tiny porch. Two marble pillars framed the open doorway. The roof was half-covered by a wild profusion of pink bougainvillaea.

In here, she sometimes sat and read to Sophie because it was secluded and cool on a hot day. Nobody else ever came to this place. Here, Juliet knew she could be alone in this bitter hour; nobody would find her.

She flung herself on a pile of garden cushions and cried and cried as though her heart was breaking; trying, finally, to renounce her love for Lucien, whilst her hope of happiness in the years ahead receded into the shadows and seemed to become extinct.

Chapter Sixteen

Happy Birthday to you!
Happy Birthday to you!
Happy Birthday, chère Sophie,
Happy Birthday to you!

JULIET, sitting at the piano in the salon, was playing the music. A crowd of guests stood around, singing the words in English. It sounded so sweet and silly with the broken accents; it made Juliet smile.

Sophie was perched on the grand piano wearing her new dress – not pink this time, but powder blue – an exquisitely tucked cotton-voile. It had been chosen by Mimi and had adorable, short puffed sleeves and a wide stiff skirt. Her dark hair was smoothed down by a blue Alice band. She wore a necklace of tiny seed pearls – real pearls given to her by her godmother. On one wrist hung a gold charm bracelet – a present from Maman. She held close to her, the little Fabergé box with the jewelled bird, on which Lucien had spent so much money. She would not be parted from it. It enthralled her.

Nobody had ever seen Sophie look so well; she was almost pretty today. She could never really be that, but she was less wizened, and sullen, and miserable-looking these days. There was a sparkle in her big dark eyes, and a smile on her lips which gave her face some life. It warmed Lucien's heart as he watched her.

He dared not look too often at the young pianist, although when he had first joined the party, one swift look had shown him that his beloved Juliet also looked her best this afternoon. She, too, wore pale blue, and she was cool and fresh and shining-eyed. Pinned to her shoulder, she wore an artificial rose (rather a frightful one) which he knew Sophie had chosen and given her. But nothing would have induced Juliet not to wear it. She was always so wonderful about pleasing Sophie, he thought tenderly.

Now, everybody made the girl repeat the English birthday song, but this time they all sang "Happy Birthday *dear Juliet*!"

Mimi was close to the piano, an arm around her small

daughter, acting to the full her role as adoring mother. She was as beautiful as always, in her favourite white – and wearing enormous aquamarine and gold earrings. She appeared to be in a singularly amiable mood. She had been very nice to Juliet all day and even given her a personal present – a silver medallion on a fine chain to wear with her pullovers. Lucien had to admit that Mimi had also chosen a splendid present for Juliet from the family (from Sophie in particular); a beautiful rawhide suitcase lined with dark-blue silk and bearing the initials 'J.B.' in one corner. It had gilt locks and its own transparent nylon cover.

It was the sort of luxury case that Juliet had often admired when she walked through the luggage department of a shop like Fortnum's or Harrod's, and knew she could never possibly afford. It delighted her. Sophie's present from Juliet was a fountain-pen and pencil in a case – something she had very much wanted – that had been a success.

So far it had been a happy birthday because Juliet had woken up determined not to allow the thought of her forthcoming exile from Roquemont to wreck the party. She had herself and her emotions well in hand. That day in the 'Folly' she had cried so much that she felt now she had no tears left to shed. Today, in particular, she would not allow herself to be depressed. This was Sophie's birthday. Although Lucien had hardly spoken to her, for he had not seen her alone, Juliet could at least feel the warmth of his love for her coming towards her in a healing wave, washing away her pain.

There were many distinguished guests at the birthday party. The Vicomte and Vicomtesse Beauvallais, who had a villa in Grasse, had come with their twin daughters, aged nine, who were friends of Sophie. There were the Americans, too, with their children. And the small son of Paul and Annette Clermont who adored Sophie.

Tea was served in the *salle à manger*. The sun was still so fierce out of doors. Everybody admired the huge white and pink cake made by the de Maureville cook. The candles for the English Mees and the little Mademoiselle were all alight.

Sophie hobbled excitedly up to the table, looked down at the shining candles, and stretched out a hand to her governess.

"Look – *look* – isn't it wonderful, Juliette?"

"Wonderful, darling."

On the fringe of the party, Simone stood with young Yves

Maillard, an arm tucked through his. For the first time in her life, Simone felt truly soft and feminine – sentimental about her future.

"You know, Yves," she whispered, "that funny girl, Juliet Browning has done something for our family. She's helped Sophie to become almost normal, and somehow she's altered *my* outlook. There used to be nothing but unhappiness in this place – what with my parents always disagreeing, and Sophie always being ill. Quite frankly I used to dread the thought of marrying and having a family. Today I feel I'd like a child of my own – a birthday party like this one for *him* or *her*!"

Yves put an arm around his girl-friend and looked at her with unashamed ardour.

"One day it will be so – we *shall* have a child of our own, *ma très chère Simone*."

"Juliette, Juliette!" Sophie's high-pitched voice rose above the general conversation. "Recite to everybody that verse about birthdays – you know. It begins '*Monday's Child is fair of face*.' I was born on a Monday, wasn't I, Maman?" she turned to Mimi.

"*Oui, chérie*."

Juliet gravely went through the recitation.

"And so you *are* – '*fair of face*'," put in Lucien coming forward and hugging his little daughter.

"And Juliette is Friday's Child, and *she* is 'Loving and Giving'" said Sophie excitedly. "She *is*, isn't she, Papa?"

"That is exactly what she is!" said Lucien in a low voice.

Juliet heard the remark and hastily started to talk about something else but there leapt through her mind the rather ironic thought: 'I think I am soon going to turn into just *Saturday's Child who must Work for its Living*.' Then, because there was a lump in her throat she made sure that all the children were being served by Hortense with the kind of drinks they liked. Most of them preferred fruit juice to tea. Juliet's cheeks were scarlet and her heart thumping. Just those few words of innocent praise from Lucien were enough to disturb her, and she didn't really want to be disturbed today.

Mimi had also heard Lucien's remark and noted the young English girl's high colour. Her lips twisted into a rather unpleasant grimace. Oh yes, she thought, her suspicions about those two were justified. She would have something to twit Lucien with later on. And something to tell her *lieber* Max. Or would it be a good idea to say nothing to Lucien and to fling those two together, then perhaps find cause one day to get rid of *him*? That would be amusing – if she could find a weak spot in the armour of the so-strong, so-chaste Lucien, instead of always being the wrong-doer herself!

A dozen unworthy, unattractive ideas flitted through Mimi's amoral mind. She talked mechanically to the other mothers but through her long lashes she kept a strict eye on her husband – and Juliet.

There was one more moment of revelation for her when Juliet and Sophie, hand-in-hand, simultaneously blew out the candles on their cake.

Sophie couldn't quite draw enough breath to help extinguish the thirty candles that were on that cake, illuminating their combined ages. She called for help from her father. Laughing, Lucien bent over to add his breath. Inadvertently, his cheek almost touched Juliet's. As though drawn by a magnet he turned slightly to look at her. Not a soul in the room intercepted that look except Mimi. Mimi, who put a tongue in her cheek and began to hum a little tune under her breath. The scheming in that twisted mind of hers continued.

When the party ended and the last guests had gone, Sophie was very tired. Juliet insisted upon taking her to bed.

The child began to protest but Juliet put an arm around her and said:

"No, *chérie*, you really *are* tired tonight. You've had a tremendous lot of excitement and you woke very early to open your parcels. Just to please me, because it's my birthday too, come along to bed, darling."

"Then you must give me my bath tonight and not Blanche. Old Blanche said *she* was going to."

"Yes, yes – old Blanche must see to you this evening, dear," put in the old nurse eagerly. "I was here when you were born, you know – nine years ago, *p'tite*."

"That's true. Do allow Blanche that privilege tonight," Juliet whispered to Sophie – much as she disliked the gossiping old nurse.

"Then you'll come later on and say good night to me, won't you, Juliette."

"Of course I will, my Princess, and I'll sit by your bed and

176

write a letter or two. I had that lovely cable from my brother, Nick, and a letter from *my* papa. I must write to them both."

"Oh, I do love you. Thank you for a marvellous, *marvellous* birthday!" exclaimed the child throwing her thin arms around Juliet's waist.

"I love you too, and thank you for *my* birthday," said Juliet. But as she kissed the child the tears stung her eyelids. (Oh, how was she ever going to tell Sophie that she was leaving her, she wondered with a sense of despair.)

While Lucien and Mimi were changing for dinner, Mimi walked into her husband's dressing-room.

"Simone and Yves want to go down to the Casino this evening to dance. I think I'll play a little *chemin de fer*. Have you any objection?"

"None at all. I'll take you down," he said courteously.

Although he felt so many miles away from this woman, so completely out of love with her now, at least he must remember that she had given him Sophie. Between them there was still that one imperishable link.

But Mimi had other plans.

"Don't bother, dear. I've arranged to meet Thérèse Beauvallais. She wants a little gamble with me. Her husband has a date elsewhere. Marino will drive me down. Why don't you have some music with the dear little birthday girl? I mean the dear *big* birthday girl, of course," said Mimi sweetly.

At once Lucien scented trouble. But he had his feelings completely under control. If Mimi was trying to get him to betray what he felt for Juliet, she was mistaken. He told her coolly that he had no time for singing tonight. He wished to drive over to see Paul Clermont. Paul had said this afternoon that he was in some kind of trouble with the tax authorities. He was not a good businessman. "He will be glad of my advice," observed Lucien.

"Oh, surely," said Mimi, tying and untying the satin bow on her chiffon peignoir, "you won't leave our little Juliet alone on her birthday evening."

"We had a birthday lunch and a birthday tea for Juliet and Sophie. That is enough."

"Is that all you think about her? I should have imagined you would want to shower her with thanks for all that she has done for our child."

Lucien bit his lip. He turned away from the light blue eyes

that glittered at him with such a mixture of malice and innocence.

"I really fail to understand you, Mimi. One moment you are damning Juliet's eyes, the next you are anxious that she should be showered with thanks and praise."

"But it *is* her birthday—" began Mimi.

"Are you suggesting that she and I have a nice cosy intimate evening at the piano?"

"Cosy, yes. I didn't use the word intimate. Would you *like* to be intimate with Juliet?"

Lucien flushed crimson. Suddenly he was on the verge of losing his temper.

"Oh, for heaven's sake, Mimi, what are you getting at?"

"Getting at?" she repeated wide-eyed. "Nothing. Why are you so cross? What have I done or said to annoy you?"

He set his teeth.

"If you don't mind, I'd like to get on with my shaving. It's nearly dinner-time; and kindly allow me to make my own plans for spending this evening."

Mimi shrugged.

"*Comme tu veux, chérie.* But I can't think why you're so agitated."

She was fiendish and cunning. She was playing some dark sinister game of her own and he knew it. His heart was very heavy. It was even more clear to him tonight than before that it was utterly necessary for Juliet to leave Roquemont.

But Mimi had not finished. Once dressed, she tackled Juliet.

"So sorry, dear, Simone and Yves and I are going down to the Casino, Juliet; it sounds mean to leave you, as it is your birthday night, but I know Lucien wants to practise his songs. *Do* suggest it to him, once we have gone. He said he did not like to suggest it to *you*, because he thought you were too tired. But I know he adores to sing when you are here to accompany him."

Juliet blushed which amused Mimi. The girl was to transparent, and it was so obvious that she was in love with Lucien. Mimi had half decided to let this affair ripen. One day she would be bound to catch them out – she might be able to put an end for good and all to Lucien's efforts to prevent *her* from seeing too much of Max. She would stop him from pretending that he was so angelic, and that *she* was the horrid, faithless one.

But Mimi's schemes this evening, anyhow, were not a success. After she and the others had left for the Casino, Juliet rather timidly approached Lucien and suggested an hour or two of music. This was coldly refused.

"Thank you. The idea has already been suggested to me, but I am going along to see the Clermonts."

"Of course," Juliet said, and felt abashed and confused, and wondered as she had been doing for a long time if her loss of control in the library that day had shocked him – despite what he had said to her.

They were alone in the hall where she had waylaid him and issued the invitation. She had wanted so much to hear him sing again. Now he looked down into the small troubled face and some of his control snapped.

"Oh, Juliet, don't you see that I can't stand the idea of an evening alone with you at the piano, or anywhere else," he said roughly. "Oh, for God's sake leave Roquemont before I come back from Majorca. Don't let me find you here any more. Get a replacement. I'm only human and I find this position intolerable. I want you too damned badly. Good night, my dear, *dear* love ..." he broke off abruptly, turned and left her standing there. The big front door slammed, reverberating through the quiet Château. She was miserable. The future looked black. But she could not help feeling utterly thankful that her fears about Lucien were without reason. He *did* still love and want her. She had not lost his love.

She went upstairs and found Sophie in bed, still awake, and calling for her.

It was plain enough to Juliet that Mimi must have suggested the evening's music to Lucien with an ulterior motive. It had upset him. There seemed little hope of putting this thing right; certainly not now that Mimi had grown suspicious and was playing a game with them.

She really *is* an evil woman, Juliet thought in horror.

She found it difficult to write happy birthday thank-you letters to her father or Nicky; but she wrote at length to her friend Phyl.

I'm coming home in about four weeks' time – for good. I'll have to find a nursing job. Possibly I'll go down to Bristol where Luke Farrell says he can always get me back on the old Wandsworth staff. I can't tell you everything fully in a letter but I'm now in your unhappy shoes, darling Phyl. Terribly in love and without one vestige of hope for the future. I'm trying to be strong because he wants me to be, and he is not finding it too easy to be strong, himself. He

179

is a man of very deep passions. The more I think about him the more terrible it seems. We could have been so happy, although I can hardly believe it's true that he loves me. But we are in sympathy – we seem to be marvellous friends, and could have been wonderful lovers.

His wife is a devil – cruel as the grave. It is killing him. And it kills me to see him suffering, but there isn't a thing I can do about it.

Oh, Phyl, I never fully realized until now how terribly hard you must have been hit when you had to say good-bye to the man you loved. It is the end, isn't it? You can't sleep or eat or think – you're just one big fire of longing.

Thank goodness you'll be coming here once they go off to Majorca. It will make all the difference to me and I want you to meet him just once – to see what I've got to give up. As for the child – that is the most awful part of it. Between us we've got to make Sophie suffer. I wonder if you know anybody nice and kindly and sympathetic, and who can speak a little French, who might take my place. I have decided to break the news to her gradually and half promise to come back, then ease out of it very gently. She will have had time to get accustomed to her new governess . . .

By the time Juliet had finished this letter, she was in tears again – having told herself that she had no more to shed. But she had . . . they poured out. She began to wonder if she would ever stop crying again.

She was awake when she heard Lucien's car come up the drive. She knew the difference between the sound of the wheels of his Jaguar, and those of the smaller car belonging to Mimi.

She pictured him walking into his lonely Château, not only tonight but after she had gone. All his old worries over Sophie would begin again. It was her sacred duty, Juliet told herself, to find the right person to take on her job.

She was quite shocked by her own passionate desire to get up, put on a dressing-gown, run downstairs and fling herself into Lucien's arms. She almost wished she was one of those girls who had no principles; that he had none either, and that they could just take what the gods offered and enjoy it to the full. Then, with a vision of herself locked in Lucien's arms . . . all his . . . *all his* . . . she buried her face on her folded arms and this time she did not cry. She prayed as she had not prayed since she was a little girl.

"Please God help me . . . *please God . . . do!*"

She felt ill and looked it the next day. Sophie was particularly troublesome. The child had got overtired and was fretful and exacting. Very little that Juliet did was right. There was much grumbling, and some reluctance to do any of the things Juliet had planned. Finally Juliet snapped and Sophie dissolved into tears. This tore at Juliet's already overwrought emotions. She gathered Sophie up on to her lap and wept with her.

"I didn't mean to be so cross. Forgive me, Sophie darling."

Sophie immediately cheered up and suggested that they should play with the little musical box. But the very sound of the tiny jewelled bird warbling his song added to Juliet's misery. She could so plainly see that box in Lucien's hands, as he had first shown it to her.

Lucien, Lucien! . . . This love was beginning to be a madness, she told herself, and felt afraid.

She was glad he was away all day, and it did not seem that he would be back tonight. He had flown to Paris on sudden business.

That same afternoon, the Maillards took the young couple to Paris on the Caravelle. An engagement was soon going to be announced, Mimi told Juliet. She was delighted. It was a good match. Simone would be rich.

"What really matters is that she seems to love the boy – so she'll be happy," remarked Juliet.

"How sentimental you are," murmured Mimi. "I'm afraid you are the type to think that love comes before anything in the world but I am afraid I can't share your romantic belief. Haven't you a saying in England about *'love flying out of the window when poverty comes in at the door?'* "

"Yes, but I don't believe *that*, Madame . . . Mimi," Juliet corrected herself.

Against her will, she was, just then, sitting alone with Lucien's wife. Sophie was in her bedroom with the physiotherapist. Juliet had been doing some sewing out on the terrace under the striped awning. It had been another dazzling Mediterranean day. Mimi lay full length, languidly, on a chaise-longue – her eyes closed while she spoke to the English girl.

"You really think if you loved a man you would put up with poverty so long as you were with him?" she asked dreamily.

Juliet looked down at her needlework.

"Certainly."

"You suggest that, if Lucien lost all his money, I ought to accept the fact and be very happy to leave this Château, give up my Paris flat, and exist joyfully with him in some cheap residence, wearing cheap clothes and, perhaps, doing my own cooking?"

Juliet hesitated. She had a feeling that she was being baited; knew that her cheeks were hot, but tried to keep cool.

She said:

"I must admit that I can't imagine you doing any of those things."

"For which you despise me?"

"No question of that. I have no right to despise anybody."

"Yet you are quite sure, that if you, for instance, were in my shoes, you wouldn't mind making any such sacrifices for Lucien?"

Now Juliet raised her head and looked steadily into the aquamarine eyes that were mocking her.

"It's such a hypothetical case, it surely isn't worth pursuing."

"But if you *were* in my shoes – what then?" persisted Mimi.

Juliet's fingers, holding the needle, trembled so that she dropped it, which Mimi, to her satisfaction, noted.

"Forgive me, but isn't this rather a senseless discussion?" Juliet asked in a low voice.

"No, it rather interests me. You admire my husband, don't you?"

Once more Juliet looked Mimi squarely in the face.

"Very much."

"Perhaps you are also just a *teeny* weeny bit in love?"

Juliet, tanned though she was, could actually feel the blood recede from her cheeks.

"Please, Mimi – let us talk about something else – it's all so – so – so stupid," she said with a laugh that held a touch of hysteria.

Mimi was quite satisfied now that she had hit the nail on the head. They *were* in love these two. Perversely, she was piqued by the idea. She could not too easily relinquish her hold on anything that she possessed. She was indignant because this unglamorous freckled-faced girl should have won Lucien's admiration and respect to such an extent; taken such a hold on Lucien's affections.

But she wasn't going to let Juliet know what she felt. She was still determined to involve Lucien – corner him – and use Juliet in the process.

Of course, in the future she must also lose Juliet Ingram's

friendship. That wouldn't matter. She could do without her American friend. She could do without everybody, providing Max married her. Well – Max had told her that the day was fast approaching when he meant to dispose of the Clinic and go to New York where they wanted him to open a much larger hospital. That suited Mimi. It looked, too, as though she would shortly get her daughter comfortably married off to Yves Maillard, so she would have no worries about *her*. Mimi herself would be happy to join that sparkling Café-society-set in New York – the Mecca of all beautiful elegant women.

Maria appeared.

"Madama is wanted on the telephone by the Herr Doktor."

Her slanting almond eyes threw Juliet a saucy provocative glance as she spoke. Mimi jumped up and followed Maria indoors. Juliet was left alone. She relaxed, dropped her needle-work and closed her eyes.

Oh, God, she thought, this is all so wrong, so unfair to Lucien. If only she were decent to him – if only all this suffering and renunciation on our part were worth while. It's so ghastly ... we've both got to lose everything and gain nothing.

Nothing but the feeling that they had done the right thing. Well, Juliet thought bitterly, maybe saints and angels could live happily in an exalted atmosphere of virtue but she was all human, this afternoon – just an ordinary warm-hearted girl, madly and desperately in love. She found little comfort in having done what was right. She was all the more unhappy because Mimi was betraying Lucien behind his back.

Only one good thing had come out of all this, she told herself; the rehabilitation of little Sophie. That in itself must be counted well worth her own pain.

Mimi returned looking flushed and excited. Mimi wasn't very often excited. She threw one of her brilliant smiles at Juliet.

"*Tiens!* I thought today was going to be a bore but it's turned out otherwise. Dr. Sternburg has to fly to Rome for a consultation. It only takes a little over one hour and fifteen minutes there by air. He has asked me to go with him. Of course I shall. We should be back late tonight – long before dear Lucien returns from Paris, so *he* won't be able to grumble because he doesn't find me at home. Men are egotists ..." Mimi chattered on as though Juliet were her best friend and confidant. "I don't know what *he* is doing in his spare time, but he always wants to know what *I* am doing ... *so* jealous! ..." She gave her flute-like laugh.

Juliet said nothing. What could she say? She was quite sure that Lucien wouldn't have wished his wife to fly to Rome with Max Sternburg; but not because he was jealous.

"I adore Max's private plane and he has a very good pilot and it's going to be quite above board. He is taking his best nurse with him. I believe he has been called to an Italian millionaire's villa for a terrible case ... a young Italian girl who has attempted suicide ... Max is marvellous with psychopaths ... He is so famous – all over the world."

Still, Juliet made no reply, but inwardly she burned with indignation. "*Above board*," Mimi called it. Yes, on the surface, with a nurse to chaperone the pair, but there were plenty of opportunities to get rid of *her* once the consultation was over. Plenty of chance for Mimi and Max to explore the *dolce vita* in Rome.

Oh, it's all so beastly for Lucien, Juliet thought indignantly.

Mimi, in high spirits, went off to change her clothes.

"You're so trustworthy, I can leave everything safely to you," she cooed.

Sick at heart, Juliet watched her drive away to the airport. How perverse life was! Here was Lucien's wife going gaily to a rendezvous with her lover while she, Juliet, would have given all the world to have been in Mimi's shoes, waiting here for Lucien to come home ... waiting for Lucien – and love.

She was not to know them, that Mimi had made a rendezvous not only with love, but with death.

Chapter Seventeen

IT was an extraordinary coincidence that about six o'clock that evening Lucien de Maureville happened to be drinking a glass of champagne in the house of a business friend in Paris, and the friend turned on his radio.

"I want to hear the news . . ." he said.

The news for Lucien was especially horrifying. Towards the end, the announcer reported that a private plane had crashed just outside Rome and that everybody in it had been killed, including the pilot. It was believed that the crash was due to the weather; possibly the aircraft had been struck by lightning as they had run into a violent thunderstorm just before they reached the airport.

The private aircraft was flying its owner, Dr. Max Sternburg, to an urgent case in Rome. It was not possible to identify the bodies of the two women who were with him, because the crashed plane had caught fire; but inquiries made from the Herr Doktor's clinic revealed that he had taken with him one of his nurses, a Mlle Duval – and a friend. The friend was Mme de Maureville, wife of M. Lucien de Maureville whose home, Château de Roquemont near Cannes, was of great historic interest to tourists . . .

At this point Lucien sprang to his feet, deathly white. The man he was with put a hand out to steady him.

"*Mon Dieu, mon cher de Maureville. Quelle horreur! . . .*"

Horror, confusion, amazement . . . every kind of strong emotion shook Lucien in that moment of revelation.

Mimi . . . killed in an air-crash; and with Max Sternburg. What was she doing on that flight? Lucien could only guess. His personal feelings for her culminated in genuine sorrow. Mimi's death was no great loss for him. How could it be? As he had so often told himself, little was left between them but the tie of their child. But it was terrible to think of that still-youthful radiant beauty being annihilated; to know that death had struck Mimi down so suddenly and finally on this golden summer's day.

Lucien had a vivid imagination. As he thought more about

the crash, he began to shiver violently. His friend made him sit down, and gave him cognac. After a few moments Lucien was in control again, and telephoning the Château.

He spoke to Juliet.

Down at Roquemont they already knew about the catastrophe. Paris radio had been on to them. Juliet had told them that Monsieur was in Paris but that she didn't know where to get in touch with him. Her voice shook as she spoke to Lucien.

"It's too awful."

"Unbelievable," he said. "I must contact Simone. She may already have heard, although as far as I know, she rarely listens to radio news. It never interests her. It's obvious that I won't be back until the morning. Look after Sophie."

"Lucien, I don't know what to say to you . . ."

"Nothing," he broke in, "At this moment, there is nothing, *nothing* to say, *ma chère*."

"The telephone has been ringing incessantly. When people ask me about . . . about Mimi . . . I just say that the doctor had been giving her a lift, and that she, herself was on her way to stay with friends in Rome."

"Thank you," said Lucien.

A little of the horror and shock he felt was relieved by the thought that that dear girl at Roquemont was guarding his reputation – trying to avert a scandal. He added:

"Don't tell Sophie."

"I haven't done so. I've warned all the staff to keep quiet, too. Maria is the only one who has had hysterics. I've sent her to bed."

"I'll think over what I must tell Sophie when I get home," said Lucien.

That was the end of their conversation.

And that was the end of any personal contact between them for some time.

The French Press, having got hold of the news of the air disaster that had killed a famous neurologist and the equally famous Parisienne beauty who was the wife of the well known M. de Maureville, found it agreeably sensational and made the most of it. The morning papers were full of it, and published a recent photograph of Mimi – looking dazzlingly beautiful at the Opera, in one of her slinky dresses, and wearing white Icelandic foxes and her emeralds.

Once Lucien got home, he decided it would be best, if Sophie did not stay at the Château. There were too many telephone calls and reporters turning up; a crowd of would-be sympathizers. It was bad for the child. He put her and her governess into Mimi's car and sent them with Marino up to Leques again.

"Stay there my dear, until this thing has blown over," he told Juliet. "Meanwhile there is much for me to do. I have to go immediately to Rome and arrange for the funeral, but I don't want Sophie to be made aware of any of the horror, or told, at the moment, how her mother died. All I have said to her is that Maman has gone away for a long time, but that I would always stay with her. Also that her beloved Juliette would continue to look after her. She seemed quite happy about this, and quite oblivious of the truth, thank God."

Juliet's heart was torn with pity for him. He looked strained and ill. She was well aware that despite the ill-feeling that had existed between husband and wife, he had once loved Mimi. The shock of her violent death had shaken him badly. And she admired him for the fact that not once did he remark upon, or deplore, the scandal Mimi had invited when she took that trip; nor did he blame her for the gossip and the publicity that followed. He had nothing to say that was not compassionate.

He told Juliet about his stepdaughter. Simone had taken the news badly but was greatly consoled by Yves. The Maillards had suggested that the young couple should become privately engaged, and that Simone should stay with them in Paris until her mother's funeral. Mimi's remains were being brought back for burial in the family vault in the little churchyard of St. Pierre in Roquemont.

Only when Lucien saw Juliet off to Leques, for a fleeting moment, did he let the mask drop. His tired eyes glowed with all the affection and appreciation that he felt towards her.

"God bless you," he said in a low voice, "and thank you just for being here and for looking after my Sophie so well. You won't leave her now, will you?"

She looked back at him steadily.

"Never, as long as she needs me, Lucien."

That was the last she was to see of him for a couple of weeks.

At Leques she had to give all her love and attention to the little girl who asked endless questions about Maman and quite naturally did not really understand why she had gone away or why she wasn't coming back. Juliet herself, still suffering from

187

shock, found it difficult to answer the child in a satisfactory manner. Somehow she managed to weave a story about Maman not being well, and having gone to a wonderful place where she would get better. Knowing the resilience of the very young and how quickly they forget and settle down, no matter how badly disturbed, she was not too worried about Sophie.

The little girl adored Leques and in time mentioned her mother only in desultory fashion. She told every fresh friend she made at the hotel about the broken bridge (there was now a new one), and how she had learned, that day of the accident, to dive.

Sophie was quite happy, especially as she was able to speak to Papa on the phone whenever she wanted. But for Juliet this was a trying period. She felt restless – and useless – leading such a lazy life up here in the mountains. She felt that she ought to be down at the Château, helping Lucien. But he kept telling her that she could help him best by staying away – keeping Sophie out of the gloomy atmosphere at Roquemont.

The day came of course when he came up in the Jaguar to fetch them home.

Juliet was thankful to see him looking more like himself, although his eyes were still tired. But the worse was over. Poor, beautiful, heartless Mimi had been laid to rest with the other de Maurevilles. Her Italian maid, Maria, had returned to Italy.

The rest of the staff seemed relieved to welcome Miss Browning back – even old Blanche had a pleasant word for her. But she upset Juliet by creeping around after her, constantly referring to *la pauvre Madame*, and when they were alone, discussing the horrific details of the crash in the morbid way of the very old.

Soon it became plain to Juliet that things could not go on as they had done before Mimi's death. She could not live alone in the Château with Sophie and her father. It would not be *comme il faut* in the eyes of the community. Added to this, she knew it would be too great a strain on both Lucien and herself.

Simone came home for a few days, but soon said that it was like a 'morgue' and she could not bear the Château. So she went back to her fiancé's family. They seemed delighted to keep her with them.

Sophie, alone, was content at home, continuing with her own little life, playing, doing her lessons, or walking with Tache, her dog. Only occasionally she asked when Maman would be back and why Killarney Boy, Maman's chestnut mount, had been sold.

But Lucien still shrank from telling the child the truth. He had decided that both she and Juliet must go away again.

"I have an idea," he told Juliet one morning in October. "Supposing you take Sophie to England for a month or so. It is not too bad, the weather in England just now. I could ask friends of mine to book a suite of rooms for you in some seaside hotel – Brighton or Eastbourne. The change might be good for Sophie and she could have her little English protégée to stay with her."

"Yes, that sounds a good idea," said Juliet.

"You know that I don't want to get rid of either of you," said Lucien with a faint smile, "but personally I am inclined to think that it would be best to shut down the Château except for a skeleton staff, and for me to go and live with the Clermonts for a while, as they have suggested."

"I see," said Juliet.

He glanced around the library where they were talking.

"It's all too full of ghosts just now," he said in a low voice.

She nodded. She, too, had felt the acute depression, although she was sure that one day Lucien would want to come back to his beloved house, and that the sun would shine for him again here. But just now, as he said, poor Mimi's ghost haunted the place. Her perfume lingered in the air. It was sad to see her big glamorous bedroom shuttered and covered with dust sheets. It seemed quiet without the click of her high heels on the polished floor or the sound of her high-pitched laughter.

Juliet did not agree with that saying about 'the evil that men do lives after them'. In her opinion the evil had died with Mimi. It was only as Sophie's mother, she would be remembered – that was good.

"I am a coward. I want *you* to tell the child that her mother will never come back. But only after you reach England," Lucien added. "Is it asking too much of you?"

"No, I can tackle it. She will naturally grieve a little, but I can tackle it. I feel sure she will be good about it."

"You can tackle anything. God knows what I would have done without you, Juliet. You are more to Sophie than her own mother."

She flushed and gave him a sudden look that betrayed all the love and longing in her overburdened heart.

"Oh, I shall miss you, Lucien. I don't want to leave you. But I think it's best for you to close this place and live with the

Clermonts for a while. You are so fond of them. It will suit me to be in England next month because my brother Nicky is expected home. It will be nice for him to find me there."

"I know you'll take great care of my darling Sophie."

"Of that you can be sure."

"The next thing on the *tapis* will, of course, be Simone's wedding. They don't want to rush into it because of her mother's death, but I expect it will be round about Christmas time. The Maillards see no reason why the young couple should wait any longer than that and it will be a relief for me to know that Simone will soon be happily settled in a home of her own. It has taken the edge off her sorrow for her mother."

"I'm terribly glad."

"Incidentally," added Lucien, "I don't think I ever told you, did I, that my erring cousin, Michel, appeared at the funeral with his mother – while you were in Leques, of course. They came back to the Château for a glass of wine. Michel seemed very shaken by the accident. I think everybody has been. Anyhow, he was very nice indeed, and even apologetic because he had upset me, and behaved so badly over you."

"Oh, really that doesn't matter. I had forgotten it," said Juliet, her cheeks red.

"Anyhow, he and I have made our peace."

"Good. Now I'd better go and find Sophie, and see what she is doing," said Juliet feeling suddenly embarrassed. But this time Lucien put out a hand, took one of hers and raised it to his lips.

"I've said so many 'thank-yous', I'll only repeat myself if I say thank-you again for your support and for all your goodness to my child."

She shook her head. The tears had sprung to her eyes. She stood there looking suddenly helpless and very very young, he thought sadly, for he had never felt older. He kissed her hand again.

"Dearest Juliet, this isn't either the time or the place for saying all that is in my heart, but I don't want to be a hypocrite. I've already told you that I love you. I don't think if Mimi hears me, she will mind, wherever she is, if I say it again now."

Juliet's heart throbbed. The tears welled over. She pulled one of his hands against her wet cheek and kissed it.

"You know how much I love *you*, Lucien."

"Yes, my darling, I know, and it's a great comfort to me. We'll work something out for the future. One day – one day I'll be able to say so much more. You will come back to Roquemont and to me, won't you?"

"*I will*," she said.

Only later, much later, when she was in England with Sophie, did she remember that answer, and smile at the memory because it was so much part of the Marriage Service. She was equally happy to think that one day Sophie would become more to her than a pupil – much, *much* more.

ALSO BY DENISE ROBINS
IN CORONET BOOKS